" I heard a groan, and going to the cottage door, beheld the figure of a
man stretched before it, while in his cloak nestled a lovely infant."

GALLANT TOM;

OR,

THE PERILS OF A SAILOR

ASHORE AND AFLOAT.

AN ORIGINAL NAUTICAL ROMANCE OF DEEP AND PATHETIC INTEREST.

BY THOMAS PREST,

AUTHOR OF " ELA, THE OUTCAST; OR, THE GIPSY OF ROSEMARY DELL;"
"ANGELINA; OR, THE MYSTERY OF ST. MARK'S ABBEY;" "THE
DEATH GRASP; OR, A FATHER'S CURSE;" "ERNNESTINE
DE LACY; OR, THE ROBBERS' FOUNDLING,"
ETC. ETC. ETC.

" The hardy sailor braves the ocean,
Fearless of the raging wind ;
Yet his heart with fond emotion,
Throbs for those he leaves behind."

DIBDIN.

LONDON:
PUBLISHED BY EDWARD LLOYD, 231, SHOREDITCH.
—
MDCCCXLI.

PREFACE.

———

This is the author's first attempt at nautical romance, and is taken from " The Penny Sunday Times and People's Police Gazette," with considerable alterations and additions. The favour with which it has been received is highly flattering to the author, and he is anxious to assure his friends of the due sense he has of their kindness. He has endeavoured to adhere as closely to nature in his sketch of the honest and hardy sailor — brimful of loyalty, love, and liberality—as possible; and he is inclined to flatter himself that he has not entirely failed in that object. At an early period he trusts he shall be once more in the field, a candidate for public patronage, when he trusts that he shall be found deserving of the same success as that which has crowned the present production.

May 6th, 1841.

" Away with the black villain to the crazy boat, secure him in it, and commit him to the waves;—this is only a just punishment for his heinous crime."

GALLANT TOM;

OR,

THE PERILS OF A SAILOR ASHORE AND AFLOAT.

AN ORIGINAL NAUTICAL ROMANCE.

PART I.—ASHORE.

" It blew great guns, when Gallant Tom
Was taking in a sail,
And squalls came on in sight of home,
That strengthened to a gale."—DIBDIN.

THE moon was shining brilliantly upon the ocean in the port of Plymouth, when a large party of Britain's hardy sons of Neptune were assembled on the benches before a small public-house, known by the sign of " The Old Commodore," and kept by a superannuated old tar, nicknamed Mat Marlinspike, whose family consisted of his wife, a motherly, comfortable-looking old dame, his daughter, the pretty Ellen, and a handsome boy about twelve years of age, named Richard, and who was supposed to be the nephew of Mat, whom he had kindly taken under his protection on the death of his only sister, about seven years before.

No. 1.

It was the evening before the sailing of the fleet, under the command of the gal-
ant Nelson, when they went to achieve the glorious victory of the Battle of the
Nile. The grog passed freely round, toasts were drunk to the success of Britain's
hearts of oak, and so merry had every one become, that the time passed away un-
heeded, until one of the party rising, said,—

"Come, messmates, it is growing late, and it is time for us to weigh anchor;
so, three cheers for Admiral Nelson and the British Navy, and then away."

The sailors charged their glasses, and drank the toast with an enthusiasm which
made the place re-echo again.

"So, my lads," said old Mat, coming forward, "you are homeward bound,
then ?"

"Why, yes," answered the sailor who had first spoken, "yer see, Master Mat,
we must pass a few short hours with sweethearts and wives, for to morrow morning yon gallant fleet sets sail to join our noble commander in the Mediterranean
to bang the Mounseers, and mayhap many of us may be towed into the port of
Eternity, and never see the fair craft again."

"Right, right, my lads," observed Mat; "so good night, and may your dreams
be of Nelson and victory."

"I say, Mat," said another of the sailors, "where's Tom Mainstay, that he has
not joined us to night ?—for when the mess is abandoned by Gallant Tom, every
thing seems as dull as a tar without flip. He is as brave a fellow, and as taut a
sailor as ever reefed a topsail."

"Why, yer see, my lad," replied Mat, "Tom has been to town to buy some
trinkum trankums to leave his sweetheart in remembrance of him, or he would
have been aboard with ye, depend upon it."

"Aye, aye," returned the tar, "must keep a weather-eye on the fair craft, Mat.
I say, what a happy lass your daughter ought to think herself, to have such a
brave fellow as Tom Mainstay for a sweetheart. But, good night ;—come, messmates."

"Aye, aye," responded his companions, and tossing off the remainder of their
grog, they departed to their homes, and the "Old Commodore" was silent and
vacated.

"Ah," said Mat, turning to his wife, "there goes as brave a set of lads as ever
mounted the quarter-deck of a British man-of-mar. Splice my timbers, it does
my old eyes good to see them. But I say, dame, you look as dull as a frigate in
a fog."

"In truth, Mat," said the old woman, sighing, "I am sad at heart. To-morrow morning, with yonder fleet, our poor little Richard will depart on his first
voyage, and when I think of the perils he will be exposed to, my heart sinks within me; for though he is not our own son, his fond endearments have rendered
him the very soul and prop of our old days."

"True, true, dame," said Mat; "Richard is a noble boy, and it grieves me to
part with him ; but he possesses a gallant spirit, and longs to distinguish himself
in the service of his king and country, and Heaven forbid that I should put the
boy's courage under hatches. Besides, will he not be under as brave a tar as ever
furled a sail, our Ellen's sweetheart, Tom Mainstay ?"

"But when he is gone," added the old woman, mournfully, "who will be left to cheer us in our old age, and to raise the drooping spirits of our daughter, in the absence of her lover?"

" Trust to Providence, dame," answered Mat, earnestly: " but, sit down, my old lass, I have something to tell you—something of importance—'tis a secret."

" A secret?" reiterated his wife, with much curiosity.

" Aye, aye," said Mat, " and one that I have long wished to confide to you. But promise, dame, never to divulge what I am going to impart to any one, for on it, probably, the very life of Richard depends."

" Mat, I promise to obey you," returned the dame, earnestly.

" Enough, then," said Mat, taking a seat on one of the benches by her side— " listen."

Just at this moment, the tall figure of a mulatto stalked round the corner, of the house, and observing Mat and his wife in earnest conversation, he drew back, and seemed determined to listen. Why he should possess any curiosity to overhear what they were talking about, remains to be told.

This man was called Saib, and was the confidential domestic of the Earl Fitzosbert, who at that time resided in the neighbourhood of Plymouth. He was looked upon with an eye of suspicion and abhorrence by every one, for he was known to be savage and revengeful, and report was busy in attributing to him and his master many deeds of darkness, but of the truth of which no one had been at the pains of undertaking to ascertain.

" You have ever thought, dame," continued Mat, addressing himself to his wife, " that Richard was the only child of my poor sister, who died about seven years ago, and left him to my care; but it is not so—the boy is no relation of mine."

" Amazement!" ejaculated Margaret, " who, then, are his parents?"

" That I do not know," answered Mat; " but certain it is, that the boy comes from a noble stock :—hows'ever I found him a long way from hence."

" Found him!" reiterated Margaret, with increased astonishment,—" you surprise me, Mat."

" I dare say I do," answered her husband; " but I shall astonish you a great deal more before I have done my story. You must know——but, hollo!—what do you want?"

" Massa Mat, good evening to you," said Saib, coming forward, when he found that the old man had discovered him.

" Humph!" returned Mat, sulkily :—oh, good evening to you. You are more free than welcome," he continued, aside. " I never look upon that fellow's face but he reminds me of the devil. If an artist wanted a correct likeness of his Satannic majesty, I don't think he could do better than get Saib to sit to him."

" Let me have a glass of grog, Massa Mat, said Saib, taking a seat. Mat made his exit into the house, beckoning his wife to follow him, and when they had gone, Saib reflected for a second or two, and then clenching his fist, soliloquised :—

" My suspicions are all but confirmed—this brat is not the relation of Marlinspike, and his striking likeness to the late earl, almost convinces me that in him exists the young heir to the estates of Fitzosbert. Mat said he found him far at sea :—it must be so ;—curses on the billows that did not overwhelm him in the wreck! Fool that I was to trust him to the ocean! Why did I not plunge my knife into their hearts, when they were in my power.   It will be a fine tale to tell my master.   But, no matter, it may be better ; this night I am resolved shall place the boy in my clutches, and if the earl accedes to my wishes, he dies !—Yes, the hand of Julia and her wealth must be my reward for the business.   Ha !. ha ! ha ! She calls me black dog.—She shall find that the dog can bite."

" Here's your grog," said Mat, returning from the house.

" And here's your money," answered Saib, vexed at being interrupted in the train of his reflections ; " and now you can be gone."

" Oh, to be sure, Master Japan," returned Mat, sarcastically, " I'm not fond of looking on the likeness of ——"

" Of what ?" angrily demanded Saib.

" The devil, to be sure," answered Mat, with a laugh, as he retired into the house.

" The Christian dog !" cried Saib, as he vanished ;—" but, no matter ; they shall find the black man as true a devil in heart as he is like him in visage."

At this moment, the voice of a boy singing at no great distance sounded in his ears, and soon afterwards a boat approached the shore, containing Richard.   Saib recognised him in a minute.

" Here's the brat they have been speaking of," said he.   " What a fool I must be not to know him before, for he is as like the late earl as ever child was like the parent.   He comes :—now, if the old man and his guests will only keep snug to the house for a few minutes, I'll spoil your singing, my boy."

Richard having stepped from the boat, bounded gaily towards the house, when he suddenly recognised Saib, and started back.

" Oh !" said the boy to himself, " there is that frightful black man,. the servant and confidant of the Earl Fitzosbert.   I don't know how it is, but whenever I look upon his sable countenance, my heart sinks with horror.   I'll run into the house, and meet my good uncle and aunt, and my coz. Ellen."

" Stop, boy," cried Saib, as he attempted to enter at the doorway ; " why do you pass me as though I were something contagious ?"

" I am in a hurry, good Saib, and——"

" Good Saib," laughed the black, sarcastically.—" Ha ! ha ! ha !   But, no matter—drink, boy, drink."

" Excuse me, Saib," said Richard, trembling ;—" I am too young to drink ; I——"

" Oh, you'll not drink with me, I suppose," interrupted the other, scowling, " because I am a black man."

" No, Saib," replied the boy, firmly, " you wrong me :—Heaven forbid that I should ever be so ungenerous as to despise a fellow creature only for the colour of his skin.   I will drink, just to prove to you how mistaken you was in forming such a supposition.   And he took the glass from the hand of Saib—" Here's victory to the British Navy."

" Would it were poison," Saib muttered to himself.

" And now, Saib," said the boy, " I must indeed be going—so, good night.

" Hold, boy !" cried Saib, suddenly starting upon his feet, and grasping his arm, " you must come with me."

" Spare me, Saib ;—don't hurt me ; I never injured you !" exclaimed the ter-rifled Richard as the black attempted to drag him away :—" what mean you by this violence?'

" Ask no questions, brat," cried Saib, fiercely :—" come, come."

" Savage man, unhand me!" ejaculated Richard, struggling hard to escape from his hold ; " you have some cruel design against me,—for what reason I know not. I will alarm the inn !"

" Boy," observed Saib, his eyes rolling savagely, at the same time drawing a knife from his vest, " utter a word that may be heard but a yard off, and I'll murder you on the spot."

But in spite of this threat, Richard shrieked with all his might, and at that moment a hearty voice was heard outside, shouting—" Hilly yeo ! hilly yeo !" and just as Saib was dragging him away, in rushed Tom Mainstay, and clutching the throat of the black with the strength of a lion, dashed him to the earth, at the same time wresting the knife from him, and holding the boy under his protection.

" Why, you black pirate," cried the sailor, " damme, if I haven't a good mind to lower your topsail in less time than a boatswain could pipe all hands ! Sheer off, yer swab, or may 1 never taste salt junk again, but I'll send you to old Davy like a shot !"

As Tom Mainstay stood over the black ruffian, and thus taunted him, the eyes of the latter rolled fiercely in their sockets, and he was almost choked with rage.

" Tom Mainstay," exclaimed he, gathering himself on to his feet, " the black man never receives an insult without having a deadly revenge. Beware, when next we meet !"

Thus saying, Saib skulked away, and the sailor laughed at him contemptuously. " Ha ! ha ! ha ?" said he; " boldly spoken, my sable land-lubber ; but Tom Mainstay has weathered many a rough tempest at sea, and it would be strange indeed, if he was now to be frightened by a puddle in a storm on shore. Why, Dick, you seem alarmed."

" Alarmed !" answered the boy, proudly ; " oh, no, Tom, you mistake me ; I am only a little ruffled,—for you know I am to be a sailor, and I should not have liked to have been deprived of the opportunity I expect to have, of helping to drub the foes of my king and country !"

" Splice my timbers !" cried Tom, shaking the boy's hand heartily, " a sailor already, every inch of him. But, weigh anchor, and steer into the fore-cabin, for see, here comes my pretty Ellen,—bless her blue twinklers."

Richard obeyed this order, and left Tom to talk to his sweetheart. Ellen was considered the flower of Plymouth. Her features were regular, and bewitchingly handsome ; her eyes were a brilliant blue, her figure was perfect, and she had the prettiest little foot, and the most gracefully turned ancle, that could possibly be imagined. To Tom she was fondly, devotedly attached, and the thoughts of being so soon separated from him, and the uncertainty of ever beholding him again, wrung her gentle heart, and clad her face in looks of the deepest sorrow.

" Now, my pretty Ellen," said Tom, affectionately throwing one arm around the damsel's slender waist, and pressing her hand fervently, " tell me, why will you persist in hoisting signals of distress ?"

" Ah, Tom, replied Ellen, " how can I be otherwise than sorrowful? Are you not going to leave me to-morrow, to be exposed to all the terrors of a dreadful conflict, and should you perish—" She hid her face in her bosom, weeping, and could not finish the sentence.

"Come, come, lass," said Tom, soothingly, "you must not founder in the ocean of despair. I have weathered many a hard fight and a rough gale hitherto, and we must trust to Providence to protect me through this."

"Oh, Tom," observed Ellen, "I dare not think of it."

"Now, shiver my timbers!" ejaculated her lover, "if you put your pumps to work, you'll set my heart going at the rate of forty knots an hour. As our chaplain says when he is about to swallow a good jorum of rum, 'Damn fear, always keep up your spirits.'

'Go, patter to lubbers and swabs, do yon see,
  About danger, and fear, and the like;
A stout British ship, and good sea-room give me,
  And it ain't to a little I'll strike!'

Come, lass, give us a kiss!—Lor' love your pretty face. Yer know this is to be my last cruise, Ellen; and after I have assisted in banging the Mounseers, I shall return home with lots of prize-money, a whole cargo of love, get spliced to you, embark on the ocean of matrimony, and in a short time, mayhap, become the commander of a little fleet of my own."

"What mean you, Tom?" inquired Ellen, timidly.

"What do I mean, lass?" answered her lover;—"why, the pretty little small craft that we shall have, to be sure." And once more kissing the blushing cheek of the maiden affectionately, he stepped with her into the house, where Mat and his wife were engaged in earnest conversation upon the late outrage committed by Saib, and in vain endeavouring to conjecture what motive could have incited him to it.

The Earl Fitzosbert had a handsome mansion near the house of Mat Marlinspike. He was a proud, haughty, and tyrannical nobleman, with a forbidding countenance, and who was universally hated. He was immensely rich; but there were strange rumours afloat as to the manner in which he obtained his wealth, which, if they were true, would make the earl a villain indeed. He had a ward, named Rosina, a beauteous girl, of the most amiable manners and disposition, and she was greatly pitied, for it was well known that she suffered much from the capricious and tyrannical disposition of her guardian, and the insolence of the black man, Saib, who exercised a singular authority over his master, and knew all his secrets.

A deep melancholy always seemed to absorb the feelings of Rosina, from which it was in vain to attempt to arouse her: it was evident that her mind was suffering from some secret grief; but no one could imagine what it was, for she carefully evaded every question on the subject.

"Why do you give way to these fits of sadness, Miss?" observed Patty, her maid, on the day upon which we commenced this narrative. (Patty was a great favourite with Rosina, and she confided to her breast many secrets.) "To be sure," continued Patty, "the earl does not behave kind to you."

"The earl!" reiterated Rosina, "oh, mention him not; his very name is odious to me. Oh, my poor father, little did you think when you committed me to the care of that man, to what misery you was consigning me. Patty, I am wretched ; even that hideous wretch, Saib, who is the confidant of the earl, has presumed to insult me with his odious passion, and the earl appears to encourage him. But this is not all that oppresses me."

" Dear me, Miss," observed the waiting-maid, " why, any one would imagine you were in love !"

Rosina sighed, blushed, and hid her face for a moment in her handkerchief. " Alas ! there it is, Patty," she replied; " I do indeed love one who never can be mine !"

" What, won't he marry you, Miss ?" said Patty ;—" then I'm sure he shews his want of taste, and does not pay any compliment to your charms and accomplishments."

" Listen, Patty," remarked Rosina, seriously, " and divulge not what I am about to tell you. He, who holds my heart, knows not of the passion he has inspired. He is betrothed to another, a worthy girl, and deeply do I repent the injury I am doing her, by encouraging an affection for him to whom her very soul is devoted. But, alas ! I cannot stifle my feelings.'

" You surprise me, Miss !" ejaculated Patty ; " but, may I ask who is the youth that has thus taken possession of your heart ?"

" You remember the night, Patty," answered her mistress, " when our boat upset at some distance from the shore, and I was immersed in the rapid tide, and was near being drowned—at that critical moment, a sailor plunged fearlessly into the deep, and at the imminent peril of his own life, brought me to shore ?"

" Ah !" remarked Patty, " well do I remember that, Miss ;—it was Gallant Tom, as he is called, one of the bravest seamen in the British fleet."

" He is, indeed," said Rosina, eagerly, and her blue eyes sparkling with pleasure at the thought ;—" from that moment, Patty, I loved him."

" Lor', bless me !" exclaimed the maid, " how you surprise me !—What, love a common sailor ?"

" Accursed for ever be the wretch !" cried Rosina, warmly, " who would despise honest poverty enshrined beneath a sailor's jacket. Oh, Patty, little can you imagine the feelings I bear towards that noble youth ; something more powerful than love seems to endear him to me ; his strange likeness to a brother whom I lost in childhood, is so great, that in spite of everything I cannot erase him from my thoughts. Mine has been a strange life. As soon as I can remember, I found myself with an only brother the inmate of a fisherman's hut some miles from hence. We thought he was our father, although the cruelty with which he treated us made us fear, if not hate him. My poor brother, who was three years older than me, loved me fondly, and his chief delight was to wander to the sea-beach, to gather the pretty shells and pebbles to amuse me. One evening he went there alone, as usual ; night set in—the next morning broke, but my poor brother never returned, nor have I since been able to learn what became of him."

" Poor fellow !" exclaimed Patty.

" A short time afterwards," resumed her mistress, after a pause, " our real father, who was rich and noble, came to claim us. His motive for so long neglecting and disowning his children, I never knew. He was wretched at the mysterious disappearance of his son ; but though he tried every means, and offered large rewards, he never could gain any tidings of him. He died three years since, and made his friend, the Earl Fitzosbert, my guardian."

" What a melancholy story :—and you say that Gallant Tom is so like your poor lost brother, Miss ?"

" The very image of him ; and did I not know it was impossible, I could fancy it was him. He haunts my imagination, sleeping or waking.—Patty, I cannot live but in his presence."

" Oh, Miss, pardon me, but I must say you talk very silly," observed Patty, " why to morrow morning you know Tom sets sail with the noble fleet, now lying at anchor in the port."

" And thither will I follow him !" suddenly exclaimed Rosina.

" Impossible !"

" You may deem me romantic, Patty," returned her lady, " but am resolved ; I can no longer endure the tyranny of the earl, and the insolence o Saib ; so I have determined to assume male attire, and get on board the same ship in which Tom is to sail. I have ascertained that there will be no great difficulty, as her number is not complete. Then, and then only will I venture to avow my love for him, and throw myself and fortune at his feet. Patty, you'll not betray me ?"

" Betray you, Miss ?—lor' bless you, not for the world. But this is indeed a romantic idea—a female sailor !—but, dear me, have you well considered the perils of the undertaking ? You know they are going to fight, and suppose you should be killed ?"

" I have considered everything, Patty," replied the lady, " and I am ready to encounter every danger. I have secured everything necessary for my design, and this night, as soon as the family are at rest, I bid adieu to this hateful house for ever."

" Heigho !" sighed Patty; " and so you mean to leave me all alone, Miss ?"

" What other alternative have I ?" answered her mistress.

" Why, I'll tell you," observed Patty, smiling archly ; " I have got a sweetheart, you know, Miss, and a nice little man he is too, only not very brave.—Toby Twitter, Miss, and he's going on board the same ship as Gallant Tom is, tomorrow ; so I have been thinking, if you have no objection, I should dearly like to put on male attire, also, and accompany you in this adventure, if it is only to watch the conduct of my poor little Toby."

" I shall be delighted with your company, Patty," said her mistress, joyfully.

" Then it's a bargain," ejaculated the maid. " From this moment consider me a sailor.—Huzza ! The blue jackets for ever ! Oh, Miss, shan't I make a jolly Jack tar ?"

" Hark !" said Rosina, putting her finger on her lip, " I hear the voices of the Earl and Saib ;—they are approaching this way ; Let us begone, Patty, and make preparations for our perilous adventure."

" Oh, yes, Miss," said Patty; " come along, for I am all impatience to put on the breeches. They do say that our sex have a peculiar *penchant* for those little unwhisperables !"

" Saib," exclaimed the Earl Fitzosbert, to his sable myrmidon, as they entered the room, having first looked cautiously around, to ascertain that nobody was observing them,—" Saib, this tale you have told me of the brat being still alive, perplexes me."

"Why should it alarm you, my lord?" returned the black: "have I not said that I have the means of ridding you of him this very night?"

"But should you again fail?"

"Psha! the black man's knife seldom misses its aim. You have known its power ere now, my lord;—the proud estates of Fitzosbert came not into your possession without——"

"I know, I know!" hastily interrupted the earl; "but should this hated boy be suffered still to survive, in time all may be discovered, and my dearly-earned power wrested from me, and ignominy and disgrace may light upon me."

"I have offered you the means to rid you of your fears," answered Saib, "will you accept of them?"

"The terms are high," said Fitzosbert;—"the hand and fortune of my fair ward, Rosina——"

"Must be mine!" rejoined his companion. "Swear that, and my dagger shall be washed in the heart's blood of the young heir of Fitzosbert this very night!"

The earl paused, and traversed the room for a few moments buried in rumination, then suddenly returning to his confidant, he said,—

"I will agree."

"Enough, then!" cried the black, his large eyes rolling with gratification; "this instant I fly to execute the crime."

"Thanks, thanks, my good Saib," replied his master, "and when next we meet, the heir of Fitzosbert——"

" Will be no more," added the black, hollowly, as he hastened from the apartment, and left the earl to retire to his chamber.

Three o'clock had chimed from a neighbouring church clock, however, before
the villain, Saib, started on his deed of darkness. He had ascertained that Richard
slept in a room on the ground floor, and he had provided himself with proper implements to force the shutters so that he might gain access to his destined victim.
All was still around when Saib arrived at the little tavern. Every one had retired
to rest, and the moment seemed propitious to his purpose. He walked round to
the back of the house, and easily scaled the paling with which it was surrounded.
He walked up to the window of the back parlour, the room in which the boy slept,
and listened : he could hear the strong breathing of the unconscious sleeper, and
was convinced that everything favoured his purpose.

" All's right, that sleep should be changed into an eternal one," ejaculated the
wretch, as he applied the implements he had brought with him for the purpose,
and forced the shutters open, with very little noise. He looked into the room,
and beheld the boy reclining, dressed, upon the bed, and no other person was in
the chamber. Cautiously, the villain opened the window, and the next moment
was seen standing over the couch of the sleeping boy, with the knife in his hand,
ready to perpetrate the hellish deed.

" I have succeeded famously," he muttered to himself. " All is still ; no person will hear his dying groans, and I may escape unperceived and unsuspected.
Now, for the deed !—Die ! die ! damned offspring of a Christian dog !"

Instantly he was about to draw his knife across the throat of the boy, when,
suddenly, his arm was fiercely seized. He looked, and beheld Tom Mainstay
standing before him, with a pistol presented at his head, and attended by several
more sailors.

" Hold ! you black shark !" exclaimed the gallant sailor, " or, damme, I'll send
a bullet through your mizen-top."

At this critical moment, the noise awoke the boy, who started from his bed in
astonishment and alarm, while at the same juncture, Mat and his wife entered the
room in a state of great consternation, which was not a little increased at the
spectacle that presented itself.

" For heaven's sake, what is the meaning of this ?" inquired the old man and
his wife in the same breath.

" The meaning, Master Mat," answered Tom,—" why, I'll tell you : I had occasion to steer past the mansion of the Earl Fitzosbert, in company with my messmates, when we saw this black lubber cruising about suspiciously on the coast ;
so we gave chase to him on the sly, and watched him here, where he was about to
lay his grapling irons on young Dick, but we were lucky enough to prevent him.

" Villain !" ejaculated old Mat, " what is your design ?"

" His life ?" answered Saib, his eyes flashing with fury.

" Why, you damned pirate !" cried Tom, " say another word like that, and I'll
send a brace of bullets through your brains !—I say, messmates, what shall we do
with him ?"

" Why, I'll tell you what, Tom," replied one of his companions ; " to prevent
him from doing any more mischief, suppose we take him on board ship, where a
shot from the enemy, or the cat will soon teach him to behave himself."

"Well said," agreed Tom Mainstay; "bind the lubber, and aboard with him."

The black tried hard to escape, and he foamed at the mouth with rage; but his efforts were all useless; a strong cord was procured, and the sailors having secured his arms, proceeded to drag him out of the house.

"Tom Mainstay!" cried the enfuriated wretch, fixing upon the sailor a look that was truly demoniacal, "for this, the curse, the bitter curse, of the black man be upon your head!—Revenge! revenge!"

"Away with him," said Tom, laughing scornfully at his threats. "Well," he continued, "we have disposed of that black rascal pretty well, I think; and now, Mat, you must bestir yourself, for day begins to peep, and already the sailors are steering down here to get the grog aboard before they bid adieu to old England for some time. Come along, I go to join my messmates outside the house. Ship a-hoy, there!"

Early as it was, the sailors soon began to bustle to the little hostelrie; and when Tom went outside, he found a goodly company assembled on the seats, and who were as merry as if they were going to a wedding, instead of upon an enterprise attended with so much danger.

"Good cheer, my lads," said Gallant Tom, when he joined them; "the morning has at length dawned when we are to bid adieu to England for a while, in search of glory; so, come, boys, pitch the blue devils overboard, and let's have a good jorum of grog at parting. Mat, you are steward of the mess, my old boy, so weigh anchor, and bring the flip."

Mat did not require to be told a second time, but hastened into the house to obey the order; in the meantime, the men who had had the charge of Saib, rejoined their companions.

"Well, Tom," observed one of them, "we have towed the black hulk on board, and he's safe enough. The lubber does not seem to relish salt water."

"Well done, my lads," said Tom, approvingly; "I'll warrant we shall soon tame him. But, here's the flip, so fill your glasses, bumpers all, and I'll give you a toast—'Here's, may the enemies of Great Britain split upon the rock of despair, and founder in the ocean of oblivion.'"

The sailors drank the toast with the greatest enthusiasm, and by that time the sweethearts and wives of several present made their appearance, and the scene became one of the most animated description.

"Here are the fair craft," said Tom Mainstay, as the females made their appearance, "bless their pretty faces, they look more beautiful than ever, although they are overcast with the clouds of sorrow at the thoughts of being parted from their sweethearts. Come, messmates, yard-arm and yard-arm with the lasses, and then once more for mirth!"

There was a general kissing and embracing of the females at this hint, and then they all seated themselves at the tables to take a parting glass.

"Ah, this is what I like to see," observed Gallant Tom, "there's nothing gives such pleasure to the sailor's heart as to have the petticoats aboard. I wonder where my little Ellen is; I suppose she hasn't got out of her hammock yet.—Ah! here she comes!"

At that moment Ellen came from the house and approached her lover. Her face was overcast with gloom, and tears escaped her eyes, as Tom affectionately took her hand.

" My pretty Ellen," exclaimed the sailor, " how it glads me to see you,—but, splice my topsails, you will persist in hoisting these confounded signals of distress. Why, any one would think I was going to a funeral, instead of on a voyage of pleasure."

" Pleasure, Tom !" returned Ellen ; " oh, can you call the horrors of war by so gentle a name ?"

" Why, look you, my lass," replied Tom, " there cannot be a greater pleasure in the world to a true British tar than fighting. The roar of the cannon is music to his ears, to which he never fails to make the enemies of his country dance against their will, and Death is only master of the ceremonies, who sometimes takes it into his head to ship a few of the actors in the ball on board his own craft. Come, come, don't give way to despair, my girl, for—

" My name, d'ye see's Tom Tough, I have seen a little service,
    Where the mighty billows roll, and loud tempests blow ;
  I've sailed with gallant Howe, and I've fought with noble Jarvis,
    And——"

" Bravo !" shouted one of the sailors ; " Gallant Tom's the lad for getting the weathergage of care. Come, my pretty lass, stow yourself alongside of your sweetheart, and be happy."

" To be sure she will," said Tom, again kissing her. " Messmates, I must give you another toast, and I know it is one in which you will all join.—' Here's to the sailor's home, the bosom of the girl he loves !' "

" Hurrah !" shouted his companions. " The sailor's home !"

" Messmates," observed Tom, as Richard approached him, " this is my pro-pro-pro-protegee, don't they call it ?—Yer see, I'm not much-used to the lubber's palaver ; and if the young dog disgraces his master, damme, I'll throw him overboard as food for the sharks !"

" Ship a-hoy !" shouted two or three voices outisde, and Tom looking towards the road which led up to the house, said,—

" Hollo ! what's in the wind, now ?—Oh, its Dick Clewline coming this way, and towing two of the most dainty-looking craft along with him that I ever seed."

The dainty-looking craft to whom Tom so pointedly alluded to, was Rosina, and her maid, Patty, in male attire, who, having left the house of Earl Fitzosbert as soon as they imagined all the family had retired to rest, had fallen in with Dick Clewline, who offered to get them an opportunity of entering on board the same vessel as Gallant Tom, if they would place themselves under his care.

" Here you are, my lads," said Dick, when they had got to the house, " safe in port : Gallant Tom, there, will give you all the information you want."

" He is there !" said Rosina, in a whisper to her attendant, " and my unsuspecting rival, too :—oh, how my heart throbs !"

" Courage, my dear lady," replied Patty, in the same low tone ; " courage, or you will betray us :—I will speak to him, be you silent."

" What cheer, youngsters ?" said Tom ; " would you speak with me ?"

" We would," replied Patty, in an assumed tone —" you belong to the Vanguard ?"

" I do; and a gallant vessel she is, too," said Tom.

" We are two friendless lads," continued Patty, " who would fain serve our king and country."

" Whewgh !" whistled Tom, pitching up the waistband of his trousers : " here's jolly tars ;—place them in petticoats, and they'd make two excellent lady's maids. Why, my lads, have you considered the danger of this enterprise ? Its no use to fear when——"

" Fear, sir !" interrupted Patty, indignantly; " we are Englishmen, and never learnt that word at school."

" Well said, youngster," exclaimed Tom; " damme, he's got some mettle in him, though ;—give us your fin."

" Wh-wh-what, sir ?"

" Wh-wh-what !—oh, I forgot ; you don't understand the king's English yet.— Give me your hand."

" Ah, to be sure I will," said Patty, extending her hand, which Tom gave such a hearty pull that he almost made the tears start into her eyes.

" What a hand for a sailor," observed Tom ; " as soft as a kid glove. But, I say, my lad, you'll splice the main brace, won't you ?"

" Splice ! splice ! I"—stammered out the bewildered female.

" Oh, you don't know our nautical lingo yet," replied Tom. " Drink, my lad, that's what I mean."

" To be sure I will," said Patty, taking the glass with much apparent glee. " Here's Admiral Nelson, the hero of the seas !"

" Bravo ! bravo !" shouted the sailors, drinking the toast.

" Won't your companion drnik ?" asked Tom, pointing to Rosina.

" No, no, thank you," hastily returned Patty, with much confusion, " he—"

" Oh, perhaps he prefers pig-tail ?—Messmate, will you take a quid ?" inquired Tom, handing his box to the bewildered maiden, who stammered out some sort of excuse. Patty then inquired whether they could not see the captain directly, and Tom having commisisoned Dick Clewline to escort them to him, they departed. Shortly after this a signal gun fired to summon the seamen on board, and the scene which then took place, was one of the most pathetic description. The young men hugged their sweethearts to their bosoms with the most fervent affection, and many a manly cheek was damped with tears, as he stole a parting embrace of his wife and children.

" Now, my pretty Ellen," said Tom, turning to his sweetheart, " the time's come ; we must part for a while, lass ; but—but—damme, I'm not crying ;—no, no, Ellen."

" Oh, Tom," sobbed Ellen, " my heart sinks : I fear we shall meet no more."

" Avast ! avast ! my poor girl," returned her sweetheart, " we *shall meet* again, depend upon it. Ellen, this handkerchief is one that I have had ever since I was a little boy, no higher than half a handspike ; when I am away, look on it, and do not forget your poor Tom."

Ellen pressed the handkerchief to her lips, and her tears flowed fast as she replied,—

" This locket contains a minature likeness of myself,—will you not wear it next your heart for my sake ?"

" I will, I will," cried Tom, in a broken tone ; " and in the battle's heat, with that dear relic next my heart, defy the deadly ball, that else may lay me low ! But I must begone ; see, the boat awaits.—Ellen, farewell !—bless you ! bless you !"

Tom pressed his lover to his heart, and kissed away the tears that flowed fast from her eyes. The poor girl's feelings overcame her, and ere the signal gun had fired for the sailors to go on board, she fainted in his arms ; and with one last look of indescribable emotion, the brave fellow resigned her to the care of her parents, pressed their hands, unable to utter a word, and beckoning to Richard, hurried away.

Bitter was the anguish felt by Mat Marlinspike, his wife, and daughter, for many days after the departure of Gallant Tom, and their adopted, Richard. The poor old dame, who loved the latter with as much affection as if he had been her own son, was with difficulty reconciled at all ; and her husband, who could not bear to witness her anguish, almost regretted having yielded to the predilection which the boy had for a nautical life.

" I cannot help thinking upon the circumstance of that wretch, Saib, attempting the life of Richard," observed Mat's wife, an evening or two after the departure of the fleet ; " what motive could induce him to commit such a crime ? and in what way could the boy have injured him ?",

" Aye, aye, dame," observed Mat, " as you say, the conduct of that black swab was rather unaccountable ; but, depend upon it, he did not act without the instructions of some superior power."

" What !" ejaculated his wife, with astonishment depicted in her countenance, " do you mean to insinuate that—"

" Be cautious, dame," interrupted her husband, in a low tone, " for we might have listeners. What I mean to insinuate is, that the Earl Fitzosbert is one of the verriest scoundrels in existence, and——"

" That Saib acted only by his instructions," added his wife ;" is that what you mean ?"

" It is."

" But why should he seek the life of the boy ?" demanded the old woman.

" I know not," answered Mat ; " only the fact of the matter is, that in my opinion Richard is no menial's offspring, and that the rascally black, and his equally rascally master, have discovered, by some means or other, his true origin, and for certain reasons, best known to themselves, may have a wish to get rid of him."

" Goodness me !" exclaimed the old woman, " whatever could have put such an idea into your head ?"

" Hark you, dame," replied Mat ; " I have before told you that the boy is no relation of mine, although till lately you supposed he was the son of my only, and favourite sister, who died some time since. As we are now alone, I will, upon your promise of secresy, tell you the truth, as far as I know about him. You will recollect that about thirteen years since, after returning from a long cruise, I had occasion to visit my sister, who at that time resided at the Isle of Wight ?"

" I recollect it perfectly well, Mat," answered his wife, " and I do not forget also, that I felt myself, at that time, rather offended at your remaining there so long."

"True," said Mat; "and I don't wonder that you did, dame; but you shall now, for the first time, hear the cause of it. You see, my sister lived near the coast, in a neat little cottage which she inherited from her late husband, who had saved a little money in th service of his country, and left her enough, with care, to live very comfortably. Well, one night' you must know, when the wind blew, and the rain pattered sharply against the casements of the cottage, I was seated in the parlour, smoking my pipe, and joking with my sister, to keep up her spirits in the midst of the storm, when, suddenly, between the pauses of the blast, I thought I heard the cries of some person, as if in distress, outside. I listened, but all was again still, and I concluded that I had been deceived by the wind moaning among the cliffs, near which the cottage stood. But, presently, the sounds again broke more distinctly on my ears, and my sister became very much alarmed; for, you must know, that like many others of her sex, she could not lay claim to being over and above courageous. I started from my seat, and looked out of the casement, but the night was dark as a funeral pall, and I could not see anything before me; but once more the low moans of some person vibrated on my ears. Determined to ascertain from whence they proceeded, I placed a light in a lantern that was on the table, and laying hold of a stout cudgel, in case of danger, for there were some querish characters, I knew, at that time, in the neighbourhood, I started forth to reconnoitre. I had scarcely got over the threshold of the door, when I stumbled over some object lying upon the ground, and holding down the lantern, what was my astonishment to behold stretched upon the earth the body of a man, bleeding profusely from a wound in the side, and, apparently, in the agonies of death, while nestling to him, was an infant, who had evidently been roughly used, and was at that time quite insensible. I called to Margaret, and with her assistance bore them into the cottage, and afterwards alarmed the neighbours, and procured the assistance of a doctor. The poor gentleman, however, never spoke, and in a short time after the arrival of the medical man, he breathed his last. The child was restored—that child is our little Richard!"

"Astonishing!" cried the dame; "but was it not discovered who the gentleman was, and who had been guilty of the dreadful crime?"

"Never, dame, never," replied her husband; "every inquiry was made, but all to no purpose. A coroner's inquest sat upon the body, and they returned a verdict of ' wilful murder' against some person or persons unknown. He was a handsome, noble-looking man, and his linen was marked with the initials ' A. F.,' but that was the only clue given to who he was. It was a foul deed, and certain it is that some day or other, the base assassins will be discovered and brought to justice, and our *protegé* restored to those rights I feel convinced some other person at present withholds from him. I made a vow to act as a father to the poor boy, until I could discover the secret of his birth, and I will not break my oath. Thinking that his life would not be safe, if I did not keep the manner in which I became possessed of him a secret, I adopted the plan of placing him under the care of my sister, whose son I reported him to be. Now, dame, you know all about the matter, and I'm certain I need not impress upon your mind the necessity of silence, until Providence shall deem fit to unravel the mystery of his birth, and bring the assassins of his father to punishment. But, come, this is a melancholy story, and I must endeavour to shake off the effects of it: I must try a verse or two of my favourite old song :—

" Merry is the sailor's life,
    Free from ev'ry care and strife,
With cheerful heart he'll o'er the ocean go ;
    Let the billows foam and roar,
    It only pleases Jack the more,
And, damme ! don't he like to thrash the foe ?
    To ev'ry foreign clime he'll roam,—
    He loves his ship just like his home,
                    With a yeo, yeo, yeo!
    Drink, drink, and kiss the lasses ;
    Drink away, let's be gay,
                    Fal de ral, de ral, lal lay !
    Drink, drink, and kiss the lasses,
    That's the way, that's the way,
Fal de ral, de lido,—fal lal de ray !"

The Earl Fitzosbert paced his chamber with impatient steps on the night the villain Saib had, by his commands, hastened to the " Old Commodore," to perpetrate the sanguinary deed.

" Yes," he muttered to himself, " my heart tells me that the suspicions of Saib are right, and that my brother's hateful brat still exists in the person of the boy Richard ! 'Tis strange that he should thus cross my path ! But, if Saib fail not, he will not long remain to annoy me. And yet," he continued, after a pause, " why should I be so eager to have the boy's life ? He, probably, knows not that he is any other than the nephew of the man who has brought him up,—and what chance has he of ever discovering his real origin ? Again, is he not going to sea, and, exposed to all the perils and vicissitudes of that life, may he not perish unknown ? I do almost repent me of having sanctioned this dreadful crime. But, what a weak, wayward fool I am getting ; the deed once done, I am secure against all fear of discovery."

Still was he doubtful and uneasy ; and he longed, yet dreaded, the return of his myrmidon, the ruffian Saib. Every sound that vibrated on his ears, made him start ; and more than once he walked on to the balcony before the window, and straining his eyes over the scenery beyond, endeavoured to discover him approaching ; but he came not ; and at that late hour, for it was then midnight, all was as still as death, save, at intervals, the wailing cry of the sea-mew, and the dashing of the waves. Another hour elapsed in this manner, and still the black came not, and the uneasiness of the earl increased to ar almost insupportable degree.

" What can detain him ?" he soliloquized ; " surely he has not failed in his attempt, and fallen into the hands of justice. I cannot bear to think of that. Should it be so, what can save me from disgrace and ignominy ? Fool that I was again to trust him, when he before was unsuccessful, or otherwise deceived me ! But, no ; there is no fear of his accomplishing his inhuman purpose : the hand and fortune of my fair ward will urge him on to desperation. Methinks, however,

he will find himself duped ; the hand and wealth of the beauteous Rosina must not be so lightly sacrificed.   I have other——but, what noise is that ?"

The sounds that had disturbed the earl seemed like the closing of the outer door, and he immediately started to the balcony, and looked over, to endeavour to ascertain if any body had entered or quitted the house. At first it was so dark, that he could not perceive anything ; but at last he could just observe, but very indistinctly, apparently, the forms of two men, who were running at a rapid rate along the high road which led from the house.

The earl was astonished at this circumstance ; for who could have had occasion to leave his mansion at such an unseasonable hour of the night ? Were they thieves ? And, even if they were, how could they have gained an entrance to the house, without alarming the family ; and, more particularly, without his hearing them, when his attention was so ready to catch the slightest sound ? Not at all satisfied, and knowing that all his domestics had retired to rest, the earl took up the lamp that was burning in his chamber, and leaving the place, he descended the stairs with silent steps, often looking back, and pausing to listen, not from any fear of encountering danger, but

" Conscience, which makes cowards of us all,"

was at work within him ; and particularly at that solemn hour, when all was so still and melancholy around him. In his progress, he two or three times suddenly paused, and trembled, for he almost imagined he heard some one groaning, and then his blood would turn cold, and the perspiration would stand upon his temples. At length ashamed of his weakness, he aroused himself, and holding the lamp above his head to facilitate his view, he proceeded to the hall, and ex-amined all the doors. The front door was bolted, and perfectly secure; but his suspicions were confirmed, when he found that a back door, which opened im-mediately upon a path that led round to the high road, was neither locked nor bolted.

Fearful that the house had been plundered, the earl was about to arouse his domestics, when a thought struck him, that probably the door had been left un-fastened in a mistake, and he therefore determined to examine the rooms below. He first, however, returned to his chamber, and brought with him a brace of pistols to defend himself, in case there should be any persons in the mansion, and then made his way to the lower apartments, where everything seemed to remain in the same state as when those who had the care of them had left.

Satisfied that thieves had not been in the house, the earl re-ascended to his own room. It was now past three o'clock, and day was beginning to break in at the windows; but Saib came not. The earl's uneasiness was most intolerable, and he formed a thousand vague conjectures as to the cause, which were rejected as soon as they occurred to him. At length, however, after racking his brain for nearly another hour, he concluded that Saib had determined to stop till morning, fearful that his return might be noticed by some of the domestics and their sus-picions aroused. Tired with thinking, Fitzosbert threw himself upon his couch, and sought to woo the drowsy god. He soon fell into a sound sleep, but it was unrefreshing to him, for his imagination was disturbed by frightful visions, the nature of which may be easily imagined.

He awoke not until the middle of the day, when he hastily arose, and ringing his bell, ordered the servant who attended, to desire Saib to come to him in his chamber immediately. The man went away to fulfil these orders, and quickly returned and informed his master that Saib was nowhere in the house, neither had he been seen by any one that morning. A chilling presentiment of something wrong darted through the mind of Fitzosbert on hearing this, and he abruptly ordered the man to quit the room, for fear he might notice his emotion: he arose from his couch in a state of anxiety which we will not attempt to describe, and descended to the breakfasting room.

" Where is your lady, Miss Rosina ?" inquired the earl, when he perceived that she was not in the apartment.

" I have not seen her this morning, my lord, replied the female attendant to whom he had addressed himself.

" Not seen her this morning !" reiterated Fitzosbert ; " this is strange !—Send her waiting-woman to me immediately."

The servant left the apartment to obey the order of her master, who arose from his chair, folded his arms, and traversed the room in the utmost state of agitation. In a few minutes the girl returned, and informed him that Patty was nowhere to be found, and that the chamber of Rosina was entirely deserted !

" Liar !" cried the earl, furiously, " it is a vile plot among the lot of ye, to dis-tract my brain !" and pushing the servant rudely away from him, Fitzosbert hur-riedly quitted the apartment, and rushed up the stairs towards the chamber of Rosina. There he found a confirmation of the servants statement ; the room was empty, and the bed had evidently never been entered the night before. Casting his eyes eagerly around the chamber, he observed on the dressing-table a note. He snatched it up; it was addressed to himself; and tearing it open, he read as follows :—

"Your tyranny has driven me to this; I have followed the dictates of my own free will; expect not to see me again, until I shall no longer be subject to your power. "ROSINA."

Scarcely had the earl perused these lines, which convinced him that the two persons that he had heard quit the mansion were Rosina and her attendant, when two or three of the men whom he had a short time before sent to make inquiries after Saib, returned and made him acquainted with what had transpired at the house of Mat Marlinspike, and the manner in which the ruffian Saib had been disposed of.

"Confusion !" cried the earl, clasping his temples, "Rosina fled !—My trusty Saib trepanned ! There is some infernal spell upon me !"

PART II.—AFLOAT.

"The hardy sailor braves the ocean,
    Fearless of the raging wind;
Yet his heart with fond emotion,
    Throbs to leave his love behind."—DIBDIN.

IT was night, and Gallant Tom and several of his shipmates had gathered together in the fore peak, and were quaffing their grog as cheerful as possible. The sea was right in the *eyes* of the vessel, and the dashing of the waves against the bends on the outside, as it was divided by the keelson, had a melancholy, moaning sound. In a remote corner of the place, and apart from the rest of the men, were seated Rosina and Patty. They both looked pale and fatigued; but there was an expression in the beautiful eyes of the former as they rested upon the handsome and manly countenance of Tom, which plainly told how truly her heart was devoted to him, and how ready she was to suffer any inconvenience, to expose herself to any danger, to be near him, to gaze upon him, to hear the tones of his voice, and witness his generous and gallant conduct.

Many were the rude remarks to which the heroic girls had been subjected since they had been on board the vessel, and often was their secret near being betrayed. Sometimes the observations made by some of the men, conveyed to them an idea that their real characters were discovered; and at such times they would blush and tremble with such evident confusion, that it was a wonder they did not beray themselves. And then the arduous duties they had to perform, so opposite to their sex, were sufficient of themselves to make the strongest minds sink under it. But, no; although often exhausted and ill, Rosina and her faithful attendant went to their hammocks, and bore up against it with a fortitude that was truly wonderful.

But, although Tom frequently joked with them on their delicacy and weakness, his remarks were never characterised by that coarseness which his shipmates indulged in ; and when he saw them go awkwardly about anything, he would seem to feel a pleasure in assisting them, and shewing them the right way to do it.

In such moments as these, she could scarcely restrain her feelings ; and often was she on the point of throwing herself on her knees to him, confessing her love, and disclosing to him her real sex, and the cause that had prompted her to undertake so hazardous a step.

" But, then," she reflected, " should I indeed acknowledge my ardent passion, would he return it ? Could I ever have the power to estrange his heart from his beloved Ellen ? Would he not despise me for attempting to win his affections from that poor girl, whose whole happiness is centered in him, and who now mourns his absence with incessant anguish ? Oh, yes, I feel he must, and that I should deserve it. Rash, foolish girl that I have been, to enter on this wild, hazardous, and indelicate adventure. But, yet will I bear every inconvenience, endure any anguish willingly without a murmur, to be near him to whom I feel my very soul cling with impassioned fondness !"

Often when she heard him speak of those he had left behind, and in ardent terms which bespoke his sincerity of pretty Ellen, calculated upon the months, days, nay, hours, which it was likely would intervene before they should meet again, a pang shot through her heart which she found it impossible to suppress.

Strange it was that a passion so ardent and sincere should engraft itself in the heart of a female so differently circumstanced, and who might have had wealthy admirers at her feet, for the plain, simple, but honest tar. But love knows no distinction. When she thought about the terrible conflict in which they would soon be engaged, and that Tom might be one of those gallant fellows destined to fall, her heart sunk within her ; and many a time she tossed restless about in her hammock ; while the weary sailor slept soundly, regardless of the ocean's roar, she would offer up the most fervent prayers to Heaven for his preservation.

The ruffian, Saib, having promised to behave himself and do his duty, had been set at liberty in the ship soon after it had left Plymouth ; but he was watched narrowly, and with eyes of suspicion by all the sailors, especially Gallant Tom, who carefully kept Richard from his clutches, fearful that the dark spirit which had before prompted him to seek his life, might lead him to perpetrate it now, in spite of the consequences that must follow.

But though the black promised to obey, it was evident he still nurtured the demon in his heart, and only wanted an opportunity to be revenged upon those who had been the cause of placing him in his present situation.

How Rosina shuddered whenever she encountered this hateful being, fearful that he would recognise her, even beneath the disguise she had assumed. Frequently, too, he had made a full stop when they had met upon deck, and fixed his large and ferocious-looking eyes upon her countenance, as though he had some recollection of her features ; and it was with difficulty she could find nerve sufficient to confront him, and prevent her betraying herself to him.

" Push about the grog, my hearties," observed Tom, as he quaffed off a stiff allowance with perfect ease; "this is what I call a snug party; and, damme, I dare be bound to say a bolder set of lads are not to be found in the British fleet!"

"Well said, Tom," observed a rough-looking tar, with an immense quid crammed into his jaw, and swelling out his cheek as if he was troubled with a violent tooth-ache; "there's not a chicken heart in this vessel, I think;—if I thought there was, shiver my timbers, if I wouldn't make one to toss him over-board as food for the sharks!"

"Fear!" said Tom, contemptuously; "who ever heard of such a thing in the British Navy, I should like to know? Why, lor' bless yer, courage comes as natural to us, as A, B, C. To be sure, we all feel a little strange and qualmish like, when we first go out; and that's how it is with Joe Gordon (the name Rosina had assumed) and his cousin, I suppose. Though they are willing lads, they are much too tender and delicate for sailors. I have often thought, that if they were put into petticoats, they would make two capital milliners, or dress-makers.—Here, my lads, drink; don't sit moping there, like a tar upon six-water grog! If you will only place yourselves under my care, bless your souls, I shall make you quite accomplished in no time. You must bustle about when we tackle the Mounseers, I can tell you: no skulking in the midst of a battle; the French swabs do not turn tail easy.—However, we are the chaps that can do it for them :—

> "'British sailors have the knack,
> Haul away, yeo, boys!
> Of hauling down a Frenchman's Jack,
> Haul away, yeo, boys!'"

We need not attempt to describe the confusion of Rosina and Patty during this speech; and they could almost imagine they beheld the eyes of the sailors fixed upon them with suspicious scrutiny; and that Gallant Tom, from the insinuations he was constantly throwing out, was perfectly well aware of their real sex. How-ever, Rosina knowing that the eyes of all the sailors were watching her, aroused herself as much as possible, and, smiling upon Tom, she placed the grog to her lips, pretended to drink heartily, and afterwards remarked,—

"You are right, Tom; it is natural for a person to feel strange and timid on their first cruise, especially when he has before mingled in scenes very different, which me and my cousin Ben, here, have. But we shall wear the rust off in time, no doubt; only wait till we encounter the enemy, and you shall find that if we want to learn how to be sailors, we want no one to teach us how to fight!"

"Bravo, Joe!" exclaimed Tom, giving the white and delicate hand of Rosina a hearty smack; "damme, you will turn out nothing but a good sort after all, I'll be bound. As for my protogee, little Dick, he is a perfect wonder in his way;—he takes it nat'ral, to be sure, and in course that's quite another thing. Besides, now, I dare say you have left some one that you love—nay, don't blush like a maid : there is no harm in owning one's feelings, when they are not wrong; and, I dare say, if you speak the truth, you will own that there is one you love, and—"

"Yes, there is, indeed, *one* that I love, even dearer than my own life!" inter-rupted Rosina, energetically; "but that *one* is unconscious of the passion it has created."

"Oh, oh!" observed Tom, with a sly wink, "a little bit of secret bus'ness, eh? Now, splice my timbers, some how or the other, I do like to hear you talk; there is something so sweet in your voice, that—I was going to say, only you are a man—reminds me so of my pretty Ellen; bless her heart, I'll be bound she is even now breathing a prayer to heaven for the safety of him, whom she knows loves her so dearly!" .

"But the sailor is exposed to many temptations, Tom," said Rosina, timidly. "In foreign climes, fresh faces meet his gaze, and those he has loved may be obliterated from his heart in the contemplation of them.—Even so, may you not forget your Ellen?"

"Forget my Ellen! my pretty, kind, and faithful Ellen!" exclaimed Tom, indignantly: "damme, Joe, if—if it had been any one else that had dared to hint at such a thing, and I thought he meant it, I—I—but, what a fool I am making of myself! Don't you see, youngster, I don't mind any subject but that; but, if any lubber dare to doubt my constancy to that dear girl, he must prove himself to be a better man than Tom Mainstay, or repent of his boldness.—Hallo! Dick, what's the matter with you? Where have you been, and why do you stand there, holding out these signals?"

"Quick! follow me, cautiously, all of you, or in five minutes we shall be in eternity!" said the boy.

Struck by the earnestness of Richard's manner, Tom started upon his feet in a moment, and followed by the rest of the sailors, obeyed the wishes of the boy, wondering what could be the meaning of his strange behaviour. Richard hurried on, with noiseless steps, and led the way to the powder magazine, the door of which was open, and Tom, being the first, peeped in, and was thunderstruck, when he beheld the villain, Saib, brandishing a burning torch in his hand, and approaching a cask, the lid of which was knocked off. Tom caught the expression of the black fellow's eyes, and he could see they were bloodshot with rage and the terrible revenge he was about to take. A moment he stood over the cask, and then laughed with fiendish malice.—

"This moment decides all!" he cried. "The black man never is insulted without having ample revenge: they have dared to tear me from my home, and thus, thus, do I——"

"Hold! you infernal black swab!" cried Gallant Tom, as he rushed upon Saib, and grasping him with Herculean strength by the throat, thwarted him in his demoniacal purpose. "For this, your black carcase shall dance a hornpipe upon nothing, for the amusement of the sea-gulls!"

The eyes of Saib rolled wildly and fiercely in their sockets, as Gallant Tom wrenched the torch from his hand, and the rest of the sailors secured him.

"Fiends of hell!" he cried, "seize upon he who has been the cause of thwarting me in my well-laid scheme of vengeance! But for this, and the black man would have immolated ye all in one scene of terrible destruction, and your dissevered limbs would have filled the air! Oh! curses light upon the wretch who has caused this!"

"Throw the black shark overboard, immediately!" shouted a dozen voices.

"Aye, overboard with me, if ye like!" exclaimed Saib. "Think not I tremble at death! no; I scorn, despise you all, and would willingly have sacrificed my own life, could I have accomplished my revenge at the same time—base, despicable, detested Christian reptiles!"

"Pluck out the black villain's tongue by the roots!" cried one of the sailors; "no tortures that we can inflict can be terrible enough to punish him for the fiendish crimes he would have committed."

"Avast! avast! messmates," observed Tom; "monster as he is, we must not take his punishment upon ourselves; he must be properly tried; and, fear not, but that he will meet with the fate he so richly merits. Away with him to confinement; and then let our officers know of the frightful charge we have against him."

"Ha! ha! ha!" laughed the wretch, scornfully; "do with me as you please; tear me limb from limb; cut the flesh from my bones piecemeal; torture me in any way that you can think of, and ye shall not hear a groan escape my lips! The black man mocks torment; he laughs at death; he is callous to pain;—my last wish shall be a curse upon ye all! Now, then, bear me to your tortures! But," he continued, as he fixed a look of demoniacal hate upon Richard, "could I only wreak my vengeance in the blood of that brat before I die—for he, I feel, has been the occasion of this—I could meet my fate with exultation!"

"Drag him hence!" exclaimed Tom; "we will not listen to his unnatural ravings—away with him!"

The sailors gave a simultaneous shout as they dragged the monster away: and Gallant Tom, accompanied by Richard, who had been the fortunate means of saving the vessel, and the whole of the crew from destruction, hastened to communicate the particulars to the officers. It would be impossible to describe the praise which was bestowed upon Richard for his intrepidity, which had saved the vessel and the lives of so many human beings from destruction, or the universal feeling of disgust and horror, which was excited against the villain, Saib. No time was lost in bringing him to that punishment he had incurred, and his fate was quickly decided.

The next morning all hands were piped upon deck, and the wretch, Saib, was brought forth, heavily fettered, to receive his sentence. He stood unmoved; his large eyes gleaming fiercely, alternately upon the officers and those men who had detected him in his diabolical attempt.

"Haul up the old shattered long boat," said the captain.

The boat was lugged on to the deck of the vessel in a moment, and every eye was fixed upon the captain, in painful suspense. He paused for a second or two, and turned and spoke in an under tone to the officers, who bowed their heads as if assenting to what he said.

"Bind the villain hand and foot in the boat!" exclaimed the captain, "and commit him to the mercy of the waves:—thus do we punish the miscreant, who would have sacrificed the lives of so many of his fellow-creatures!"

There was a slight murmur of satisfaction from part of the crew on this sentence being announced; but it was quickly stifled in the solemnity of the moment, and the awfulness of the punishment they were about to inflict upon the hardened wretch. But a smile of contempt passed over his sable features, when he heard it, and he resigned himself to the hands of the sailors without a word. Another minute, and he was bound securely in the boat, and then another pause ensued, and the sailors looked earnestly at their officers, as if uncertain, and hesitating how they should act.

"Overboard with him!" cried the captain, "and the Lord have mercy on his soul!"

A death-like silence followed: the boat containing the unhappy wretch was dragged to the side of the vessel, and let down with ropes; a second only, and there was heard a loud splashing in the water, and directly afterwards (a strong gale of wind blowing at the time) the boat was seen dashing on amidst the rolling billows, with the most impetuous fury, until it became a speck, and was seen no more. At this juncture, a piercing shriek was heard, which made every person present start, and look around them with astonishment.

"What noise was that?" demanded the captain, hastily.

No one answered; and the sailors seemed to be looking upon each other with mute astonishment. That shriek was uttered by Rosina, who, after the appalling sight she had just witnessed, was so much overcome, that it was a matter of astonishment she did not betray herself. Fortunately, Patty, who did not lose her self-possession, was by her side at the time, and before they could be observed, hurried her from the deck.

PART III.—THE BATTLE OF THE NILE.

It was on the 1st of August, 1798, that the Vanguard discovered the French fleet at anchor in the bay of Aboukir, in line of battle, which was instantly communicated by signal, with their numbers. All was bustle and eagerness immediately among the British, and none displayed more anxiety for the contest than Gallant Tom. He breathed a prayer for a blessing on his dear Ellen, kissed her miniature, and then hastened to give some instructions to little Richard. But, how shall we attempt to describe the situation of Rosina and Patty? Much as the former dreaded and shuddered at the scene of carnage and bloodshed of which she was shortly to be a witness, and to mingle in, her principle anxiety was for him for whom she had ventured so much. Many were the prayers she breathed to heaven to protect him in the deadly strife, or that if it had destined that he should fall, she might not be suffered to survive him.

The Admiral having hauled his wind, was followed by the whole of the British fleet with the greatest alacrity, The signal was made to prepare for battle: and it was made known that it was the admiral's intention to attack the enemy's van and centre as they lay at anchor, according to a plan which he had sometime before communicated to the captains of his squadron. The admiral's idea in this disposition of his force was, first, to secure the victory, and then to make the most of it, as circumstances would permit. A bower cable of each ship was immediately got out abaft, and bent forward. The fleet, carrying sail, and standing in close line of battle for that of the enemy's, which appeared to be moored in a strong and compact line of battle, close in with the shore, their line describing an

obtuse angle in its form, flanked by numerous gun-boats, four frigates, and a battery of guns and mortars on an island in their van.

The position of the enemy presented the formidable obstacles; but the heroic Nelson viewed these with the eye of a seaman determined on attack; and it instantly struck his eager and penetrating mind, that where there was room for an enemy's ship to swing, there was room for one of his own to anchor.

At sunset, which was at thirty-one minutes past six, the deadly engagement commenced, with an ardour and vigour that British seamen had never before surpassed : soon it raged fiercely, and nothing could be heard but the tremendous roar of the cannon, the shouts of the sailors, and the groans of the dying. On both sides they fought bravely, and the slaughter was dreadful.

But where were the two adventurous females during this awful scene? They were compelled to keep their post; and every moment they expected would bring to them the herald of death.

As well as her eyes could penetrate through the dense smoke, poor Rosina watched the object of her affection; and one moment her heart sunk with horror as she beheld him exposed to the most imminent danger, and expected to see him stretched a bleeding corse on the deck; while the next, it swelled with gratitude and hope, as she beheld him released from his perilous position, and, apparently, sheltered from harm.

About seven o'clock, total darkness came on ; but the whole hemisphere was, at intervals, illuminated by the fire of the hostile fleets. The battle now raged with unremitting fury. In less than twelve minutes, *Le Guerrier*, the van-ship of

No. 4.

the enemy, was dismasted; and in ten minutes after, the *Conquerant* and *Le Spartiate*, the second and third ships, shared the same fate. At half-past eight, *L'Aquillon* and *La Souverain Peuple*, the fourth and fifth ships in the enemy's line, were taken possession of by the British. Victory evidently fought on the side of our lion-hearted tars.

Suddenly, there was a hollow cry on board the ship to which our hero belonged, and which quickly passed through the whole of the fleet, that the French admiral's ship was on fire; and soon the flames were seen to issue from the after part of the cabin with such rapidity, that the whole after-part of the ship was soon involved in flames. About ten o'clock, *L'Orient* blew up with a terrible explosion. It was a dreadful sight. An awful pause, and death-like silence for about three minutes ensued, when the wreck of the masts, yards, &c., which had been carried to a vast height, fell down into the water, and on board the surrounding ships. Just at this dreadful moment, a loud scream sounded in Tom's ears, and, turning suddenly round, Rosina fell bleeding into his arms. She had been struck on the head by a portion of one of the masts of the unfortunate *L'Orient*, and had become completely insensible, and apparently dying.

Anxious to know to what extent the supposed youth was injured (for he had become attached to him since he had been on board), Tom bore the insensible Rosina to a place of security, and raising her in his arms, unbuttoned the collar of the shirt he wore, to give him air; but who shall attempt to describe his astonishment and emotion, when he discovered the beautiful alabaster skin, and gracefully moulded neck of a female? He could scarcely credit the evidence of his senses. Again he looked: he parted the hair from her temples, and he was then not only convinced that it was a woman, but one of the loveliest creatures he had ever seen before.

"Poor girl! poor girl!" said the honest tar, as he gazed on her pallid features, and re-arranging her dress, "what can have tempted you to this?—Some love affair, I'll venture my life. Well, well, God send that your magnanimity may be rewarded as it deserves; but, much I fear that you are summoned up alott. Well might I say, that she looked as delicate as a dressmaker, poor lass; but little did I suspect this. How lovely she looks, although so pale; almost as pretty as my Ellen. But, shiver my topsails, while I am thus talking, she is probably dying: let me hasten to get her assistance."

With these words, Tom threw the senseless maiden over his shoulder, and made the best of his way to the surgeon, under whose care he placed her, after having informed him of the singular discovery he had made. The news of this romantic adventure spread like lightning through the fleet, and the general astonishment was not a little increased, when her companion was also discovered to be of the same sex. The blow which Rosina had received, was not dangerous, and had merely stunned her; with the skilful treatment of the medical man, she was soon recovered, and found her maid, Patty, attending upon her; and her surprise and confusion may be easily imagined, when she was informed that their sex was known, and that the discovery had been made by him, to be near whom, she had assumed the disguise she did.

"Good God! what shall I do?—What can I say in excuse for this strange behaviour?" she ejaculated, when her and Patty were alone. "My real name and rank must be discovered; and what will be the suspicions they will entertain of my conduct?—What will he, too, think? Should he by any chance ascertain the motives that have stimulated me to this rash, this foolish act, will he not despise, detest, upbraid me, for seeking to obtain that heart which is already in the possession of another?—Yes, yes, he will, he must—I feel he must.

"Oh, no, Miss," ejaculated Patty, "you wrong the young man by such a thought; I know you do; he has too noble, too generous a mind to do as you say; he may pity, but can never hate or despise you."

"Alas!" returned Rosina, weeping, "how poor a reward will pity be for one who loves him with the fervour that I do; methinks I could rather endure his scorn. But, since it has come to this, I will no longer keep my unfortunate passion a secret locked within my own breast. No; to him I will impart the truth, unravel all my thoughts, and, having thus disburthened my mind, and thrown myself upon his generosity, what more will then be left me than to die?"

"Oh, my dear lady," exclaimed Patty, "do not talk so, it grieves me to hear you. Let us hope for the best, and happiness may yet be yours."

Rosina shook her head.

"Happiness!" she repeated; "oh! no, no, no; happiness will ne'er again be mine. Indeed, I have known but little from my childhood; and since the loss of my poor brother, my path has been one of thorns. There will be no peace for me but in the grave."

"Lor', Miss," observed Patty, "how you do talk! why, it is enough to make a person melancholy to hear you. But, do not give way to despair, for there is no knowing what Providence has in store for you, and——"

"Nay, my good girl," interrupted her mistress, "do not deceive yourself, nor think to deceive me; I know the goodness of your motives; but with me they must fail in having the effect you wish they should. However, I will no longer act the hypocrite: no; the object of my affection shall be made acquainted with the passion he has excited, let whatever may be the result."

The glorious battle was now over, and the immortal Nelson and his gallant men added largely to the laurels already upon their brows. Tom, who felt a deep interest in the fate of the female whom he had a second time rescued from death, for he soon became acquainted with her real rank and name, took the liberty of requesting an interview with her. Rosina complied with his desire immediately.

He found her seated alone in her cabin, and her face, which was very pale when he first entered, became suffused with blushes, as he looked compassionately upon her, and in a tone of more than usual gentleness, inquired after her health.

Rosina shook her head, sighed, and replied, "that she was as well as she could ever expect to be;" and, after having expressed her thanks to him for his kindness to her while she had been on board, she became silent, and her feelings were evidently undergoing a severe trial. Several times she looked at Tom, and tears trembled in her eyes: she tried to speak, but the words died away in her throat; she turned away her head, and hid her face in her handkerchief.

Tom felt embarrassed and confused at this strange behaviour, and fearing that his longer intrusion might be considered impertinent, he expressed his pleasure at finding that she was getting better, and was about to leave the place, when Rosina, aroused by his actions, rushed suddenly forward, with convulsive emotion, and throwing herself at his feet, clasped his knees, and exclaimed,—

" Do not leave me thus !—nay, you shall not go, until I have made you acquainted with my weakness, and revealed to you the unhappy wretch my headstrong and ungovernable passion has rendered me !"

The honest tar was completely thunderstruck ; he could scarcely believe that he was awake. Then he thought that Rosina was suffering under the effects of madness from the blow she had received. The earnestness of her manner deeply affected him ; and, raising her from her knees, he led her towards a chair, and retiring respectfully at a short distance, he begged her to inform him in what manner he could assist her.

" Nay," exclaimed the distracted damsel, " do not look so coldly upon me ! I know I have done wrong to encourage this unhappy passion, when I knew that your heart was engaged to another : but, still let me not hear that you hate me, and I will endeavour to be content. If you really love the fair maiden you have left behind, you can feel for me, and will know how powerful, how irresistible, is a sincere affection."

Tom looked confused and incredulous ; he twisted his hat in his hand, held down his head, blushed like a maid, and scarcely knew what to say. As for Rosina, she appeared to be more composed, and perfectly prepared to hear his answer. She had divulged the secret which she had so long (with the exception of Patty) confined to her own bosom : she had confessed it to the object who had inspired that passion, and she felt as if a heavy burthen had been removed from her heart. She looked at Tom, and perceiving his embarrassment, fixed upon him a glance of the deepest affection, and said,—

" Think not wrong of me for making this disclosure, or that I have overstepped the bounds of female modesty by so doing. Alas ! love, such as I feel, admits of no such restrictions as would bind the tongue. Yes, I repeat, I love you ; that for your sake I assumed this disguise ; to be near you, I braved all the perils of the ocean, the terrors of the battle ; and, even now, would I willingly make any sacrifice, could I obtain a return of the affection I entertain for you : but, no ; it must not be ; your heart is already engaged, and I do the poor girl wrong by——. Oh, Tom, for by that familiar name I must for once be permitted to call you, from the moment I was saved from an untimely death by your bravery, my heart has throbbed towards you ; but it is no common passion that has moved it ; it is a mysterious, an indescribable love, which but increases in strength the more I attempt to vanquish it."

" I ask pardon, Miss," said the honest, plain spoken tar, who still continued to twirl his hat upon his thumb ; " yer see, th' fact o' th' matter is this—I—I—I mean to say, that I am not much used to fine palaver, and, therefore, cannot make you such a reply as I ought. You do me a great honour by th' good opinion you are pleased to have of me, and I'm sorry you should have been put to such an inconvenience in consequence : as for loving me, why, you know, Miss, the difference of our stations would forbid me to encourage any idea of returning it, even if my pretty Ellen did not present a still greater obstacle. I am only a poor sailor, with no other fortune than a strong arm, a willing heart, and a clear conscience ; while you, a lady, and——"

" Oh, what is rank—what is fortune?" ejaculated Rosina, fervently ; " I value them not. But, enough of this ; I have relieved my mind, and I appeal to your honour not to betray the confidence I have reposed in you."

" Betray you, Miss!" cried Tom, emphatically ; " never !—I would suffer myself to be hauled up to the yard-arm first. Nay, more, Miss, if the friendship, the esteem of a humble being like me, should be considered of any value by you, rest assured that they are yours ;—indeed, that I will love you as a brother."

" A brother!" reiterated Rosina, and tears filled her eyes. " Ah! I had a brother once, a kind, a gentle brother,—I lost him in his childhood !"

" Did he then die, Miss?" inquired Tom, whose interest and curiosity were excited

" No ; he did not," answered Rosina ; " he disappeared in a most mysterious manner, and I have heard no tidings of him since."

" And how long, say you, is it since this occurred ?" inquired Tom, eagerly.

" As near as I can recollect, it is about eighteen years since," answered Rosina ; " but I can recall the features of my poor brother, as clearly to my memory, as if I had gazed on them but yesterday. It was the strong likeness which you bear to that lost brother, which first drew my heart towards you, and——"

" This is strange !" interrupted Tom. " I was stolen from my home, when a boy, by gipsies, from whom I afterwards escaped, and having lost all clue to my friends, I entered on board a ship, and have been ploughing the waves ever since."

" But, had you a sister ?" demanded Rosina, breathlessly.

" I had," answered Tom : " I can well remember her ; she was a pretty blue-eyed girl, like a little fairy, of whom I was fond, and used to take such a pride in gathering for her all the fancy shells and pebbles on the sea-beach. Many a time has that sweet child haunted my imagination, and——"

" Was your father living when you were stolen away ?" asked Rosina, as a strange, indefinite feeling came over her.

" He was ; a fisherman was his calling ; and, though it becomes me not to speak ill of him that gave me being, he was such a morose, harsh, and cruel man, that neither me nor my sister could love him."

" His name ?—quick ! quick ! for Heaven's sake !" gasped forth Rosina.

" Will Brandon !" replied the astonished Tom.

Rosina uttered a scream of astonishment and joy, and threw herself into the arms of Tom.

" Merciful God !" she exclaimed, " Thy ways are wonderful !—My brother !—my long lost brother !"

It would be utterly impossible to describe the astonishment and agitation of Tom, as he held the beauteous Rosina to his bosom, she having fainted, and remembered the words she had uttered. He parted the silken locks, from her pale temples, gazed steadfastly upon her countenance, and scrutinized minutely its every lineament ; and, as he did so, he felt as it were his heart bound towards her, and he was convinced that they were as nearly related as she had mentioned. His emotion became excessive ; he sought to arouse her to sensibility, called her sister, and pressed his lips upon her cheek with all the fervour of brotherly love.

" Yes, it must be so," he cried, as he gazed upon the pale countenance of the insensible maiden ; " my heart tells me that the poor lass has spoken correctly.

and that she is the same dear sister with whom I have so often frolicked in child-hood, and whose innocent smile I can never forget. Ah! there is the same fairy locks, the beautiful mild blue eyes, the—the—oh, shiver me! I am so ove joyed I don't know what to do with myself. SISTER!—Damme, I could repeat the name a thousand times, I am so fond of it. And, then, to think that the dear girl should feel such an instinctive affection for me, and to expose herself to so many dangers to be near me, while I was so blind and so silly that I did not know her—it seems to be impossible! My eyes! here will be a tale to tell old Mat and my pretty little Ellen ;—that—that—I have got a sister !—that I am rich ; and that—splice my timbers, if my Nell sha'n't ride in her carriage, and have servants to wait upon her !"

Here the honest tar was so overcome by the power of his feelings, that in spite of all his manly efforts to the contrary, he could not help weeping upon the pallid cheek of his newly discovered sister.

" But, what a fool I am to stay here, with my pumps at work, and she is, per-haps, dying !" he suddenly ejaculated, dashing the tears from his eyes, raising her in his arms, and putting his ear to her lips, to ascertain whether or not the dear object of his care and anxiety still breathed. " Poor girl ! I do think it would break my heart if you were to be taken from me, just as you have discovered that you have a brother living to protect and love you. The more I look upon her coun-tenance, the stronger my heart warms towards her, and methinks I see *sister* stamped upon every feature. Dear, dear, girl!—But, avast ! this will not do; I am ashamed of myself; I shall become a child again in a few moments, if I do not put a stop to it."

As Gallant Tom gave utterance to these words, he placed the insensible form of Rosina carefully over his shoulder, and bore her hastily into a cabin, where he placed her under the care of a female and the doctor ; but would not leave her until he was satisfied that there was no fear of her recovery, and that her feelings, being overcome by the sudden surprise, had caused her merely to swoon. Tom then pressed two or three more ardent kisses on her lips, and departed to his duty.

Tom had scarcely got upon deck, when he was startled by loud cries, and upon inquiring the cause, he was horror-struck to learn that the boy, Richard, had that moment accidentally fallen overboard, and had disappeared beneath the waves. Like a madman, Tom rushed forward, and inquired the spot where his *protegé* had fallen ; but ere the answer could be given, he saw him rise upon the crest of one of the billows, and, without waiting an instant for consideration, the heroic tar sprang overboard, and, catching hold of the jacket of the boy, almost immediately afterwards sunk with him under the waves.

The persons who had watched the action of the intrepid Tom, which was all the work of a moment, and done before they had time to render any assistance, which they might otherwise have done, were in a state of the most dreadful suspense, fearful that he would perish in his brave attempt to save the life of Richard ; but, ere they could take any steps to rescue them, Tom was seen to rise again on the waves, with the senseless body of the boy held firmly under his arm, while, with the other hand, he made a desperate effort to reach the boat, which had been lowered ; it was a narrow chance ; another moment, and the gallant fellow must have sunk exhausted, when the boat fortunately was drifted towards him; he caught hold of it by the gunnel, and succeeded in getting into it, with the boy. The sailors set up a loud shout of joy, when they beheld their esteemed messmate in safety, and immediately assisted them both upon deck.

Richard was insensible with his immersion in the water, and Tom was quite exhausted with the exertions he had undergone. However, the former was put to bed, and being immediately attended upon by the doctor, was soon pronounced to be out of danger; while the latter speedily recovered, and, after changing his clothes, and swallowing a glass of good stiff grog, he declared that he was as well as ever he had been in his life, and overwhelmed with joy to think he had so fortunately succeeded in saving the life of Richard.

Rosina had regained her senses, and acquainted Patty with the wonderful discovery she had made, whose astonishment, as may be naturally expected, exceeded all bounds. She, however, was strictly enjoined by her mistress to keep it a profound secret, until her and Tom had consulted what was the best plan to adopt. When the poor girl was informed of his late adventure, and his perilous escape, her emotions were strongly excited, and she returned thanks to Providence for his preservation, with the most unfeigned earnestness.

Tom sought the earliest opportunity of seeing Rosina again, and their meeting was of the most affectoinate description. They hung around each other's neck, and mentally breathed a prayer of thanks to Omnipotence, who had so miraculously brought them together again, after they had been so long separated, and vowed that no power on earth should part them again. If anything had been wanting to confirm the truth of Tom's being the brother of Rosina, two peculiar marks on his left wrist did away with every doubt; besides, the name of the man who had brought them up, the place where they had lived, and the different scenes which they had been in the habit of rambling to, and which Tom perfectly well recollected, did away will all possible suspicion.

Rosina related all that had happened to her since Tom's abduction, to which he listened with the utmost surprise, more especially when he learned that Will Brandon was not their father, and that their real parent was wealthy and noble. But his heart throbbed with indignation, when she recounted to him the conduct of the Earl Fitzosbert towards her, and the presumptuous insolence of the wretch, Saib.

"The infernal shark!" exclaimed Tom, his eyes sparkling with rage; "let me but reach Plymouth again, and I will pull his house about his ears :—to dare to insult and ill-treat a woman, and that woman, my sister, too !—oh, damme, if I would not make mincemeat of his proud carcase!"

Rosina beheld with love and admiration the honest energy of her long lost brother; and, as she hung upon his neck, and looked into his features, all the happy days of childhood rushed into sunny vividness upon her memory, and she wept; but they were tears of joy she shed. Many were the earnest prayers or thanksgivings she offered up to Heaven for the miraculous preservation of her brother, who had twice been made the happy instrument of saving her from an untimely death.

To prevent the excitement that such an event would cause on board, and likewise the more securely to forward their designs as regarded the earl, it was determined between Tom and Rosina, that they should keep the discovery they had made, a secret, till after they had got on shore.

So singular were the events of the last few days, that Tom could scarcely persuade himself that it was not a dream. His heart was overflowing with gratitude to Omnipotence for the restoration of his sister ; and, if the idea of the alteration there would be in his circumstances made any impression on his mind, it was to fill him with delight, to think that he should be able to make his Ellen not only happy, but rich.

"Yes," cried the gallant sailor, as he pressed the likeness of his sweetheart to his lips, "if I were to become a prince, no other but you, my pretty Ellen, should become my bride. What care I for wealth, were it not to make you happy ?"

After giving vent to these sentiments, elated with joy, Gallant Tom joined his mates on deck, and laughed and joked with the merriest of them.

"That was an awkward fall, young Dick had," observed one of the sailors; " and had it not been for you, Tom, some shark would ha' made a meal on him to a certainty ;—if he meant to try his skill at diving, I think he might just as well have stayed to undress himself first, at any rate."

"Ah, Will Johnson was the chap to dive," remarked Ben Binnacle, a rough weather-beaten old tar, with one side of his jaws converted into a miniature mountain, with a huge quid of tobacco; "he was a surprising lad,—and such a one to jump ! Why, he used to think nothing of jumping from the maintop gallant yard into the sea, just for amusement."

"Lor' love yer, what's that ?—I could beat that myself," said Tom ; " why, when I was on board the Alexander, we had a man as would do that a dozen times a day, just for exercise ; and something else that would beat Will Johnson all to nothing."

"What was that, Tom," asked Ben.

"Why, he would jump back again, to be sure," answered the sailor.

"Ha ! ha ! ha !" laughed the sailors ; " well done, Tom ;—beat that if you can, Ben."

"Oh, I'm no use to Tom," answered Ben ; " when he does begin to throw the hatchet, he puts everybody else into the shade. But, here comes old ' Fiddler Sam,'—what do you say to a dance, my lads ?"

"Aye, a dance, a dance, my lads," cried Tom ; " and, as I am very merry, why, I don't mind giving you a bit of a jig by way of a beginning. Strike up, Sam, and go your hardest ;—

' For laughing, quaffing, dancing, fighting,
  Singing, loving I delight in ;
  Let old fools grow grave and sad,
  Damme, Gallant Tom's the lad !'

Off she goes, messmates !" and the merry sailor's feet moved like lightning in the fantastic mazes of a nautical hornpipe, which he danced with remarkable skill, to the no small delight of his companions, who afterwards joined him, and the scene became one of the most happy, since the battle in which they had so distinguished themselves.

PART IV.—ASHORE.

It was a beautiful evening; a refreshing breeze was wafted from the bosom of the deep blue ocean, and the crimson glow of the setting sun caught the white spray, and gave it the appearance of molten gold. Many a gallant vessel was floating in the port; and from their lofty mast heads, Union Jacks waved proudly and triumphantly in the air. The town of Plymouth presented an unusual scene of gaiety; people were moving to and fro, attired in their best clothes, and all the different public-houses were full of sailors, old and young; the fiddle was going merrily in many of them, while in others might be observed groups of old sailors, and anxious females, listening to one who was reading from the *Gazette*, the account of the Battle of the Nile. At the end of every sentence, the pride and delight of all present demonstrated itself in the most enthusiastic shouts: the females looked sadly on; mothers wept at the uncertainty of the fate of their sons, and young women trembled when they reflected that probably those they loved were among the slain.

"The Old Commodore" public-house, was more than usually thronged, and Mat Marlinspike and his dame had enough to do, to wait upon their numerous guests. As for Ellen, she was too deeply affected, and her heart was too heavy, to suffer her to take any part in the business; and she listened to the account of the engagement with feelings of terror and apprehension. When the grey-headed old veteran, who was reading the paper, came to "The Vanguard," and the number of the killed and wounded, she turned ghastly pale, and was obliged to lean for support against the porch.

"Come, come, Ellen," said her father, "don't be down-hearted; your lover may be safe enough after all; and, if not, he has met the death of a brave fellow, as many one has done before him."

"Oh, my dear father!" exclaimed Ellen, shuddering, "for Heaven's sake, do not mention that dreadful probability; it smites my heart with horror. If Tom is slain, my happiness will be at an end, and death would be a mercy to me."

"Do not despair, my dear girl; there are many chances and mischances for a man at sea," observed her father; "perhaps he may have been sent aloft; perhaps he is quite well; and mayhap he is wounded. I say, Nell, what would you say if your lover was to come back to you with a timber toe, one eye, or an iron hook instead of a hand?"

"Heaven preserve him from any such calamity!" exclaimed the damsel, fervently; "but, if he should come back maimed and disfigured as you have described, think you it would alter my sentiments towards him? Oh, no, no: although he might be frightful to look upon, in my eyes he would be all that he ever was; the same kind, the affectionate, the brave, the constant Tom; nay, if it be possible, I would love him still more ardently for his misfortunes."

"Well spoken, Nell; well spoken, my lass," said her father; "God send that your best wishes may be realized, for you are an honour to your sex, and every way worthy of becoming the happy wife of such a brave fellow as Gallant Tom. Richard, too—I wonder if he is safe? Oh, how anxious am I to see them both again. See, yonder goes the Earl Fitzosbert, looking as moody as usual. Since he has lost his worthy confidant, that black rascal, Saib, and the strange disappearance of his ward, Miss Rosina, together with her servant, Patty, he has become more stern than ever, and he looks upon everybody with an eye of suspicion, and seems if he could willingly cut all our throats. Well, let him enjoy his whim; there is no love lost, I reckon.—Coming, messmates."

With these words, Mat bustled into the house to attend upon his customers.

The Earl Fitzosbert stood for a few moments at some distance, with folded arms, and gazed upon the group. His brows were contracted, and the contemptuous curl of his lip, shewed the dark thoughts that pervaded his mind. He frowned, and walked slowly on in the direction of his house, with his eyes bent upon the ground, and seeming completely absorbed in his own gloomy meditations.

Vain had been all the endeavours of the earl to learn what had become of Rosina and her maid; and, after instituting inquiries for several months, and offering a large reward to any one who could give him any information upon the subject, he at length gave it up in despair. The account of the engagement brought the business more immediately to his mind. He wondered if Saib still lived, and if he would return to England: if he did, then would hope once more revive in his bosom, for he knew that the zeal of his faithful myrmidon would never rest, until he had discovered the retreat of Rosina, and placed her once more within their power.

It was about a month after the news of the Battle of the Nile had reached England, that the earl was seated in his study, when the door was suddenly thrown open, and his astonishment may be readily imagined, when Saib, in a sailor's dress, stood before him.

The earl started, and could scarcely believe the evidence of his senses, while Saib folded his arms, and stood gazing upon his master's demonstrations of astonishment in solemn silence.

" Is it possible !" at length, exclaimed the earl ; " and do I again behold Saib, my faithful Saib, or is it only some delusive vision ?"

" It is no vision, Earl Fitzosbert," answered the black, in his usual harsh, grating tones, " but the same Saib to whom you are so much indebted."

" Indebted !" repeated the earl, with a shudder, as the dark deeds of the past arose upon his recollection, and he could not help feeling a momentary sentiment of disgust at the wretch who could thus make a boast of his iniquities : but he stifled the feeling as well as he could, and soon forgot everything in the surprise he experienced at the unexpected re-appearance of his faithful myrmidon.

" This, indeed, affords me pleasure," said the earl ; " welcome once more to England. I much need your aid and counsel. But, tell me, whither have you been ?"

" I have a tale of wrongs to tell you," said Saib, " which will make your blood boil with rage to listen to : but the injuries that have been done me shall be amply avenged. Yes, now I once more tread this shore, nothing shall foil me in my designs. Let the Christian reptiles tremble ; they have aroused a spirit that will not rest until it has heaped destruction upon them all. I suppose you heard how I was trepanned on the night when I sought to rid you of that hated obstacle to your peace ?"

" I did," answered the earl.

" And yet you sought not to avenge the deed ?"

" On whom was my vengeance to fall, when those who had done the wrong were far away ?" demanded the earl.

" True," returned Saib ; " but the blackman's wrath would have led him to have wreaked his revenge upon all those who had in any way been connected with the objects of his hate ; and it shall do so yet, or may my arm wither from my body !"

The villain related the manner in which he had been frustrated in his diabolical attempt upon the life of Richard, and afterwards forced on board " The Vanguard." He continued :—

" I cannot describe to you sufficiently the passions of deadly malice and hatred that inhabited my breast ever afterwards. I exhausted all my execrations in breathing curses upon the heads of those who had been the means of placing me in such a situation, and was determined that I would have a dreadful and sanguinary satisfaction. But I was forced to dissemble, or I should have been kept in irons, and totally deprived of all power to put my wishes into execution. I, therefore, pretended to compunction, promised obedience to the rules of the vessel, and expressed contrition for what I had been guilty of. Need I tell you, how this tortured me ? I could endure no greater punishment, than even to shew the semblance of repentance towards those whom I only longed for an opportunity to sacrifice to my vengeance. But it had the desired effect ; the officers were deceived ; I was released from my fetters, and permitted to take my seaman's station in the ship. No sooner did I thus find myself at liberty, than my heart yearned to put my plans into execution. I watched my opportunity with the same vigilance as the Minerali does for his booty. But an infernal spell seemed to be upon me, and something always occurred at the very moment I was on the point of gratifying my wishes, to render my stratagem abortive. Yet was it not fear of detection that prevented me; no, I never calculated for a moment, to escape that punishment which the deed would entail upon me; but I was willing to lose my own life, could I but first witness the dying agonies of my victims, and be convinced that I did not fall for nothing. Several times, when the brat, Richard, was sleeping in his hammock, I have stood over him with gloating eyes, and been about to draw my knife across his throat, when I have heard the voices of some of the crew near me, and my arm has fallen nerveless by my side, I have concealed the murderous blade in my bosom, and fled from the spot. More than once I have stood behind that sailor, Gallant Tom, as he is vauntingly called, with my arm upraised, ready to bury my knife in his heart, when, at the very moment he has turned, and some others of the men have made their appearance, and my design has been rendered in a moment futile. These repeated disappointments drove me to madness and a state of ungovernable fury, and at last I determined, by one desperate effort, to immolate, not only those whom I had cause to detest, but myself, and the whole of the crew. To be brief, I resolved to set fire to the powder magazine, and blow the whole of them into the air."

Even the earl could not help shuddering as the villain, Saib, detailed the manner in which he made the diabolical attempt to destroy the vessel and her crew; and he unconsciously admired the interposition of Providence, by which means, it had been saved in so miraculous a manner. After a pause, during which it was evident, from the convulsive workings of the muscles of Saib's countenance, how great was the rage that struggled in his bosom, as he recalled to his memory this circumstance, and the punishment to which he was sentenced for it: he continued,—

"The wretches bound me hand and foot in their shattered boat, and consigned me to the mercy of the waves. As I was tossed like a straw, sometimes nearly to the clouds by the mountainous billows, and at others, buried deep in their foamy crests, I felt as though I had lost every feeling of humanity, and become a fiend. All the devil was raging in my heart, and I uttered the most terrible maledictions against the authors of my fate. Death, I knew, was inevitable; for, even if the boat should be able to battle with the fury of the ocean, I must die of hunger. Had my limbs been free, I thought I would at once end my tortures by plunging into the sea, and I wished that every wave would swallow me up. With the apparent nearer approach of death, my strength seemed to increase, and, after innumerable efforts, I succeeded in getting my arms at liberty. Of course, it was not long before I released myself from the ropes altogether; I stood upright in the boat, and, folding my arms, looked sternly around me upon the dark blue waves, on the surface of which I was whirled at a furious rate. I was about to take the fatal leap, when a sudden thought darted across my brain, and arrested my purpose. A voice seemed to whisper in my ear, that there was yet hope, and that I might still live for vengeance on the objects of my detestation. I resolved to make a violent struggle to save myself. But how?—Exposed in an open, crazy boat, with nothing but the ocean and the sky to be seen, and without any knowledge of whither the impetuous billows were driving me? For six hours was I tossed about in this manner, expecting every moment would be my last; at length the crazy vessel was swamped, and I found myself immersed in the ocean. I rose again upon the waves, and struggled hard for life. I saw a rock at no great distance from me, to which I endeavoured to make my way. After some difficulty, I succeeded in my design, and, weak and exhausted, clambered up the craggy side of the rock, until I reached its lofty summit. I gazed around me, and the scene presented nothing but despair to my eyes. The rock was entirely barren. Here, then, must I remain to starve : but, still the hope of future revenge sustained me. I crouched down in a hollow of the rock, and, completely worn out with fatigue, fell into a sound sleep. I must have slept many hours, for when I awoke it was quite dark, and the gnawings of hunger and thirst upon me were intolerable : but yet, though I several times approached the verge of the rock, with a determination to end my misery, some inscrutable power seemed to withhold me from my purpose. A deadly cold, like the icy grasp of death, was upon my limbs, and yet I felt my eyes like two red-hot balls of fire burning in their sockets.

" That night I passed in the same state ; the next day, hunger was so intense upon me, that I gnawed the flesh from my arm, and sucked with frenzied greediness the blood as it flowed from the wound. Suddenly, my eyes rested upon the white sails of a vessel, at no considerable distance, and which seemed to be approaching in the direction of the rock on which I stood. In a delirium of joy, at the hope of deliverance, I tore the shirt from my back, and, waving it over my head, shouted till I felt the blood rushing to my head with the exertion. The ship approached quickly ; at length they gave a signal that they saw me, and a short time afterwards they put off a boat, with three men in it, to my assistance. I could scarcely wait till the boat reached the rock, and was almost tempted to plunge into the water to swim to it. At length it reached me ; I was released, and conveyed safely on board It turned out to be a Spanish vessel. I told them that I had sailed in a trading vessel, which had been attacked by a pirate, who destroyed the captain and all the crew and passengers, I only escaping my fate by precipitating myself into the sea. The captain received me kindly, and conveyed me to the port to which he was bound, where I was turned adrift, penniless and helpless. What was I to do ?—I could not tamely lie down and perish. One night, I stopped a gentleman, and demanded his money. He resisted, and paid for it with his life. For this crime I was apprehended ; but I escaped from prison, and, after enduring the most dreadful privations, I contrived to get on board a vessel bound to England, in which I arrived but yesterday. Now, tell me, Earl Fitzosbert, has not your *slave* endured enough in his endeavours to serve his master ?"

When Saib had thus concluded his narrative, the earl remained silent for a few minutes, and appeared to be wrapped in deep rumination ; while the former folded his arms, and traversed the apartment, brooding over the facts he had first recited, and contemplating the means of gratifying his revenge. At length the earl broke the silence, and said,—

" Saib, you have, indeed, done much, for which I hope you will receive ample satisfaction; nor have I been without my share of trouble since you have been away. Rosina——"

"Ah! what of her?" interrupted the black, eagerly; "speak—tell me!"

"Immediately after you were taken away," replied the earl, "I missed Rosina, and her maid, Patty; and from that time, although my search has been most vigilant, I have not seen or heard anything of her!"

"Damnation!" exclaimed the enraged black, his eyes rolling fiercely in their sockets, and his broad chest heaving with the intensity of his feelings; "Rosina fled! my hopes crushed!—hark, you, Earl Fitzosbert, do not attempt to deceive me, for you know how much you have cause to dread me, and how little I care about risking my own life, to be revenged on those who do me wrong. This is a stratagem of your own, to avoid the fulfilment of the promise you made and swore to me.—You know where the girl is situated!"

"By heaven, I do not!" ejaculated the earl; "you wrong me, by such a supposition, Saib. But, even if Rosina was still in my power, you have not yet fulfilled your compact, and, consequently, have no claim upon her."

"Indeed!" sneered Saib; "so, this is your gratitude, Earl Fitzosbert, for all the risks I have run, the services I have rendered you? Well, well, I ought to have expected it; but, beware. Seek not to tamper with me, or to cross my expectations, or, by all the powers of evil, you shall repent it!"

"Oh! dare you threaten?"

"Dare I threaten!" repeated the black, with a contemptuous smile; "aye, and perform, too. Do you know, Earl Fitzosbert, that one word from me, would level all your present wealth and power with the dust, and place you—yes, you—upon the scaffold? Seek not to exasperate me, for, when I am once aroused, it is no easy matter to appease my wrath."

"Nay, my good Saib," said the earl, shuddering at his threats, and truckling with all the weakness of a child; "this is madness; *we* should not quarrel, who——"

"You know where the girl is concealed!"

' I swear to you, Saib—solemnly swear, that I do not!"

"And could no one in the neighbourhood afford you any information? Did no person see them on the morning of the flight?"

"Nobody. Indeed, it is a mystery which I have pondered over for hours, in a vain attempt to elucidate it. A note I will show you, was left behind by Rosina; but it gives no explanation."

"This is strange!" muttered the black, biting his lips, and pacing the room with hurried steps;—"but her fortune?"

"Is still in my power," replied the earl.

"'Tis well," said Saib, with a look of exultation; "at any rate, if the flight of the girl prevents you fulfilling one part of your agreement, the possession of her property enables you to perform the other."

"Her money is not at my disposal!" exclaimed the earl.

"'Pshaw!" cried the black, "you were not wont to be so nice about trifles!"

"Is she not out of my jurisdiction?"

"What of that?—Who is there to ask any questions about the appropriation of the money? If she should ever return to England, have you not an excellent plea in her clandestine flight, when she was placed under your protection?"

"We will talk more of this anon, Saib," said Fitzosbert; "at present, we must devote our whole attention towards the discovery of the retreat of the fugitive; and, now that I have the aid of your sagacity, I entertain a hope that we shall yet be successful."

"Well, be it so" said Saib; "but, say, have our foes returned to England yet?"

"They have not; but are expected every day," answered the earl."

"If those I hate have survived the bloody carnage," ejaculated Saib, "I will not rest until I have had a deadly revenge for what I have suffered!"

"And what of the boy, Richard, as they call him?" asked the earl.

"He shall not escape," returned the black; "the brat has became my bane, my spell, my curse. Did he not thwart me in my scheme of vengeance?"

"True; but is that your only motive for wishing to despatch him?"

"Why do you ask the question, when you know it is not?" returned Saib. "Do yo wish to retain the estates of Fitzosbert?"

"But do you still think that this boy is——"

"Your brother's son, Julian, the right heir to the proud earldom and estates of Fitzosbert. I am certain of it. Oft have I watched his countenance narrowly, and traced every lineament of his father's features, and almost fancied I could see the eyes of the murdered man beaming with an expression of reproach through his."

"This is a theme I like not to converse upon," said the earl, in a state of agitation; "we will postpone all farther conferrence upon the subject till to-morrow. You need refreshment; and when you have finished your repast, divest yourself of that apparel, and appear as you were wont to do."

"Aye," exclaimed Saib, as the earl quitted the room, "I will not only appear, but be what I have hitherto been, and, if possible, a more hardened villain! conscience—bah!—I do not understand the word!"

We will now leave the black to the discussion of his meal, and return once more to the honest inhabitants of "The Old Commodore."

At length the joyful news arrived, that such of the vessels as had returned after the engagement had reached Portsmouth; and there were many anxious hearts in Plymouth on that occasion, and many hopes, and doubts, and fears, lest those dear to them should not be among the number of those who had survived the battle.

"Cheer up, my lass, cheer up," said old Mat Marlinspike to his daughter, on the evening that they received this intelligence, as they were seated on the bench outside the house with the dame, "I feel confidant that those wel ove are quite safe, and that they will soon be with us : it is a strange thing, that I seldom make up my mind to anything in which I am afterwards disappointed."

"Heaven send that your prognostications in this instance, at any rate, may be realised!" ejaculated the dame.

Ellen responded to her prayer.

"Damme, how I long for the moment," said Mat, "to see our little Dick once more, and to hear from the lips of Tom how he has acquitted himself. I dare say he has grown apace ; and, as for Tom, wont he be able to give an account of this glorious victory? Come, come, I must not have any dull faces this evening, for I know that we shall have no occasion for sorrow."

But Ellen was not so sanguine as her father ; in fact, a melancholy presentiment tormented her mind, which she in vain endeavoured to shake off, and she longed, yet dreaded for the moment to arrive, fearful that her unaccountable forebodings might be verified.

All that night Ellen slept but little ; and when she did, dreams of the most perplexing description haunted her imagination. She arose at an early hour, and walked down to the sea-beach. Her eyes watched with the greatest interest the noble vessels in the port, and her thoughts were wholly occupied with the image of her lover. She was suddenly aroused from thought, by the sound of loud shouts of merriment ; and, on looking in the direction from whence they seemed to proceed, her heart leaped with joy and expectation, when she perceived a posse of sailors and females going towards her father's house.

With hurried steps, she made her way home, and looked anxiously among the group which had by that time assembled on the benches outside the house ; but the object of her search was not among them, and her heart sunk with despair. Mat, however, would scarcely allow the gallant fellows to seat themselves, before he sought the gratification of his curiosity.

" What ship, messmate ?" inquired he, of the first one to whom he could get an opportunity of speaking.

" The Vanguard," was the reply.

" Oh !" exclaimed Mat, " then, mayhap, you can tell us, whether Gallant Tom and Dick——"

" They are both safe and hearty, and on their way here by this time, I day say," answered the sailor.

Ellen uttered a scream of joy, and raised her head in thankfulness to heaven.

" Ah ! his sister, I suppose," said the sailor.

Some person whispered that it was Gallant Tom's sweetheart.

" Oh, no, no ; avast, there !" cried the man ; " that can't be, for didn't we leave Tom at Portsmouth with his sweetheart,—and precious loving they seemed together, too ; and, no wonder, either ; for, damme, she must be a woman every inch of her, or she would never have assumed the disguise of a man for the purpose of following him !"

A piercing shriek prevented the sailor from saying any more, and Ellen sunk insensible into the arms of her father.

" Good God !" cried Mat, in a tone of agony, " this intelligence, whether true not, has killed my poor girl !"

Mat Marlinspike bore the insensible form of his daughter into the house, and the dame, in a state of the utmost agitation, sought every means to restore her ; but for sometime all her efforts were ineffectual ; and when she did partially recover, her brain wandered, and, looking vacantly round the apartment, she exclaimed,—

" Where is he ?—the deceiver ! He dare not meet my gaze !—and she, too !— ah ! there she stands !—She mocks and laughs at me !—And now she presses her lips to his with all the fervour of impassioned fondness ! By Heaven ! I cannot

endure it! Do not hold me!—I will tear her from him!—he is mine; sworn to me in the face of Heaven!—Off!—off, I say!"

And, as the poor girl thus spoke, she struggled so violently, that it was with the utmost difficulty she could be held in bed. In this pitiable state she continued the whole of that day; but towards night she became more composed, and at length dropt into a tranquil sleep, in which she remained for several hours: when she again awoke, the delirium had entirely left her, and she was enabled to talk dispassionately upon the cause of her suffering. Her tears flowed fast, as she recalled the happy hours her and Tom had passed together, the many vows of constancy he had made to her, and the fond hopes and anticipations her sanguine and ardent imagination had formed. Those hopes, those anticipations, were now crushed for ever. The sun of her earthly happiness had set. Yet, still so fondly did her early passions cling around her, that she felt, although Tom's heart might be given to another, her's could never be estranged from him.

Her father tried hard to persuade her not to place any confidence in what the sailor had said, who, probably, only intended it for a joke, seeing the anxiety she had betrayed when he mentioned the name of her lover; but Ellen shook her head mournfully; and Mat himself, was too doubtful that the sailor had spoken the truth, to urge his opinion further: in fact, he had, after Ellen had been removed, questioned the man more particularly, and he related all the circumstances that had occurred on board the vessel, in the same manner as we have detailed them before, with the exception of the one important fact, that Rosina had discovered in Tom her long-lost brother; but with that, none were acquainted but themselves, and thus the inference the sailors had drawn, was a reasonable one. The companions of the man also confirmed his statement; and Mat, upon the testimony of so many, could not do otherwise than believe, although he could not yet reconcile it to his knowledge of Tom's honest and generous character, to think that he could so heartlessly abandon that girl, whom he had made such solemn protestations of affection to, for another; and he hoped that he would yet be able to give some satisfactory explanation of his conduct.

Willing as Ellen was, and anxious, also, to receive any idea that might palliate his conduct, she could not admit this hope into her mind:—the delay in his return, seemed more than all to confirm her worst surmises. Had his heart remained true, oh, how anxious would he have been to have flown to the object of his affections at the earliest opportunity. These thoughts racked the brains of the poor girl, and her tears flowed fast, more particularly as she took the handkerchief which Tom had given her at parting from her bosom, and gazed upon it. At that moment, the voice of one of the sailors, who were assembled below, singing Gay's beautiful ballad of Black-eyed Susan, met her ears, and the following verse particularly struck her:—

> " Believe not what the landsmen say,
>   Who'll tempt with doubts your constant mind;
> They'll tell you seamen, when away,
>   In ev'ry port a mistress find.
> Oh, yes, believe them when they tell you so,
> For thou art present wheresoe'er I go!"

" No, no, dear Tom," cried the poor girl, bursting into a paroxysm of tears, " I will not believe you are false, until I hear the confirmation from your own lips; I will not do you the injustice to suppose you capable of acting with such heartless deception towards her to whom your vows have been so often, so fondly plighted. It was very wrong for me to entertain such a suspicion for a moment;—it was cruel, it was ungenerous."

Thus did Ellen endeavour to soothe the violence of her thoughts, and once more to engender hope in her bosom; and she succeeded better than could have been expected; so well, in fact, that she was enabled to leave her bed the same day, and appeared to be perfectly firm and composed.

The day passed away, and still Tom or Richard did not return. Mat and his wife became very uneasy, and began to think that the sailor had either deceived them, or was mistaken, and that they had both fallen in the engagement. It would be impossible to do adequate justice to the sufferings of the good old couple, as this idea darted across their imagination; but they took especial care to conceal their fears from Ellen, whose life, they felt convinced, would yield to the shock.

In the meantime, Tom and Richard, with Rosina and Patty, had been in the vicinity of " The Commodore" for the last two days; but until they had finally arranged the important business which occupied their minds, and Rosina had been placed in a secure retreat for the present, Tom judged it prudent not to make his appearance to his friends, notwithstanding he was so anxious to see them. They had imparted the secret of their consanguinity to Richard, but strictly enjoined him to silence.

At length, Rosina succeeded in getting apartments in the house of a lady with whom she was acquainted, and upon whose friendship she could depend, and then Tom, with a heart full of hope and extacy, hastened towards the residence of her on whom his very soul doated, accompanied by Richard.

"Hilly yeo! hilly yeo!" shouted the elated tar, when he reached the door, and gave it two or three hearty knocks with his fist; "house! house! The pretty Ellen, ahoy! Shiver my timbers, Dick, how my heart throbs as I gaze upon the old spot again; it is just the same as when I last saw it :—no, it is not the same, for then there were sad faces to be seen around; but now, all looks cheerful and sunny. Ah! there is the old honeysuckle still climbing the casement; the same bench where I cut my name, and that of my darling, Ellen, and a couple of hearts, with a cupid's arrow, about the length of a marlinspike, thrust through them : and, hark! there's the old clock ticking in the parlour, as though it were uttering a welcome to me, and——but, damme, what a fool I am to stand palavering here ; —what, ho! ship ahoy! Mat——"

Ere the honest tar could finish the sentence, the door was thrown open, and Richard was locked in the arms of Mat and the dame.

"Mat! dame!" cried Tom, in a transport of delight, grasping the hands of the worthy old couple, and the big tear of joy stealing down his manly cheek, "let's shake your fins—I am so glad to see you;—I—I—ah! Ellen—my own, my pretty Ellen!"

The poor girl could not speak, but, uttering a cry of uncontroulable delight, she rushed into the arms of her lover.

"Ellen! Ellen!" exclaimed the overjoyed tar, as he pressed warm kisses on her lips, her cheeks, and her forehead, and parting the silken tresses from her forehead, looked into her eyes with intense adoration ; "oh, what a happy moment is this! I—I could laugh—I could cry—I—I—damme, what a fool I am making of myself! But, eh!—why, you are pale;—you look ill! Why do you not speak to me? Not a word to your own Tom—your faithful Tom, after so long a separation? Why do you look so strangely at me? Mat! Dame! speak to her; —tell me, what does this mean?"

Ellen withdrew herself from his arms; she gazed upon him with mysterious earnestness; she tried to speak; her lips moved, but the words were stifled in her throat, and, uttering a groan of agony, she fell senseless to the earth. In a state of distraction Tom rushed towards her, and raising her frantically in his arms, called wildly upon her name.

"Mat! Dame!" he cried, "do not drive me to madness!—what does this mean? What has happened?—Tell me, I beseech you."

"Bear her into the house," said Mat to his wife. "Tom, a few words will explain this; and Heaven send that it may be in your power to quiet our doubts and apprehensions, or it will break the heart of my poor girl!"

"Doubts! apprehensions!" repeated Tom ; "Good God! what——"

Mat interrupted him, and, drawing him aside, in as few words as possible, informed him of what they had been told.

"Ah!" exclaimed Tom, when he had concluded, "is it so ?—I did not foresee this!"

"Tell me, Tom," said Mat, with extreme emotion, "have we been told aright ?"

" You have, you have—but not all; the—the—I shall choke !"

" And you love this female ?"

" As my own soul," answered the distracted sailor; " it is my duty to do so. But, Heaven can bear witness that my sentiments are unchanged towards Ellen: that—but I cannot explain any further at present ! I——"

Enough, enough, Tom," interrupted Mat, with a look of agony and reproach . " Heaven pardon you; but the death of my unhappy girl is upon your head !"

As the old man thus spoke, he rushed into the house, and left Tom paralyzed to the spot with astonishment and agony.

Tom stood for a few minutes, after the old man had left him, in a complete state of stupor ; his brain seemed to whirl round, and a mist to float before his eyes ; at length, starting, he exclaimed,—

" Damme ! surely I have been dreaming ! My mizen-top is out of order; my—my—oh, shiver my timbers, I cannot stand this !—I will rush into the presence of Ellen, and explain all. Fool! how can I, unless I would break my oath, and, perhaps, render all the plans to gain retribution for my sister and a restitution of her rights abortive ?—And, without I unfold everything, how can I do away with the suspicions of the poor girl ?—It will break her heart. No, no; I will not seek an interview with her until the violence of her grief is somewhat calmed, and she may then listen to me dispassionately. Oh, Ellen ! Ellen ! never could I believe that you would doubt the faith of him who would readily sacrifice his life to secure your happiness."

As the noble-hearted youth thus soliloquized, he cast his eyes up towards the casement of the apartment which he knew was appropriated to Ellen, and, breathing a sigh, walked slowly from the spot.

" Alas ! Tom," he ruminated, as he bent his steps he knew not whither, " little did you expect such a reception as this when you returned to England. You thought to meet with nothing but welcome smiles and open hands; and, above all, to be greeted with the fondest delight by that little craft to which your heart has ever been as true as the needle to the pole. But the gallant vessel which my ardent affections had launched upon the sea of hope, has struck upon the rock of disappointment, and threatened to founder in the ocean of despair. But—but what a lubberly swab I am making of myself; it will only be a few days, and I shall be enabled to explain everything, and we shall once more be happy. Oh, yes; our happiness will be tenfold ; for I shall be rich, and able to make the dear girl a lady ! Yes, my Nell shall ride in her carriage ; and—oh, damme ! won't she look as handsome as a seventy-four scudding lightly before the wind ?"

Thus did the gallant sailor commune with himself as he proceeded : one moment his heart seemed to leap for joy, and the next, to sink in despair. He took the miniature of Ellen from his bosom, where he had worn it next his heart ever since the morning she had given it to him, and, gazing upon it with rapture, ejaculated,—

" Yes, there is her sweet, pretty, smiling face, for all the world like the figure-head of an angel : her two pouting lips, that seem to coax a hearty kiss, and eyes, damme, that sparkle upon me brighter than a couple of stars. Bless her heart—I could gaze on this for ever ; and yet, when now my heart feels as though it would overflow with the unbounded love I bear towards her, they doubt my truth !

Why, I could sooner submit to be hauled up, and flogged to death—the flesh being torn piecemeal from my back, by the claws of the hateful cat, than I could ever prove faithless to my pretty Ellen !"

In the meantime, the object of Tom's anxious thoughts remained in a most pitiable condition confined to her chamber. At times she would rave of her lover, and accuse him of infidelity, in the most wild and afflicting manner; then she would be more calm, and speak of him and their love in the most heart-rending terms of affection.

"Hark !" she would cry, in one of the latter fits, "hark ! do you not hear how merrily the bells ring ?—There ! there ! oh, how beautiful ! But, don't you know why they ring so merrily ?—I'll tell you ;—it is for the wedding of me and Tom. Yes, we *are* going to be married, although they said he was false to me, and loved another ! But the wretches wronged my poor Tom—I knew they did while they spoke, and I believed them not—for never could he love any other than his faithful Ellen. Hush !—not a word ! See, he comes ! Oh, don't he look handsome in his wedding clothes ! Ring on, ring on, a merry peal—a merrier still ! Ring on, ring on !"

Then the unfortunate girl would sink into a state of torpor, and seemed to be totally unconscious of what was doing around her. Sometimes, however, she would be calm and rational, and in such moments she would have but a confused recollection of what had taken place, and would inquire with the utmost solicitude after her lover, and request to know the reason he did not visit her ; but, suddenly a faint recollection of what the sailor had said would dart across her memory, and she would wring her hands and burst forth into hysterical sobs and tears until completely exhausted with the poignancy of her sufferings, sleep would happily fall upon her eyelids, and afford her a temporary relief.

We need not attempt to describe the anguish of her friends at the sufferings she was thus enduring. A thousand times did they upbraid the cruelty and infidelity of Tom, who, they believed, could thus coolly render himself the cause of bringing Ellen to a premature grave. Narrowly, did Mat and his wife question Richard on the subject ; but he was faithful to the promise he had made to Rosina and Tom, and would not divulge anything that he knew, but earnestly endeavoured to convince his benefactors that they wronged him, by supposing for a moment that his sentiments were in the least changed ; and that a very short time, probably, would explain everything to their satisfaction. Mat shook his head incredulously ; and, after once more urging Richard to tell him all he knew, and expressing, in severe terms, his disapprobation of what he called the lad's obstinacy, he left him to himself.

Notwithstanding all that Richard had said, and Tom's own protestations, Mat could not help believing that their suspicions were too well founded, not only from the hints which Tom had himself thrown out, but from the circumstance of his not visiting the house since the first interview that they had had since his return to his native land. Yes, he knew himself to be guilty, and he could not face the poor girl whom he had so cruelly made his dupe, or offer anything in exculpation of his conduct to her parents.

Several days passed away in this manner, and still they heard nothing of Tom. The delirum had entirely left Ellen, and her grief had settled into a calm melancholy, which showed at once that, although she had tried hard to stifle her real feelings, and to put on the semblance of resignation, her heart had received a blow from which only one circumstance could restore her, namely, indubitable proof of his constancy.

She was enabled to leave her chamber, but she most sedulously avoided society, it being her delight to wander forth alone, and to ramble in the fields for hours. Her parents tried every means they could think of to arouse her from this state of feeling ; but their efforts were unsuccesful : it seemed the only source of enjoy-ment left her.

At that period, there was at no great distance from the town, the mansion of a nobleman, which had a beautiful park and gardens attached to it, which were open free to the publc. This was Ellen's favourite place ; and there for hours would she remain, rambling beneath the umbrageous foliage of the stately trees, or seated upon the green sward, give herself up to melancholy rumination.

It happened, that one day, about a month after Tom's return to Plymouth, the damsel having been taking her customary walk in the park felt tired, and conse-quently seated herself on a bench fixed to the trunk of one the trees to rest herself. She had not been many minutes there, when she heard voices proceeding from be-hind the very tree at which she was seated. Some strange and unaccountable foreboding darted across her mind, and caused her to listen with breathless curiosity. The first words she could distinguish were spoken in the voice of a female, and were to the following effect :—

" Oh, dearest Tom, would, indeed, that the happy moment of which you speak had arrived ; but, alas ! even now, although I have hitherto been so sanguine, I fear that something will occur to thwart our wishes."

" Nonsense, my dear girl," replied the man ; " this is a weakness of which I did not think you capable ; depend upon it, that a few days only will elapse ere we shall see the realization of our fondest hopes, and then we shall be indissolubly united."

The heart of Ellen beat heavily against her side ; her brain seemed to be on fire ; and she felt a sensation as though she should be suffocated. She could no longer delay the gratification of her painful curiosity ; but, gazing from behind the tree, beheld Tom, pressing to his heart the tall and elegant form of a female.

Paralyzed to the spot with astonishment, the hapless damsel stood and gazed upon them ; but she uttered no sigh,—she showed no sighs of emotion : no ; her sentiments in that moment seemed to undergo a terrible change : she felt as if her heart was frozen into stone, and bitter hate and revenge took possession of the place which had previously been occupied with such gentler passions. She felt that if she had had a weapon about her, she would not have hesitated or shrunk from destroying her supposed rival. It seemed almost impossible that the feelings of any one could in so short a time undergo so extraordinary a revolution.

The back of the female was turned towards her, so that she could not observe her face, but she thought that the voice sounded familiar to her. She was all anxiety to see her features ; but she did not turn, and Ellen could not go from her place of concealment without revealing herself to Tom, which she did not wish to do at that moment. She listened attentively for some time, thinking she might be enabled to overhear some more of their conversation ; but it was carried of in such a low tone, that she could only catch a word here and there, and they were not of a description to afford her any information. Shortly afterwards they moved away, and she watched them till they left the park, when they were suddenly hidden from her view.

As they disappeared, Ellen stood still for a second or two, and gazed vacantly in the direction she had taken, burst into a wild hysterical laugh, and turned towards the path which led to her home.

She hastened on with the greatest precipitation ; and any one to have seen her, would have supposed that she was going on some particular and urgent business. Suddenly, she paused. She was near a favourite spot to which her and Tom, in their days of happiness, when they never dreamed that anything would ever occur to interrupt their peace, or to fill their minds with the doubts and suspicions that Ellen was now indulging, used to love to repair. Well did she remember every little particular connected with this place ;—it remained unchanged as when they had last visited it. As the poor girl gazed upon this place, every circumstance of the past returned to her memory with tenfold power ; and, in spite of the feelings that had just occupied her mind, she could not help sighing, and tears stole gently from her eyes.

" Yes," she ejaculated, " 'twas there he breathed vows of eternal constancy in my ears, and appealed to Heaven to bear witness to them. 'Twas there, our trysting place, I acknowledged to him the feelings he had inspired, and pledged my faith with his. Oh, little did I then imagine how he would break those solemn vows! Fool, fool that I was to believe him : but, oh, who could doubt one who seemed so true, so honourable? But, 'tis over now ; he no longer loves me. He could never have regarded me with affection, or he would not thus have abandoned me for another. He was only mocking me all the time ; and, blind as I was, I could not see it. But he shall not triumph completely :—no ; he shall not have an opportunity of laughing at my weakness. I will learn to despise, to——"

She could not finish the sentence, and her grief overcoming her, she sunk down upon the green sward, and wept hysterically. It was sometime before she could recover herself sufficiently to enable her to proceed, when, with melancholy steps, she bent her way towards home.

*　　*　　*　　*　　*　　*

In the meantime, while the events we have just recorded were going forward, the Earl Fitzosbert and his myrmidon, the hateful black, had been indefatigable in their endeavours to discover the retreat of Rosina, but without success ; and Saib's impatience and disappointment became almost insupportable. So fully had his mind been occupied in the above-mentioned manner, that he had not a moment scarcely to turn his thoughts to anything else ; but, when he had, they were devoted to a dark scheme of vengeance he was forming against those whom he detested, more especially Tom and Richard. Their return had soon been made known to him ; but the story which had reached the ears of Ellen and her parents in so fatal a manner, concerning the female who had followed Tom in the ship in disguise, he had fortunately not heard of, or else, perhaps, his suspicions might have been aroused, and he might have discovered the retreat of Rosina, and committed some daring outrage, before proper steps could have been taken to frustrate his designs.

Notwithstanding all the precautions Saib had taken to keep his return to England a secret for the present, it very soon became known, and created no little astonishment in the minds of Tom and the other sailors, who never thought it could be possible that he could escape with his life, from the fate to which he had been consigned for his diabolical attempt.

A fortnight had now elapsed since the sailors had returned to Plymouth ; and, during that interval, the earl and Saib had experienced no change, neither could they hear anything of her they sought. The earl, in fact, was very well contented that the affair should remain as it was, hoping that something had happened to her, so that her fortune, which was in his keeping, would be entirely his. At times the impatience of Saib alarmed him, for he would throw out his suspicions that he (the earl) was trying to deceive him, and that he knew what had become of Rosina. The earl dreaded Saib, for he was in his power; and he knew full well, that if his revenge or hatred was once aroused, he would not hesitate to risk his own life to gratify it. Often since his return, and the account he had given of his narrow escape from death, he regretted that he had not perished, for he was the only person who knew of the dark deeds of his early life ; and, had he have died, all fear of detection would have ceased to torment him. What need he fear from the boy, Richard, even supposing him to be what he suspected ? He was ignorant of it, and who dare accuse him of a crime of which there was no living evidence ?

It was evening, and the earl and Saib were seated in the library. It was very evident that they were both much excited, and had been quarrelling. At length Saib, who had been traversing the room with disordered steps, turned to his master, and said,—

" 'Tis well, my lord: methinks since you are attempting to deceive me, it is time that we parted : but I warn you ; the separation will work you no good : on the contrary;—bitterly may you have cause to repent your conduct. You have experienced many services at my hands, and now——"

" Saib! Saib !" interrupted the earl, whom his threats had alarmed, " I swear that I have not deceived you ; but your own suspicious nature will not suffer your eyes to penetrate the veil of prejudice that obscures them. Have I not given you sufficient proof that I am as anxious as yourself to discover this proud and froward girl, by the manner in which I have aided you in the search ?"

" Bah !" cried the African, with a look of scorn ; " then, as we have failed to succeed, she is most likley dead, and you will hear no more of her, why hesitate to give me my fair share of the money you now hold in your hands ?"

" Divide that which is not mine ?"

" Aye.—But you are growing scrupulous, my Lord Fitzosbert ; you were not wont to be so, or the title and estates of your noble name would not now have been yours. I ask you nothing but what is fair. I have run many risks to serve you, and am still willing to run more ; and, surely you cannot have any reasonable objection to give me half of that of which I should have had the whole, had Rosina been made my wife ?"

The earl, whom the reasoning of Saib bewildered, had not time to return any answer to this speech, for, suddenly, the attention of both was drawn to a loud noise which seemed to proceed from the hall, accompanied with the confused sound of several voices all speaking together. Hasty footsteps approached the

room; the next moment the door was thrown back on its hinges, and, bowing ironically, and hitching up his stock, Gallant Tom stood in the presence of the astonished Earl Fitzosbert and Saib.

"Tom Clewline!" exclaimed the black, while his eyes rolled fiercely upon him, and he felt in his bosom for his knife, as though he contemplated the satiation of the mortal hatred which he entertained for the sailor; but he was unarmed, while Tom had a brace of pistols in his belt, and was every way prepared for anything that might occur, and to meet any danger with resistance.

"Yes, my black shark, it is your old *friend*, Tom Clewline!" answered the latter, with a sarcastic grin. "I have come to pay my respects to you, although I never expected to have the pleasure of coming athwart your hawse again. Earl Fitzosbert, your most obedient; you and I have got a little business to settle together, and so I'll just take a seat, if you please."

With these words, Tom cooly drew a chair opposite the earl, and, sitting down, gazed with the utmost nonchalance, alternately, upon him and Saib.

"What means this insolent intrusion?" at length demanded Fitzosbert, haughtily. "Leave the room immediately, fellow!"

"Don't be in a passion, Earl Thingamyjig—damme, what's your name?—You noblemen have such devilish long ones, that it takes a fellow a day nearly to pronounce half a dozen of them. As for your palaver about insolence, you can better belay it as soon as possible; but, as regards calling me a fellow, you're not much out there, I believe; for, if I am to believe what my messmates tell me, they say I am a fellow, and as honest and jolly a fellow as any in the ship's company.

No. 7

Now, your lordship, if you can truly state as much in your log-book, I am very much mistaken, that's all."

The earl was so complelely taken by surprise at the abrupt entrance of Tom, and the singular boldness of his behaviour, that he could not speak a word for a few moments; but the rough sailor, placed one hand upon each knee, clapped his tarpaulin hat on the table, and with a smile on his weather-tanned, but handsome countenance, he seemed to regard their astonishment with infinite delight and amusement. At length, Fitzosbert somewhat recovering himself, his first impulse was to ring the bell for the attendance of a servant, which Tom observing, jumped from his chair, and resolutely prevented him, saying,—

" Avast! there, avast! no piping all hands yet; our conversation must be of a private nature; unless you like to let that black lubber, there, to be made acquainted with the nature of it, why he can stay;—I believe he has a pretty good knowledge of all your secrets !"

" My lord !" cried the enraged black, " can you—will you tamely brook this insolence from the uncouth varlet ?"

" Varlet ! you damned figure-head of the devil ?" cried the indignant sailor, darting towards Saib, and his eyes glancing fiercely upon him; " you—you—but, damme, you are not worth wasting as much breath upon as would put out a rush-light; I only caution you not to make use of such a term again, or, may I never be able to crack a biscuit again, if I don't make a passage through your skull in the twisting of a handspike !"

" Ruffian !" exclaimed the earl, as Tom presented the pistols with which he armed himself at the black.

" Better language, my lord," said Tom; " for even your proud station is nothing in my eye; and I would as soon resent an insult upon a nobleman, as I would upon his slave."

" What do you mean by thus forcing yourself into my presence ?"

" Because I wished to see you, to be sure."

" And your business ?"

" Oh, you shall soon know it," replied Tom; " and I hope you may be able to settle it without any bother."

The earl felt a strange trembling sensation, and placed his hand upon the back of a chair to support himself, while Saib, with arms folded, and leaning against one of the pillars which supported the roof of the spacious apartment, listened with sullen silence, but eager curiosity to what Tom uttered.

" What can be the nature of the business you can have with me ?" said the earl.

" Do you know a person of the name of Rosina Burlington ?" inquired Tom.

" Ah ! Rosina !" exclaimed the earl, while Saib's eyes seemed as though they would start from their sockets; " how dare you — what have you to do with her ?"

" More than you expect," answered Tom. " You was her captain, I believe —that is to say, you was her guardian ?"

" This is past endurance," cried Fitzosbert, his blood boiling with rage at the boldness of the questions put to him by Tom ; " have you come here to insult and intimidate me ?"

" I came here for justice," returned Tom ; " and it's very strange if I don't have it before I leave you. But, come, come, belay your wrath, and take it coolly, for it's no more use getting out of temper with me, than trying to batter in the sides of a seventy-four with a pop-gun. Your charge has slipped her cable for some time—deserted, eh ?"

The earl made no answer.

" Silence gives consent. Well, she must have had a bad captain, or she would never have deserted from him. I come to tell you news of her," said Tom, emphatically.

" News of her ?" ejaculated the earl and Saib in a breath ; " but," continued the former, " you mock me."

" If I do not tell the truth, may I never splice the main brace again," said Tom ; " I have not long since left her."

" Impossible !—but, where has she been all this while ?"

" Under the protection of her brother," replied Tom.

The earl turned ghastly pale for a second, and reiterated Tom's words ; but, then recovering himself, he turned upon him a look of the most ineffable contempt.

" Aye, you may scorn my assertions," observed Tom ; " but it shall not be long before you shall be convinced of their truth. I repeat, that she has been, and is now under the protection of her long lost brother, who always thought that they were the children of the fisherman, Brandon :—you know the rest, and, therefore, I need not tell you. You seem thunder-struck, Earl Fitzosbert ; and, well you may ; but I have not half done with you yet."

" This is only a plan to extort money from me, and shall not go unpunished," said the earl ; " the boy you speak of was lost many years ago, and has, without a doubt, long since been dead, or he must have been restored to his father after the many inquires that have been made about him."

" It is false ; he lives !" cried Tom, rising from his chair ; " he lives, to protect his sister, and to tell the Earl Fitzosbert that he is a villain !"

" Ah ! dare you ?"

" *Dare I*—to such a land lubber as you ? Why, I have dared to meet the enemy, when death and horror surrounded me on every side, and it would be strange, indeed, if I was now to be afraid to call such a thing as you by his right name ! You now hold in trust, property that of right belongs to the persons I have named : are you prepared to restore it, or to render a good account of it ?"

" Unparalleled insolence !" cried Fitzosbert ; " and, what right have you to demand it ?'

" A brother's right," replied Tom.

" You—you !—" gasped forth the astonished earl, while the agitation of Saib was plainly visible in the distortion of his frightful countenance.

" Why, you seemed surprised, my worthy swabs," exclaimed Tom, sarcastically, " but, do not doubt me, for you will too soon, most likely, have cause to know that I am speaking the truth. Earl Fitzosbert, in me, I repeat, you behold the long supposed fisherman's son, who was lost when a boy, and never expected to be heard of again, But, you see, Providence has kept a watch over me, and I am still afloat, and prepared to give that poor girl whom you supposed to be quite friendless, the protection she so much needs. Nay, you may frown ; but, damme, I care nothing for your black looks ; you have acted as a cowardly, unmanly villain, and would now, if you could, rob her out of that which 'ustly belongs to her : but, if you don't render a good account of yourself, and restore every coin, may I never chew pig-tail again, if I don't pull your house about your ears, and——"

"Ah ! am I to be insulted in my own house, by this impudent ruffian ?" exclaimed the earl, in a great passion.

"I shall not take your titles angrily," said the honest tar, with the utmost coolness, "for a bad word from the mouth of such as you must be taken as a compliment ; but, otherwise, if I did, I should make you cry peccavi in no time. I tell you what it is, I came here for the purpose of seeing whether you are prepared to pay this money without any fuss, to save the trouble of employing a lawyer ; and, moreover, to see whether you were willing to make an apology to me for the manner in which you treated my sister ; but as you have not shown any intention of doing one or the other, why——"

"By Heaven ! I will not put up with this !" cried the enraged earl, whom the coolness and perfect *sang froid* of Tom, exasperated more than all :—"and there, Saib, you stand, as though you were paralyzed, and do not offer to aid me. Leave my house, or you shall deeply repent of your insolence and attempt at imposition !—Leave the house, immediately, I say !"

"Then I shall just do no such thing," replied Tom, re-seating himself. "I have not seen you for a long time, therefore you need not be surprised if I should make my visit rather a long one. I have a good many affectionate inquiries to make, and also some few particulars to relate, which, perhaps, may be rather interesting to one of you. Perhaps you would like to know where Rosina has been all this time ? if so, I will inform you :—on board the same vessel—mark you, my black pirate—on board the very same vessel in which you sailed, until you was so justly punished for the monstrous crime which you would have committed. Yes, disguised as Joe Gordon, she followed me throughout the voyage, and was as often by your side as any of the rest of the crew ; and yet you see, with all your penetration, you could not discover her !"

"Curses light upon my stupidity !" cried the black, in a hoarse, gutteral voice. "Yes, it must have been her, and that accounts for the strange feeling that came over me whenever I was near her, and the deep impression her features had upon me :—fool that I was, not to know her !"

"And, now, Earl Fitzosbert," said Tom, rising "I shall leave you : the next you will hear of me and Rosina, will be through the lawyer ; and you may thank your lucky stars that I have not taken summary vengeance on you for your villianous conduct to that poor girl, whom you had a right to protect. As for you, you black swab, the next time you are caught at any of your tricks, look out for squalls; for, damme, if I don't keep a good look out after you, and if I catch you doing anything wrong, I'll rob the gallows of its due, and send you to Davy Jones on the spot."

Saib bit his lips, but said nothing; while Tom, rising from his chair, hitched up his trousers, and, bowing sarcastically to them both, moved towards the room door.

" Hold !" suddenly exclaimed the earl, in a voice of much agitation ; " you shall not leave this place, until you have given me further particulars of this affair."

" I have told you all that I think proper to do at present," said Tom : " as for my not going away, who's to prevent me, I should like to know ?"

" Saib, your aid !—I command you !" cried the earl, as he rushed furiously towards Tom, who deliberately taking his pistols from his belt, presented them at him and Saib, and held them both at bay, at the same time saying, in a determined manner,—

" Earl Fitzosbert, again l warn you to keep off; for, may I never go aloft again, if either you or your black companion advance but one inch further, to prevent my departing from this house, that same moment shall be your last !"

After giving utterance to these words, Tom fixed upon the earl and his creature a look of defiance, and gradually retreated from the room. The earl and Saib were about to follow him ; but they heard a hearty laugh, which made the walls re-echo again, and looking over the bannisters, they found that Tom had come fully prepared for anything that might take place—for in the hall stood, at least, seven or eight jolly and hardy sons of Neptune, who had given utterance to the laugh of derison and exultation which they had heard, at a signal given by Tom. The latter once more cast his eyes up towards the spot where Fitzosbert and Saib were standing ; then, beckoning to his companions, the door was opened, and they quitted the house.

For a moment after Tom and his companions left the place, the earl and his guilty myrmidon were transfixed to the spot, and gazed upon each other in speechless astonishment ; at length, the former starting suddenly, and looking towards the staircase, exclaimed,—

" Why was the villain, the bold-faced beggar suffered to escape? Have I, indeed, sunk so low, that even a low-born wretch, like this sailor, shall presume to beard me in my own house ; and——but I had forgot ;—he said he was the brother of Rosina, did he not ?—Impossible ! It is all a vile plot, for the purpose of extorting money from me, but it shall not succeed."

Saib shook his head, and replied,—

" I am afraid, my lord, Tom's words are true ; and you may perceive that the likeness between him and Rosina is very strong, when you come to look closer to them. A thousand curses light upon the chance which made this discovery ; or, that I had not contrived some means to silence him for ever, while we were on board the same vessel together !"

The earl bit his lips, and, folding his arms, paced the room with hasty and disordered steps ; at length, turning suddenly to Saib, he said,—

" If, then, this is really the brother of Rosina Burlington, and, no doubt, he would not make so bold an assertion without being in possession of unquestionable proof that he is so, all our schemes, as far as the damsel is concerned, are at an end, and the readiest way to escape the public odium that would be sure to fall upon me is, to pay over the money at once, and for you to resign all hopes of Rosina, whom you could never have anticipated getting possession of, but by force."

" Resign Rosina ?—never ! By hell, I would sooner lose my life, after what I have hazarded to gain the consummation of my wishes ! Earl Fitzosbert, you are becoming a coward! Resign not a farthing, I beseech you, until it has been fairly sued for. What . would you give this bold and insolent youth the means of boasting that he had frightened you out of it ? Psha ! become a man again ; and, doubt not, it will yet be your fortune to triumph ;—at any rate, it shall not be any fault of mine if you do not."

"Alas ! Saib," replied the earl, in a gloomy tone, " lately, a heavy weight has seemed to press upon my heart, and I have not the spirit that I was wont. My thoughts have been haunted with terrible forebodings, and I have had dreams——"

" Dreams !" interrupted the black, with a bitter sneer ; " bah !—my lord, I am ashamed of you ; you are worse than a child. Come, you must banish these sickly ideas from your memory."

" I would I could do so," observed the earl ; " but they gain more strength every day. You mock me, when I talk to you of the visions that haunt my pillow. Oh, would that I could treat them as lightly, Saib ! You cannot form any conception of their horror. Last night, I dreamed, too, that my——I cannot, dare not, speak the name—was alive, and had come here to hurl me from my ill-gotten grandeur, and to demand retribution upon my head !"

" I have no patience with this preposterous nonsense !" cried Saib ; " and yet you are continually bothering me with your idle fears and imaginations ! I tell you, from your brother you have nothing to fear : long ere this, he has become nothing but dust. Come, come, you must arouse yourself, my lord, from this weakness, and learn once more to be a man. At any rate, I am determined not to resign my prey so easily as they probably imagine I will; and if I cannot accomplish my wishes, I will take care that I will not fail in having vengeance."

" There has already been too much bloodshed; and I would that what we seek could be effected without adopting such sanguinary measures," observed the earl.

" Why, my lord," returned Saib, " the visit of this sea-shark seems to have quite unnerved you.—What have we to fear from him ?"

" If he is really the brother of Rosina, everything," answered Fitzosbert.

" Psha !" ejaculated the black, impatiently ; " this is ridiculous. Should Tom prove himself to be the brother of the girl, what more can he do to you, than compel you to restore the money you now hold in trust, as Rosina's guardian ?"

" And where will then be your hopes ?" demanded the earl.

" Leave that to me," returned the black ; " for the present, let us endeavour to devise some means to discover the retreat of Rosina."

" That will avail us nothing, if we do," said the earl ; " for she has now an efficient protector, and any outrage committed by us, would sure to be punished."

" Punished !" sneered Saib ; " well, be it so ; but I'll take especial care that they do not punish me for doing nothing :—my enemies shall have good cause to repent of having aroused my wrath. But, for the present, I will leave you, my lord, as you are in no very fit mood to discuss this subject. When we meet again, I hope you may have recovered from the nervous debility which at present afflicts you."

Saib uttered the last words with a sarcastic smile, and an expression of countenance, which showed that he held the earl in utter defiance and contempt ; then, bowing formally, left him to his reflections.

*   *   *   *   *   *

In the meantime, Ellen, in the solitude of her chamber, gave way to the violence of her anguish, caused by the supposed faithlessness of Tom, and was deaf to all the endeavours of her parents to console her. Her mind was tormented with the alternate passions of grief, indignation, and revenge. One moment her gentle spirit would be overwhelmed by the turbulence of that feeling occasioned by the manner in which she had been deceived, by one whom she had fondly imagined could never have been untrue, and against her who had dared to supplant her in his affections; the next, she would melt into sobs and tears, and reproach the cruelty of Tom towards her, who would have thought no sacrifice too great to secure his love. Then she would endeavour to doubt that she had really beheld a confirmation of his infidelity, and tried to persuade herself that she had been labouring under some painful delusion all the while. But this, while it gave her temporary relief, only made her anguish the more poignant, when the reality was again presented to her mind. Many, many were the ideas that racked her brain. Sometimes she thought she could gather resolution sufficient to treat him with contempt, and to forget him altogether; but very soon her feelings told her, that he, to whom her young affections had been given, must hold them still, even although he deceived her, and mocked her. She felt that his image was so deeply engraven upon her heart, that that heart must break ere the impression could be erased from it.

In the midst of this bitter suffering, her mother entered her apartment, and presented her with a letter. Her heart throbbed violently against her side, and her hand trembled as she took the letter from her mother, in whose countenance there was a mingled expression of anxiety, hope, and fear. She looked at the superscription; her heart seemed to rise to her throat, and she had the utmost difficulty in breathing. Well did she know the hand-writing—the letter was from Tom. For a moment or two she stood hesitating how to act. One moment, her woman's pride prompted her to return the letter unopened. "What could he write in extenuation of his conduct?" she reflected. He could but add insult to his cruelty, by either maintaining his innocence, or acknowledging the truth, and confess that he had never loved her. But, then a sudden ray of hope, which beamed upon her mind, tempted her, at any rate, to see what he could say in his defence, and the melancholy wish to trace those characters, and peruse those sentiments from one she still so fondly loved, probably, for the last time, prevailed, and she broke the seal. For a moment, a mist seemed to rise before her eyes, and she could not read a word; and, in a voice choked with emotion, she said, putting the letter in her mother's hand,—

" I—I cannot read it : dear mother—you——"

She could not finish the sentence; but her mother understood what she meant, and she proceeded to read the *billet doux*. It was couched in the most affectionate terms, and, after energetically expressing the sorrow he felt at the suffering he had caused her, owing to his not being at liberty to enter into an explanation before, he protested, in glowing terms, the strength, the unabated ardour of his passion for her, and then went on to give a full explanation of what has already been related, concealing, however, the name of his sister, but promising to present her to Ellen, on an assurance of her forgiveness.

The poor girl listened to this letter with profound astonishment, and fixed her eyes vacantly upon her mother without uttering a word ; but when she had come to the conclusion, she suddenly snatched the letter from her, and with eager eyes retraced every sentence.

"Yes, yes, it is so," she said, in a voice of delirous joy; "he is still faithful to me ; my Tom could never deceive me :—oh, what an injustice have I done him !"

With frantic extacy she pressed the letter again and again to her lips, and placing her head on her mother's shoulder, the intensity of her feelings found relief in a copious flood of tears.

Her mother did not offer to interrupt her ; and, indeed, her joy was so great at the prospect of a reconciliation being effected between Ellen and Tom, that she was too overpowered to speak.

"But why do I stand here?" exclaimed Ellen, suddenly starting from her mother's side, and wiping away the tears that glistened like drops of chrystal on her eyelids; "let me hasten to him, to assure him of my love, and crave his pardon for having ventured to doubt his faith. I cannot, will not rest until I have seen him."

As she spoke, she hurried down the stairs, followed by her mother ; she reached the parlour, and scarcely had she done so, when the door was thrown open ;—there was a cry of joy, and Ellen found herself locked in the fond embrace of her faithful lover.

"My Ellen, my dearest, my pretty Ellen, look up, and smile upon me !" exclaimed the gallant sailor, as he pressed still closer to his bosom the form of his lover, and imprinted kisses the most impassioned upon her lips ; "It is Tom, your own faithful Tom, who has been as true to you as the needle to the pole. Poor girl ! her feelings have overpowered her; she does not hear me—she is prettier than ever :—even now, she looks like a sleeping angel, or a moonbeam upon the ocean ! I—I could look my senses away in gazing upon her. Ellen, dear, dear Ellen, speak to me !"

But Ellen still remained unconscious of all around ; and with difficulty her mother persuaded Tom to resign her to her care ; but nothing could induce him to leave the room until she was recovered.

A few minutes served to revive her, and, opening her eyes, and looking vacantly into the countenance of her mother, she said,—

"Oh, mother, I have had such a sweet dream ; too delightful, indeed, to be realised. Methought that Tom had returned to me, and assured me of his constancy, and that——"

"My dearest lass, it was no dream," exclaimed her lover, rushing forward, and once more enfolding her in his arms ; "your Tom is here to assure you of his constancy, and kiss his reconciliation upon your lips."

"Ah ! then you have not deceived me, Tom ?" ejaculated the damsel, while her countenance beamed with love and transport; "you are still the same true and faithful Tom that you professed to be ?"

"Still the same, Ellen," returned Tom ; "oh, how could you doubt me ? How could you imagine that I could be the villain to deceive you ?—that I could suffer another to supplant you in my heart ? This, this was not like my Ellen. Oh, my dear girl, nothing could ever have induced me to suspect your constancy. No ;

never would I have done you the injustice to suppose that, after the many vows you have pledged to me, you could prove untrue ! Oh, Ellen, did you but know my feelings—could you but read my heart, as I can yours, in your pretty eyes that twinkle upon me with such lustre, you would see how fondly, how sincerely, how devotedly my heart is attached to you, and you alone. Though many miles have separated us, still have you always been present to my thoughts ; nothing could erase you from my memory. In the dreary watch—in the raging storm—in the battle's heat, my Ellen was never absent from my mind ; and it was her dear image which nerved me on to deeds of valour, and to smile at danger. When sleep closed my eyelids, then would delightful visions take me back to this loved spot, and imagination would give me a repetition of all my former happiness—and, yet, my Ellen, to imagine that I could prove untrue to her, and——"

"Oh, Tom," interrupted Ellen, while her eyes beamed with all that ardent affection which her heart prompted, "reproach me not, although too well do I feel that I deserve it. I should not have doubted you; I ought to have known my Tom better ;—but some strange infatuation took possession of my senses—and, then, that dreadful tale, and the female with whom I saw you, all conspired to make me think you perfidious, although my heart was almost broken in admitting what I thought to be the fatal truth."

"Ah ! did you then see us together ?" asked Tom, eagerly.

"I saw you with a female, in the gardens of Sir Richard Overton," answered Ellen ; " nay, more, I overheard you breathe to her words of the utmost tender-

No. 8

ness and love;—I saw you press your lips to her's; judge, then, Tom, whether your Ellen had not a sufficient cause to imbibe suspicion?"

" You said you heard all this," said Tom, " and yet the female was not recognised by you?"

" Her back was towards me, so that I did not see her features," replied Ellen. " Oh, Tom, how shall I describe my feelings at that time? I shudder, even now, when I recollect them;—a dreadful change had in a moment come over my heart; and—yes, Tom, well may you start—at that moment I could, had I had the means, have become a murderess !—I could have plunged a knife into the heart of my supposed rival, and have exulted at the deed !"

Tom did, indeed, shudder when he reflected upon the dreadful, the awful catastrophe which might have taken place; and a thousand times did he feel grateful to think that the time had arrived when he was allowed to explain himself, and which would be the means of preventing circumstances he could not contemplate without the deepest horror. Again, he pressed his lover still more closely to his bosom, and imprinted kisses of gratitude and delight upon her lips.

" Ellen," said he, " you had, indeed, plenty of occasion to hoist the yellow flag; you had, apparently, sufficient cause for suspicion; but, had you overheard the whole of the conversation that passed between us, you would have ascertained that that female was my newly-discovered sister."

" Your sister?"

" Aye, my dearest lass," returned Tom, " my own fond sister, whom, next to my Ellen, I love with all the ardour that can possibly be felt; that sister, who is prepared to love the destined bride of her brother with that strength and sincerity which only such noble minds as her's is capable of feeling."

" Her name?" anxiously gasped forth the maiden.

" She is here to answer for herself," said Tom, throwing open the parlour door —" behold !"

" Rosina Burlington !" ejaculated Ellen, with mute astonishment, as the latter bounded into the room, and advanced to embrace her, with looks of the utmost extacy and attachment.

" Yes, it is Rosina," answered she, " the cause of all your late anguish; but whose constant study shall be to repay you, by her future love and attention; regarding, as she does, with admiration and pleasure, the fidelity of your love for a dear brother, from whom she has been so long separated."

As Rosina said this, she offered to embrace Ellen; but the latter shrunk back, timidly, when she remembered the differences of their stations, which Rosina perceiving, encouraged her by a look of sweetness which was perfectly irresistible; and the next moment the two beauteous females, like twin graces, were locked in a fervent embrace.

" Hurrah !" cried Tom, in a transport of delight, and tears of joy rushing to his eyes; " yard-arm to yard-arm. Oh, shiver me, if this job wont be the death of me, through downright pleasure ! What a happy fellow I shall be, to be sure, to have to divide my affections between two such dear creatures. But, eh—what's the meaning of that cloud passing over your lovely countenance, Ellen? You sigh, too?—come, come, belay that, lass; the storm has all passed over, and there is no cause for sorrow now."

" Alas ! Tom," said Ellen, "your good fortune will be my only cause for misery ; you will now be rich, and move in that station to which your birth entitles you, while the humble Ellen——"

" Ellen," interrupted Tom, hastily, " think you, that any change of circumstances can alter my sentiments towards you ?—By Heaven ! if riches were to be purchased only by the forfeiture of my Ellen, I would sooner be condemned to poverty and the meanest hovel. No, no, my dearest girl, you alone it is that forms the principal charm of my life, and, without you, all else would become completely valueless to me !"

The manner in which Tom spoke this, convinced Ellen of his sincerity, and her bosom, which had lately been the abode of such poignant misery, became light and buoyant. Rosina, whose affable manners never failed to engage the admiration of the most insensible person, did all that she possibly could to convince her of her esteem, and, in time, succeeded in dissipating that air of restraint which the difference of station occupied by Rosina had caused her at first to evince.

A happy evening was passed at " The Old Commodore," among Mat, his wife, Ellen, and their two guests, the house being closed against public visitors, and Rosina particularly keeping out of sight of any one that knew her, fearful that the knowledge of her being in the neighbourhood, might reach the ears of those she had, at present, some cause to dread. The heavy care which had formerly pressed so heavy upon the heart of Ellen, and clad her features in an aspect of gloom, had entirely disappeared ; and, happy in the confidence of her possessing the love of Tom, she had not a thought besides, which could cause her the least uneasiness. As for Tom and Rosina, they seemed sufficiently happy in seeing the good effects, this reconciliation had upon Ellen ; and Mat, and his dame, did all that they possibly could to contribute to the pleasure of those around them.

It was late when Tom and Rosina took their departure, and Mat and his family were about to prepare themselves to retire to rest, when they were suddenly surprised by hearing a loud knocking at the outer door.

" Who can that be, at such a time as this ?" said Mat, as he went to the window, up stairs, and looked out.

" Who is it knocks ?" he demanded.

" A traveller, who is weary and footsore, and claims the indulgence of a night's rest and shelter," was the answer.

" Humph ;" said Mat, " it's a pity you could not come before, master ; we are just going to retire, and I don't know what to say to you. I do not recollect your voice—who, and what are you ?"

" A stranger to you, I rather think ; and, doubtless, to most persons in this neighbourhood, now," answered the man.

Mat stretched his head out of the window as far as he could, but it was so dark, that he was unable to make out more than that it was a tall figure, apparently enveloped in a mantle, which stood in the doorway. Mat hesitated, and looked at his wife and daughter, who did not encourage him by the expression of their countenances, to comply with the applicant's wishes.

" For goodness sake, do not keep me standing here in suspense, or I shall faint with exhaustion at your door," said the man. " I assure you, you have no cause to fear."

" As for fear, master," returned Mat, " you mustn't come to an old seaman to talk about that. Well, I'll e'en chance letting you in ; and, if you play me false, only mind that you are not taken in, that's all."

Having thus spoken, Mat took the lamp in one hand, and grasping a stout stick with the other, descended the stairs, and unbolted the door.

The person who entered was enveloped in a long mantle, and presented the tall figure of a man, apparently about fifty years of age, and of noble appearance, but whose clothes were very old, and whose countenance, which had evidently once been handsome, had an expression of deep melancholy and care. Mat, having eyed him minutely, and discovered all these particulars in a moment, handed him a chair in the chimney corner, in which the stranger took his seat, and, as he did so, sighed deeply.

" Thanks, my good sir, for this kindness," said he. " I was, indeed, afraid, that I should not have obtained a shelter this night ; and, weary as I am, I should never have been able to support it. I am very much obliged to you for your goodness."

" Oh, I need no thanks, sir," returned honest Mat ; " it is, indeed, seldom that any one is turned churlishly away from ' The Old Commodore.' "

" The Old Commodore !" repeated the stranger, thoughtfully ; " ah ! I remember now—but, so near ?"

" You seemed to have travelled far, sir," said Mat, inquisitively, after having ordered his wife to hasten for a glass of good stiff grog, and afterwards to bring forward such refreshment as they had in the house, of which there was always an ample store, plain, but the best quality.

" You are right," answered the stranger : " I have, indeed, walked many weary miles, and am fatigued and footsore."

" You are a stranger in this neighbourhood, methinks," observed Mat ; " at least, I never remember to have seen you before."

" For many years I have been a stranger to this place," replied the man, with a sigh ; " but, well do I—no matter, the time is past, now ; and it is, perhaps, imprudent of me—ah ! the grog !"

With these broken and unconnected sentences, the stranger, who seemed anxious to avoid being questioned, took the glass from the hand of the dame, and, politely pledging Mat and her, raised it to his lips, and drank heartily, seeming to be refreshed by it.

Mat observed the behaviour of his guest with much curiosity : there was something in his appearance and manners which deeply interested him ; and from his noble demeanour, he was confident that he had moved in a higher sphere of life. His features, too, particularly struck him ; and there was something in their expression which was quite familiar to him ; but he could not at the time call to mind whether he had seen them before, or where. Some heavy affliction evidently weighed upon his spirits ; for, at intervals, he seemed perfectly abstracted from all around him, and he frequently sighed deeply. He partook greedily of the refreshments which the good dame placed before him, and seemed as though he had been long fasting.

The curiosity of the dame was not more excited than that of her husband ; but she had no means of gratifying it, for the stranger seemed too taciturn to lead them to suppose that they would be able to elicit anything from him.

Having finished his repast, he looked up, and, addressing himself to Mat, said,—

"Does the Earl Fitzosbert, *as he calls himself* (laying particular emphasis on the latter words,) still reside in this neighbourhood?"

Mat answered in the affirmative, and added,—" You know the earl, then?"

" Know him," cried the stranger, with much emotion ; " oh, God ! have I not reason to know the——"

" Villain, you would add, I know," remarked Mat ; " and, indeed, you would only speak the truth, if you did, for he is well known to be such here. Respectable persons of his own rank avoid him ; and those beneath him hate and despise him. If you should see him, tell him, this is the character old Mat Marlinspike gave you of him, who cares no more about him, than he would about cracking a biscuit, or swallowing a mouthful of salt pork."

" He is, indeed, a villain, a most blood-thirsty, treacherous villain !" exclaimed the stranger, warmly ; then, suddenly checking himself, he added,—" but, it is growing late ; with your permission, I will retire to rest."

Mat immediately took up the lamp, and, preceding the stranger up the stairs, shewed him into the clean and neat chamber in which he was to pass the night.

" Did you not notice the extraordinary likeness ?" observed the dame, when he came down stairs again.

" His face is familiar to me ; but, for the life of me, I can't call to mind where I have seen him before," answered Mat.

" Why, how foolish you must be, not to discover it in a moment, Mat," said the dame, priding herself upon her own penetration ; " why, he is the very image of our Richard : goodness me, when he came in——"

" You are right, dame, by jingo !" interrupted her husband ; " he is exactly like the boy, now I think of it ;—but, what of that ? There is nothing at all wonderful in that circumstance, for there are many faces alike in this world."

Mat, however, did feel more than he thought proper to acknowledge, and he could not get the stranger out of his thoughts the whole of the night ; even in his dreams, his form was again presented to his imagination, and he awoke in the morning more anxious than ever to know who and what he was.

The morning's repast being ready, and the stranger not having yet descended from his chamber, Mat hastened to summon him to attend. Shortly afterwards he came down stairs, and, after paying the usual compliments of the day to Mat and his wife, he prepared to take his seat at the table, when his eyes suddenly encountered Richard, and, no sooner did he behold him, than he gave a convulsive start, and turned red and white alternately. Mat and the others noticed his agitation with astonishment, but did not offer to interrupt him. For several minutes he remained as it were petrified to the spot ; but at length, without speaking a word, took his seat at the table, and, fixing his eyes upon Richard, never removed them from him during the repast, and his mind seemed totally abstracted from everything else. He ate but little ; and he also seemed to be violently agitated. Mat and his wife watched him narrowly, and exchanged mutual glances of significance. At length, when the breakfast was over, the stranger arose, and,

turning to Mat, requested him to favour him with a few minutes conversation
alone. Mat readily complied, and led the way into another apartment, where
they remained closeted for some time; and when they returned to the parlour,
the emotion visible upon both their countenances, plainly showed that the subject
of their discourse had been something important. There was a mingled expression of joy and surprise in the face of Mat, which not a little increased the wonder
and anxiety of his wife, who eagerly waited till they were alone, thinking that
the former would divulge what had taken place between him and the stranger.
She was, however, doomed to be disappointed, for the latter, shortly after their
return to the parlour, quitted the house, and, instead of Mat furnishing her with
the information for which she was so anxiously waiting, he strictly enjoined her
to be secret upon the subject of the stranger having visited their house, and firmly
refused to reveal to her anything that had taken place at the interview. He told
her, notwithstanding, that in a very short time he should, probably, be permitted
to disclose to her everything, and she would then find that the subject was one of
rejoicing instead of misfortune.

With this explanation the dame was forced to be satisfied for the present; but
she murmured a good deal about it. Mat was particularly cheerful the whole of
the day; and it was noticed that he paid more than usual attention to Richard,
and seemed to be very uneasy when out of his presence.

*   *   *   *   *

When Saib left the Earl Fitzosbert, after the scene which we have described
that took place between the two mentioned persons and Tom, he walked immediately from the house. The interview he had had with the gallant sailor, and
the scorn, the triumph, and threats of the latter, together with the assertion he
had made with regard to Rosina being his sister, filled the bosom of the savage
African with the most unbounded rage and distraction. He clenched his fist as
he walked along, and gnashed his teeth. He felt at that moment capable of com-
mitting the most hellish deed to gratify his revenge; and curses, deep and horrible,
frequently escaped his lips, when he thought upon the manner in which he had
invariably been foiled in his diabolical schemes, and always when so near the
attainment of his object :—foiled, too, principally through the instrumentality of
Tom Clewline (the name by which our hero had always been known in the navy,
and to which he seemed more attached than that which really belonged to him).
In the first instance, when he had discovered by the conversation he had overheard to take place between Mat and his wife, that the right heir to the proud
estates of Fitzosbert, still existed in the person of the boy, Richard, and his life
was in his hands, the latter had been rescued by the sailor at the very critical
moment. The second attempt he had made, was also, not only thwarted by the
same individual, but he was punished by being impressed on board ship, and hurried away from the theatre of his crimes, his wishes, and his prospects; treated
like a dog; mocked at, and reviled by the very man against whom his bosom
glowed with the most sanguinary feelings of revenge; and when brought up to a
pitch of madness, and ungovernable hatred of every one, and tired of his own life,
he had determined upon sacrificing it, and immolating the whole of the crew, his
design had again been frustrated, at the very moment that the spark was being
applied to the train, which would have sent them all into eternity, by Gallant

Tom, who had been directed thither by the other being he had so much cause to hate,—the boy, Richard. With the thoughts of a demon, he recalled to his memory the punishment he had undergone for that offence: the dreadful sufferings he had endured; and, as he did so, the blood seemed to rush scalding hot through his veins, and his whole frame was convulsed with the power of the furious passions they gave rise to. The appearance of the African at that time was frightful in the extreme, and was sufficient to strike terror into the most resolute heart. He paused:—his eyes, which were fixed on vacancy, became terribly blood-shot; his hideous features were awfully convulsed with passion; his lips were closely compressed; his teeth were firmly clenched; and his black shaggy brows fiercely contracted. His broad chest heaved with the fury of the tempest that was raging at his heart; and, with his clenched fist raised in the air, he looked the prototype of the fiend of darkness. The waves dashed furiously at his feet, but he heeded them not; the wind howled among the hollow cavities of the rock, like the sepulchral moans of some troubled spirit, but he heard it not; his whole thoughts, his every idea was fixed upon the manner in which he had been invariably baulked, in the machinations he had formed, and the probability which there appeared to be of his being still farther disappointed. The turbulent passions of hatred, malevolence, and vengeance, raged with uncontrollable power in his breast, and completely monopolized the place of every other thought or feeling.

" An eternal curse, one universal malediction, light upon the heads of all those whom I so fiercely hate!" he exclaimed, in a voice hoarse with rage. " May they never know a moment's peace,—never experience one minute's happiness, for the torture, the disappointment, they have caused the despised, the detested black man! But, I will be avenged!—Yes, deeply, dreadfully avenged! Nor heaven, nor hell, shall ultimately thwart me in the gratification of my desires! The black man fears no danger to gain his ends; and, by all the infernal host, they shall yet tremble at my power, and writhe beneath the agonies it shall be my delight to cause them! Oh, how I will glut over the work of my hands! Their groans of anguish will be as music to mine ears; and their cries for mercy be met by me with the scornful laugh of exultation! Yes, Tom Clewline, Richard Fitzosbert, Rosina, all, all shall feel the full terrors of the deadly vengeance they have aroused. Rosina must and shall be mine!—The proud, scornful beauty, shall become the mistress of the hated African; and her brother shall know of her disgrace, her shame, her destruction, without having it in his power to assist or to save her. Fool! blind idiot that I must be, not to recognise the girl under the disguise she had assumed on board the vessel! What a famous opportunity for the gratification of my desires did I lose; and, even had I been foiled in that, I would have taken care that she should not have lived for another to revel in those charms I covet:—no; the deep bosom of the ocean should have formed her grave!"

Saib here paused; and, folding his arms across his expansive chest, leaned his back against a rock, and gazed over the ocean with an expression of countenance which showed that his mind was intent upon the perpetration of some diabolical scheme. Suddenly, he fixed his eyes upon a vessel which was lying at anchor, at no great distance, and, as he did so, his features relaxed somewhat from their sternness, and a smile of exultation overspread them, as a sudden thought seemed to dart upon his brain.

"Ah! I have it," he cried, in a voice of pleasure ; " a scheme of vengeance rushes in a moment to my mind, which cannot fail of succeeding. Yonder lies the "Nancy ;" she is thought here to be a fair trading vessel ; but little do the fools suspect her real character. It is strange that this idea did not occur to me before !—But it is not too late. I must see Will Barnsley directly, and no doubt he will readily fall into my scheme. This Tom must be disposed of in some way or the other, to prevent his urging his claims in behalf of his sister and himself; and I have this moment thought of a plan, which will not only effectually accomplish that object, but do away with all fear of his ever coming here to trouble us again. Once having got him out of the way, it shall not be long ere Rosina shall be in my power, and I will amply repay myself for the past. Now, revenge, thou art securely in my grasp !"

As the black man thus spoke, he hurried on his way, fully bent upon the immediate execution of the diabolical scheme which had entered his mind.

In the parlour of a low public-house, known at that time by the sign of " The Blue Anchor," and which was greatly resorted to by the sailors, their lasses, crimps, Jew pedlars, &c., sat a strong party of sailors, with several females. They were all of them doing ample justice to the tobacco, for the objects in the room were scarcely distinguishable, owing to the dense clouds of smoke by which it was filled ; and the tables were loaded with grog, the merits of which the guests were fairly discussing. There was a very mixed assemblage of merchantmen, men-o'-wars-men, &c. ; and some of them, it must be confessed, were by no means prepossessing in their appearance. The females present, were of the lowest description ; and the language that occasionally was made use of by them, was anything but calculated to afford pleasure and satisfaction to ears polite.

At a small round-table, near the fireside, and apart from any of the rest, with the exception of two or three rough-looking individuals, to whom he addressed his conversation, sat a square-built, middle-aged man, with a dark, swarthy countenance, large, fierce-looking eyes, and huge black whiskers. He was dressed in a large P jacket, a broad-brimmed, tarpaulin hat, and a very capacious pair of boots, which reached up to his thighs. He was smoking, and holding a conversation, in an under tone, with his companions, over whom he seemed to exercise considerable authority. The appearance of this individual could not fail to fix the attention of the beholder in an instant; and there was something so peculiarly expressive in his countenance, that few could gaze upon it without a sensation of disgust and horror. The other persons in the room seemed to take but little notice of him and his companions ; while they, on the other hand, did not appear to be at all anxious to associate with them. Sometimes, indeed, they would respond to a toast, or join in the laugh, which ever and anon the tough yarns the sailors were spinning to one another would excite; but then it did not seem to be done spontaneously; and they immediately relapsed into their previous behaviour, and entering into conversation among themselves, did not appear to be taking any notice of what was passing around.

It was night, and the blaze of the fire, and the smoking tumblers of grog, was by no means a cheerless or unpleasant sight. The moon was shining above, over th

sea, like a pale girl gazing into a looking-glass; and the white sails of the different vessels lying at anchor, reflected upon by her silvery beams, looked like so many fluttering spirits of the air. But the sailors took no notice of the weather or the moon, their thoughts were entirely engrossed by the stories they were narrating to one another, and in quaffing deep potations.

In the midst of a group of attentive listeners, sat a handsome, weather-beaten sailor, about forty years of age, with a huge quid in his mouth, a long pipe in his jaws, and a pig-tail of such an enormous length, that the end of it nearly swept the floor. He had been spinning several yarns, much to the amusement of his companions, and was evidently about to treat them with another, for they were all most eagerly watching him, with their mouths wide open, and silence had more than once been proclaimed, and peremptorily enforced, by a loud knocking on the table.

" Well, I say, messmates," began Dick Taffrail—for so was the sailor alluded to called—" I was going to say, as how, I'll be bound that there is not many that are seated here, as have cruised on board a pirate?"

At the mention of this name, the man whom we first described, and who before did not seem to be paying any attention to the conversation, jumped suddenly upon his feet, his companions following his example; and they fixed their eyes fiercely and intently upon Dick and the others, who observed their behaviour with considerable astonishment.

" Hallo! captain," exclaimed Dick Taffrail, addressing himself to the man in the Packet. " what's in the wind, now?—Why, damme, you look as——"

"As what?" shouted the captain, fiercely; "hark ye, my fine fellow, I would advise you to belay your lingo a little more, and mind how you call honest men in future, pirates!"

"Why, shiver my timbers, captain, you are off like a sky-rocket," said Dick, with perfect coolness, ; "but, avast, avast, you are all abaft for once. I accused no one—not I; God forbid that I should call any man out of his right name!"

The captain, as he was called, exhibited a great deal of confusion, and seemed to recollect himself, looked significantly at his companions, and resumed his seat without saying another word. Dick Taffrail then turned his quid, took a hearty swig of the grog, and resumed as follows :—

"Well, as I was about to say, messmates, it was once my ill-fortune to get amongst pirates, and to be forced to sail with 'em for some time. The vessel to which I belonged, was a merchant ship, called 'The Saucy Peggy,' and we were bound to St. Domingo,—this was in 1769, or 1770, I'm not sartin which : hows'ever, that's no matter. We were sailing right in the wind's eye, when, suddenly, one of the men discovered a strange-looking vessel bearing down upon our larboard tack, and, at such a rate, that she must be on to us in no time. She was a black-looking brig ; and, as she swept over the ocean, looked as gloomy as a hearse. We hoisted our colours directly ; but she did not return the compliment.

" 'I don't much like the appearance of this craft,' said the captain, addressing himself to the purser, who happened to be standing by. ' Port helm !' he shouted, running towards the forcastle; ' we will get out of her way, if possible !' His orders were obeyed, but it was no use ; the vessel neared us like lightning, for a rare fast sailer she was ; and it was not long ere she had got so close to us, that we could distinguish her build very distinctly.

" ' By G—!' ejaculated the captain, ' this is a pirate, as sure as I live !'

"And sure enough it was ; and a rare saucy one, too ; for the next moment they hoisted the black flag, and fired a gun as a signal for us to heave to. This polite request our captain, hows'ever, thought fit to decline, and again ordered us to stretch every stitch of canvas we could, and endeavour to elude the enemy ; for we were in a very poor condition to resist it, and any chance was better, he considered, than falling into their hands. It was no use ; the pirate fired after us, and struck our vessel in the waist, but did not do her much harm. It was now very clear, that we must either quietly submit, or fight for it; and, as the latter was by far the most pre-*fer*-able, we made all the preparations which we could in so short a time ; and every man was in an instant at his post. My eyes ! I shall never forget the first salute the pirate gave us ; it made every timber in the ship tremble ! ' She carries some heavy metal,' said the captain; ' but we have justice on our sides ; so let us do our best. We did do our best; but it was all to no purpose. The pirates boarded us, and me and Joe Atkins, Ned Binnacle, two other men, and a boy, being all that survived, were taken on board the Pirate Brig. Our ill-fated vessel was then stripped of all its cargo, and burnt. These swabs, the pirates, were the most desperate set of ruffians I ever knew, and they delighted in murder. The captain of them was a fellow who stood six feet two inches high, and stout with it ; his features were large and ferocious ; and his eyes were enough to frighten any one to look at them. He ⸺ ⸺The Sea⸺

Devil,' and a very proper name for him, too, for a greater devil than him there could not be. His men were all afraid of him; for, if they offended him, their life was sure to pay the penalty of it. Only the day after I had been on board their vessel, one of the crew having murmured at obeying some orders which the pirate captain had given him, he had him stripped immediately, and lashed to the gratings; and he was flogged so severely, that when they went to release him, the poor devil was a corpse. So, you see, my lads," continued Dick, " we could not expect to have a very pleasant berth among 'em; and we was not disappointed, neither. We was obliged to be very cautious in our behaviour, and to do many things which made our blood boil again, or else we should very soon have been sent to Davy Jones's locker. But the poor boy was worse off of us all; for, from the very first moment that we was taken on board, the pirate captain seemed to have taken a dislike to him, and he knocked and kicked him about shamefully. The poor lad could not do anything to please him; he was constantly at him, and made him do more heavy and laborious duty than any of the crew. He was a very delicate-looking boy, with a melancholy countenance, and of a meek disposition; but no one of any feeling could be off liking him, for he was so civil, and so willing to do anything he was told. One day, poor Ben happened to be sitting on the bowsprit, when the pirate coming upon deck, and observing him, seized hold of a marline-spike, that was just handy, and dealing him a violent blow, knocked him overboard. Horror-struck at such an event, I rushed forward, with an intention to endeavour to save the boy; but the captain held me back fiercely, and threatened to serve me the same, if I offered to move. I was compelled to obey; but I looked upon the spot where poor Ben had disappeared with feelings of horror. There was a pool of blood upon the crest of one of the waves, and in a second afterwards (although any one would have thought that the violent blow which he had dealt him must have killed him), he arose again, the blood streaming over his ashy face. He was quite erect, as though he was standing; and, although it was but an instant before he sunk to rise no more, in that brief space of time, I saw him, as plain as I see one of you now, fix his eyes solemnly on his murderer, in a manner which I shall never forget. I turned away with a shudder, and said to myself, ' For this cruel deed, the spirit of poor Ben Walton will haunt you, or my name is not Dick Taffrail !' "

" And, did it, Dick ?" eagerly inquired about a dozen of the anxious listeners.

" Did it !" reiterated Dick; " aye, aye, indeed it did, my lads, or may I never eat salt junk again. What I am relating, is as true as the Bible. I witnessed it with my own eyes, and I can, therefore, vouch for its being correct. Ben's ghost was almost our constant companion ever after that."

" How was that ?" asked one of the sailors.

" Why, I'll tell you," returned Dick. " The night after this shocking affair—I think it was the sixth watch—when I was on duty, that I suddenly heard a deep sigh, which seemed to be breathed close behind me; but, thinking it was the wind, I took no notice of it, at first; but, in a very few seconds it was repeated, and, starting round, I proceeded forward. The moon was shining brightly, and everything was as clear upon deck as if it had been the middle of the day; and, casting my eyes towards the bowsprit, you may guess how alarmed and astonished I was, when I beheld poor Ben seated across it (or, rather, it was his ghost), with his face looking so pale, and the blood streaming down it, just the same as he had looked when he appeared in the water, for the last time. At first, I was so surprised, that I had not the power to move; but, in a minute or two, I called to the other men who were on duty, and who saw it also. It did not remain on the bowsprit; but, all in an instant, it would disappear, and would be seen on the extreme point of the jib-boom. Sometimes it would be seen standing in the ratlines; then seated on the top of the companion; or, on the binnacle; but there was no way of shutting it out from our sight; turn which way we would, the ghost of Ben Walton was sure to be before us. It was an awful sight, and such as I do not wish to see again; and the pirates showed the terrors of men who knew the crimes of which they have been guilty, and, therefore, the more unprepared for a circumstance of the kind. They looked at one another with ghastly faces, and shook their heads, as much as to say, that they dreaded some accident would happen to them after this, and that a spell would rest upon the ship as a punishment for the savage murder of the unfortunate boy; and, indeed, I thought so, too: for, surely, such a savage, cold-blooded crime as this, would not be suffered to go unpunished."

"But, did the captain see the ghost?" inquired one of the sailors.

"Yes, he did," answered Dick; "in fact, he was never out of his sight from that time, and he became a complete mad man. It was quite awful to hear him swear; and then he would lay hold of anything that was handy to him, and deal such heavy blows in the air, as if he was striking at some object. We were all afraid to come near him, for he would not bear to be spoken to; and he looked so dreadful, it was enough to make a person shudder to gaze upon him. Well, the vessel continued on her course, without falling in with any more prizes; and, indeed, if we had, the men were so spiritless at the constant appearance of the ghost of poor Ben Walton, that they would not have had the courage to have made any resistance, and we should sure to have been defeated. That such an event should take place, you may be sure I was constantly praying; for I was in a most wretched state of mind, while I was on board that damned piratical craft. Shiver my topsails, if I had had any half dozen of the swabs to deal with, and fair play, I could have beat them as easy as I could snap a biscuit. But, then, yer see, there was no chance of that. Well, my lads, it was only a few days after the murder of Ben, that it came on a precious storm, and we were tossed about like a cork in a heavy sea. It blew great guns; and, as for managing the vessel, it was quite unpossible. Ah! thought I, this is the penalty for the cold-blooded murder of poor Ben. We shall none of us outlive this storm. And so the pirates seemed to think; for they were all of them very dull; and, as the captain madly dashed amongst them, and gave his orders in a hoarse voice, and with eyes flashing like those of a fiend, they treated him with indifference, and seemed to be callous as to what became of them, and did not exert themselves but very little, appearing as though they had made up their minds to meet with a watery grave. Two nights and three days we was tossed about in this manner, expecting that we should founder every moment. We had thrown all our guns overboard, and done everything we could to lighten the brig, so that if we had encountered an enemy afterwards, we should have been captured, there could not be the least doubt. During this time, at least, on each night, Ben's ghost was constantly present to us all, no matter in what part of the vessel we were, there he was sure to be. Separate, or together, every person on board was sure to see him; and every night he would look more ghastly than ever. I shall never be able to scratch that from the log-book of my memory the longest day I am afloat. Every now and then he would raise a pitiful, wailing cry, which might be heard above the howling of the tempest, and the roaring of the waves; and then his eyes would glare so frightfully, that it was enough to freeze the blood to ice to gaze upon him. As for the captain, he had become quite un-manageable; perfectly mad; and it was terrible to see him rushing to all parts of the vessel, covering his eyes with his hands, and trying, but in vain, to shut out the awful object which haunted him continually. And then his groans were ter-rific to hear! The curse of his murdered victim was upon him; and he was suffering all the torments of hell. Monster as he was, I could not help pitying the poor wretch; but his punishment was no more than he deserved. On the third day, I could perceive a strange change in the behaviour of the pirate crew; they watched the movements of their captain with suspicious looks; and, alternately, they collected in groups together, and consulted with one another in whispers. The captain had become totally incapable of giving any orders; in fact, he had completely lost his senses, and had stretched himself at full length in the fore-castle, where he groaned and writhed in mental and bodily agony, without any one going near him, to offer to render him any assistance.

" During this time, the ship was almost entirely neglected, and it was a won-der how she could live so long in such a storm. Our pumps were choaked, and most of the crew stood looking at one another in despair, or with an expression of countenance which I could not very well understand. Hows'ever, I was very soon made acquainted with the meaning of it. All at once, I noticed a signal made amongst about a dozen of the pirates, and in an instant they rushed to the fore-castle, from which the groans and curses of the captain could be distinctly heard. In a minute or two, they returned with him in their arms, and his struggles were terrific; it was as much as they could do to hold him; and then his face did look so awful;—his complexion had become leaden, like that of a corpse; he was foaming at the mouth like a mad person; and his eyes shone with a fierceness that made them appear as if they could not possibly belong to a human being. He called loudly upon the name of Ben; and, with many horrible curses, begged of those who held him, not to allow him to gnaw at his heart, and to remove the red-hot coals from his brains. But the pirates heeded not his cries; their minds seemed to be made up: they bore him, struggling desperately, to the side of the vessel :—I covered my eyes with my hands, to shut out the horrible sight; and the blood ran coldly through my veins. A moment more, and I heard a loud splash in the ocean, which was followed by such a piercing shriek that I shall never forget. I removed my hand from my eyes :—the sea-devil was gone! but a supernatural light illumined the deck, and shone upon the dark countenances of the pirates in such a manner as I never saw the like before, nor do I believe that the oldest man in the fleet ever did before me. Justice had been done—the captain was tossed overboard to the sharks; and, as I heard from the pirates afterwards, the moment the waves received his carcase, the ghost of Ben Walton appeared above the spot where he had disappeared, and laughing exultingly for a second or two, became lost to the sight.

" Well, Dick," said the sailor, who had before interrupted the narrator, "that here is sartinly a tough yarn o' yourn, and I think you had better splice the main brace before you proceed any furder. Drink, shipmate, and destruction to all pirates !"

" Ditto, repeated, as our chaplain used to say, on board of the ' Thunderer,' when he was swallowing off his sixteenth jorum of grog," observed Dick Taffrail, taking the glass in his hand, " and a sound drubbing to them either on shore or at sea."

As the other sailor and Dick thus plainly gave expression to their sentiments, the man, whom they had designated captain, and his companions, looked round fiercely, and seemed half inclined to quarrel with them ; but, after frowning upon them darkly, which the former returned with a look of perfect coldness and contempt, they removed their gaze, resumed the conversation they had been carrying on amongst themselves, and suffered Dick Taffrail and his friends to enjoy themselves in the way they thought best, without offering to interrupt them.

" I s'pose," said the sailor before mentioned, addressing himself to Dick—" I s'pose, arter th' death o' th' captain, th' ghost didn't trouble yer agin, an' that th' storm abated ?"

" No such thing," answered Taffrail ; " to be sure, we didn't see no more o' Ben ; but the vessel soon afterwards split upon a rock, and went to pieces, and me and two others, were all that contrived to get into the long boat ; all the others perished. I was driven about for three days in the boat, before I was picked up by a vessel homeward bound ;—but my two companions had expired of hunger and fatigue three hours before, and thus I am the only survivor of that ill-fated vessel."

" And, is that the whole of your yarn, Dick ?" inquired another sailor.

" Th' whole of it !" reiterated Dick. " To be sure it is, and a very tidy yarn, too, it is, I think ; and ev'ry word on it is as true as if the parson o' the parish had told it yer."

" Talk about a shipwreck," remarked one of the companions of Dick Taffrail, " th' loss of th' ' Sea Lion,' eighty-four, in 1764, *was* one, when Sam Belson and I was exposed in a open boat for four days-and-a-half, without any purwisions whatsomever, but half a dozen biscuits !"

" And survived arter all ?" queried a rough-looking old tar seated in the corner, with an incredulous leer.

" I did," answered the sailor ; " but Sam didn't,—he committed suicide !"

" Committed suicide ?—That's rather an uncommon thing for a sailor to do.—But, how was it ?"

" Why, I'll tell yer," observed Jack Spicer, which was the name of the speaker ; " it was a very sing'lar death, as Sam met with, an' I wos very careful in entering it in the log-book o' my mem'ry. Sam and I, as I said afore, was exposed in a open boat, and it was so cold that we could not speak to each other ;—the words were actually frozen in our mouths ; and I recollect when I was picked up, and placed before the galley fire, as soon as I began to thaw, the conversation as I had intended to have addressed to Sam, came from me so fast, that I was almost choked, and the sailors didn't know what to make of me."

" I dare say, that's not at all unlikely," said Dick Taffrail, blowing a very stiff cloud, and wagging his right leg, which swung over his left knee.

" Well," resumed Jack Spicer, " it was very hard lines for us, and die, I certainly thought we must. We eat the biscuits in no time; and then we was so precious hungry, that we was ready to eat one another. Howsomever, I had rather a delicate appetite at all times, and I could sooner starve than do as my shipmate did. On th' second day, I see him look at his shoes very greedily, and, presently, he takes 'em off, one at a time, and crunched 'em up before I could cry Jack Robinson. His trousers was the next thing; they was canvas; but it was no matter to him; he tore the right leg away, and swallowed that in no time; and he seemed to like the flavour on it, too, for he tore th' left leg away, and that went as quick as th' other. He didn't eat any more that day; but the next, he swallowed his jacket, shirt, and hat, while I sat and looked at him with an empty stomach, but couldn't follow his example, for th' life o' me. When the third day came, he looked very suspiciously at his feet, and he soon went to work upon them !"

" Avast! avast! there, mate," said Dick; " you don't mean for to go for to say, as he devoured his feet?"

" But I do, though," said Jack Spicer; " they were only a bit of a snack to him, for his legs followed in a very short time afterwards. Th' next day, he swallowed both of his arms, an' part of his trunk, and, on the fifth day, he finished the latter !"

" And, what then ?" asked several, in a breath.

" Why, he swallowed his head, to be sure; and, arter that, jumped overboard in despair !" was Jack Spicer's reply. The sailors looked at each other, winked and laughed.

At this moment, the parlour door was opened, and the faces of all the guests were turned to see who was the person about to enter. It was Saib, the black, who, upon seeing the man in the P jacket, made his way over towards the table at which he and his companions were seated, without seeming to take any notice of any of the other inmates of the room.

" Captain Barnsley," said the African, speaking to the man whom we have before described, " I would have a few words with you."

" I am ready to hear you, Saib," said the former;—" be seated."

" Not here," added the black : " our conference must be alone. Can you attend me in another room for a few minutes ?"

" Lead the way," said Barnsley, " I will follow you.—I shall be with you again shortly," added he, addressing himself to the unprepossessing men who were his companions.

Saib immediately left the parlour, accompanied by Barnsley, and proceeded to a small room at the back of the premises, which he had previously bespoken of the landlord.

" So, you have returned again," said Saib, after he had closed the door: " what success have you met with on your last voyage ?"

" Oh, glorious!" answered Barnsley. " Fortune never smiled more bounteously upon me, since I took possession of my noble craft."

" What would you ?"

" You shall quickly hear," answered the black; " and when 1 tell you, that you will be handsomely rewarded for your trouble, I do not think that you will refuse me."

" You say right, Saib," said Captain Barnsley. " What risk is there, I should like to know, that Will Barnsley, the pirate captain, would not run to obtain the bright yellow gold? But, what is it you would have me do ?"

" First of all, you must swear, that if you decline my request, that you will never betray me."

" Avast! avast! there," exclaimed Barnsley; " there is no need for so much caution :—you know me. As for swearing, if you cannot take my word, why there's an end of the matter, and you had better get somebody else to do your business."

" No, there is not any necessity for that, Barnsley; I know I can trust you, and will, therefore, open my mind at once to you. You know ' The Old Com- modore.' "

" Know it!" cried Barnsley; " I should think I do; and many a time have I been there, if it was for nothing else than to look at and admire old Mat's pretty daughter. She is a fine lass, and I shouldn't care if she was entered along side o' me in the log-book of matrimony."

" Of course, then, you know her sweetheart ?"

" What, Tom Clewline, who has not long returned home ?" said Barnsley.— " Indeed, I do ; and a fine fellow he is, every way worthy of the lass, although I envy him his good fortune. I like his acquaintance vastly, and wish we could nab him aboard our vessel ; we want experienced hands, and he's an excellent seaman, and a good navigator."

" That is the very thing I want you to do," said Saib, an expression of pleasure passing over his sable features. " You know that this fellow, this Gallant Tom, as he is called, is no friend of mine ?"

" Aye, aye," returned the pirate captain, " I know all about that ; — you would have him out of the way !—and I would have him on board my ship."

" Exactly so."

" The task, mayhap, will be rather difficult to accomplish," observed Barnsley. " What reward would you feel disposed to give ?

" Fifty guineas," answered the black.

" Fifty guineas!—I am at your service," cried Barnsley, eagerly ; " and I am much deceived, if in less than a week he is not aboard my vessel."

" Bravely said," exclaimed the African ; " and I hope your surmises may prove correct; I may then not mind making an addition of a few pounds to the reward I have offered you. But, has Tom any suspicion of your real character ?"

" Suspicion," repeated Barnsley; " not the least.—How should he ? I have always managed to make myself very agreeable while in his presence ; and, although we have been within hail of each other but a short reckoning, and met by accident aboard ' The Old Commodore,' he has often told me, he thought me a good fellow—one who would like to do a good turn to any one in distress ; and we have drank many a glass of grog together. I have often longed to entrap him by some means or the other ; and, before this, have frequently thought of getting

the grog aboard, trying to saw up his daylights, and getting him into such a condition that he would have neither eyes to see with, nor ears to hear with. Hitherto, however, I have not had an opportunity of putting my wishes into execution; but I feel confident, that in a very few days, not only will Tom Clewline be in my power, but his sweetheart, the pretty Ellen."

"What! and do you mean to seize upon the girl as well?" inquired Saib.

"To be sure I do," answered Barnsley; "what's the use of doing things by halves?—I want the lass equally as much as I do the sailor."

"Ah! that will be more glorious revenge, still," cried the African. "But, how do you purpose accomplishing your task?"

"Leave that to me," answered the pirate captain. "I have already a stratagem in my mind; and, do not fear but that I shall meet with success.—But, you remember your agreement?—Fifty guineas, or more, if I am successful?"

"True."

"Your hand—it is a bargain: but, mind you do not deceive me, or you may guess what the consequences will be."

"Psha!" ejaculated Saib, impatiently; "why should you doubt me?—We are no strangers to each other:—the moment the deed is accomplished, the gold shall be yours; at least, as soon as I am made acquainted with it."

"Enough," observed the other: "and, now, will you not join me and my companions in the other room, and have a glass of grog over the business?"

"No, not now, Barnsley," replied Saib; "I have other business to attend to,
No. 10.

and must depart immediately.   Do not lose any time in setting about putting your designs into execution—delays are dangerous."

"Leave me alone for that," said Barnsley.   "You will not find me any dawdler; besides, I must not remain here, for fear the real character of my vessel should be found out.   Good night, Saib, since you will not accept of my invitation."

"Good night!" responded the black, and, having shook the pirate's hand, he stalked from the house, and pondering with satisfaction upon the ready compliance of Barnsley (or, "Grim Barnsley," as he was more commonly called) with his wishes, he hastened on towards home.

Rosina, who had known the business Tom was going upon to the mansion of the Earl Fitzosbert, and had tried to dissuade him from it, became uneasy at the length of his absence, and, at last, unable to endure the surmises, doubts, and apprehensions which rushed upon her mind, she requested Patty to hasten to 'The Old Commodore,' to see whether he had stopped there on his way.

Patty readily complied; although, to tell the truth, she would much rather it had been at any other time, for she had just sat down to write a letter to her sweetheart, Toby Twitter, full of bitter reproaches and remonstrances, inasmuch as she suspected that he was faithless to her, as he had not been to see her more than twice since their return to Plymouth; and she had good reasons to suppose that he had placed his affections on a certain little black girl, who was on board the same vessel with them, and who was called Cheeti.

Patty walked along in a melancholy mood, her thoughts occupied by the reflections which her jealous feelings gave rise to; and she had got to within a short distance of 'The Old Commodore,' and was walking up a lane which led to it, when the voices of a man and woman, in conversation, in the field, met her ears.   She listened, and her heart throbbed violently, when she recognised in the voice of the man that of the faithless Toby, while the broken accents of the female convinced her that it was the sable object who had excited her jealousy.   So great was her agitation, that it was with the utmost difficulty she could support herself.   She looked through the hedge, and by the light of the moon, beheld them seated on the grass, and so near, that she could plainly distinguish every word they uttered.

"Ah! Massa Toby," said Cheeti, in a tone of reproach, "you berry much little naughty man; you win poor Cheeti's heart, bring her ashore, and den you want to desert her."

"Why, the truth is, my darling Miss Black-pudding," returned Toby, laughing, "something tells me, that I have not acted right, after the vows I have made to Patty, and the risk she run in following me to sea; and, therefore, I think our acquaintance had better cease at once.   But, what's the matter, my delicate powder puff?"

"Ah! Massa Toby," said Cheeti, "you berry bad man, and great deceiver. You promise, when me get to England, to make me your chum-chum."

"Well, so I did, to be sure," remarked Toby; "and—why, I will not be worse than my word; that's all about it."

"Den you will make me your chum-chum?"

"Yes, my delicate little angel," said Toby, "as soon as we can make the necessary arrangements, and I have broken off with Patty, you shall be made Mrs. Twitter. But, where's the money you was speaking about?"

" Money! money!" answered Cheeti; "me tought you hab de money, Massa Toby."

"Nonsense," returned Toby, in altered accents; " did I not acknowledge to you, that I was as poor as a church mouse?—and, did I not make it a particular condition of my marrying you, that you should give me all the money that you said you had saved up?"

" Me know dat," said the black girl; "but dere be reasons for my not doing so."

"What, because you have not got any, I suppose."

" Iss, iss, massa."

" And did you expect that Mr. Toby Twitter would be so unfashionable, as to marry a wife without money?"

" Me tought you one ob dose generous English dat——"

" Oh, then you are much mistaken," rejoined Toby, in a tone of disappointment, "being English, is no reason for a man not making money one of his conditions when he intends to marry."

" I tought, Massa Toby——"

" Look you, Cheeti," said the faithless Toby, " that individual has very little right to the name of man, who, when a *fine* girl, like yourself, throws herself upon his honour, casts her off, because she can't pay her way into becoming a wife :—but, still, those four letters, G, O, L, D, do make a wonderful difference in a case like this."

"Iss," replied the black girl; " but dere be four oder letters dat make amends for dat, L, O, V, E ; and dat is followed by two oders as is much better still."

" What are they?"

" Good wife, massa," answered the girl, laughing archly.

" Come to my arms, my pretty snowball," cried Toby, embracing Cheeti with much apparent rapture, " I believe if you have not wealth, you have good sense; and, if your fortune consisted of your clothes upon your back only, from this moment I take you for better, for worse; and I should feel a pleasure in converting some of my own wardrobe to your use, upon this condition, that you never think of wearing the breeches."

" Den I am you chum-chum for ebber?" cried Cheeti, joyfully: " I try wedder him heart in right place, and now I find it is, I tell you, me hab lots of money."

"No!—Have you though?"

" Iss, I hab."

" You take away my breath with surprise," said Toby.—" Come to my arms once more, my little angel."

Again, Toby Twitter embraced the sable damsel, while Patty looked on, in a state of mind which only those who have felt the torments of jealousy can imagine; but it was not a little increased, when they commenced singing a duet, which she had not the least doubt they had well studied together, from the correct manner in which they sang it. As it is rather a novelty in its way, we transcribe it here, for the amusement of our readers.—

DUET.

CHEETI.—Cheeti den be buckra's wife,
    Ching-a-ring, ching-a-ring, chickaboo, chickaboo;
Happy den she be for life,
    Ching-a-ring, &c.
Wat, dough black as 'm coal 'm skin,
    Cheeti hab *fair* heart within:

BOTH.   Ching-a-ring, ching-a-ring,
          Chickaboo, chickaboo,
       Ching-a-ring, ching-a-ring, chickaboo!

TOBY.—Come, my pretty angel black,
    Ching-a-ring, &c.
Your lovely, pouting lips I'll smack,
    Ching-a-ring, &c.
What though black as mud you be,
    You never will *look black on me!*
          Ching-a-ring, &c.

CHEETI.—How bery much happy we will be,
    Ching-a-ring, &c.

TOBY.—With a lot of little whitey-browns on our knee,
    Ching-a-ring, &c.

CHEETI.—Den we will make de bargain right.

TOBY.—We'll hab it all in *black and white!*
          Ching-a-ring, &c.

Having finished this splendid specimen of poetry, which they shouted rather than sang, they commenced dancing to the chorus in the most extravagant style, and in that manner retired from the spot, leaving poor Patty completely paralyzed with astonishment, grief, and indignation.

For some minutes Patty was unable to move from the spot, she was so confused and thunderstruck; but she did what most females would have done under similar circumstances, viz:—she burst forth into a paroxysm of sobs and tears; called him "a nasty, deceitful, good-for-nothing fellow;" said she would never so much as look at him again, and left the place with her heart more full of love for him than ever.

It was with a heavy heart that Patty made her way to 'The Old Commodore,' revolving in her mind the scene she had witnessed between her faithless lover and Cheeti.

"But, to abandon me for an ugly, thick-lipped black girl!" said she:—"this is intolerable. After all that I have undergone, too, for his sake!—Oh! I could tear his eyes out, that I could! There's my new white dress of no use at all, now!—But it shall be, though!—Yes, I will marry the first man that offers himself to me, if he is nothing more than a tinker!—that I will, just to spite him!"

And, with these words, Patty sobbed more violently than ever, and her tears flowed fast and unrestrained until she reached 'The Old Commodore,' where her grief was noticed; but she evaded the questions put to her, and, having ascertained that Tom had been there, but had departed a few minutes before her arrival, and must have gone a different way, or she would have met him, she hastily left the place, and returned home, with a heart so full, that it was almost ready to burst. To her mistress, she imparted all that she had seen and overheard; and Rosina sympathised with her, and endeavoured to console her. Patty, however, was inconsolable, and ultimately retired to her own room, first, to give free indulgence to the feelings occasioned by vexation, disappointment, and indignation; and, afterwards, to write a letter to Mr. Toby Twitter, reproaching him for his base misconduct, and concluded in words of severity, which the circumstances dictated.

Will Barnsley, the pirate captain, and Saib, saw each other by appointment the following day, and concerted their infamous plot against Tom and Ellen; and it was agreed to endeavour to accomplish it without delay.

"The boy, Richard, too," said the African, on this, their second interview, "you know him?"

"Aye, to be sure I do," answered Barnsley, "and a fine lad he is: I only wish I could come athwart his hawse;—he'd make a fine fellow for our business."

"Could you but manage to entrap him as well as the others," said Saib, his large, fierce eyes glowing with fire, "I could promise you one hundred guineas more to the sum I have already agreed to give you."

"Ah! say you so?" exclaimed Barnsley, eagerly; "but, why should you wish the boy to be placed under hatches?—What can the boy have done to make him obnoxious to you?"

"That matters not to you," answered the black; "it is enough that I wish to get rid of him; and I care not what becomes of him, so that he is not allowed to set his foot in England again."

"It shall be done, you may depend upon it; leave Will Barnsley alone for succeeding in any plot he may have fixed his mind upon. But, hark ye, Master Saib, no deceit in this affair. The money must be all forthcoming at the time specified; and, if it is not, you—but I have no occasion to threaten yet; you know me before to-day."

"Right, right," answered Saib; "you have no occasion to doubt me; there will be no treachery on my part; but I hope you will use all the expedition you can in this affair."

"Aye, aye, you may be sure I shall do that," said Barnsley, "for my own sake, I do not want to lie here, wasting my time any longer than I can help; but I am anxious to be upon another cruise. The ocean is my home, and I feel like a sea-gull in a puddle when I am not upon it. Not many days shall elapse ere those I want shall be safe aboard my brig, and then away we go like lightning before the wind, bidding defiance to any of the Government cutters to overtake us, for we outsail them all."

They departed, and Saib sought the presence of the Earl Fitzosbert, whom he had not seen since the scene which took place between them and Tom. He found him in a gloomy mood, his mind evidently affected after the interview above alluded to; and he was labouring under that state of doubt, suspense, and perplexity, which constantly rendered him so truly wretched. He was pacing his apartment with uneven strides, when Saib entered; and, upon beholding him, he started, and seemed confused and violently agitated.

" My lord," said Saib, sneeringly, and with a look that showed he held Fitz-osbert in his power, and felt for him the most superlative contempt, " when I left you, yesterday, I expressed a wish, when next we met, you might have re-covered from that nervous debility which at that time afflicted you. But I per-ceive that my wishes are not gratified. Bah ! my lord, this weakness would dis-grace a whining, love-sick girl ;—I am ashamed of you !"

" You talk rather boldly, methinks, Saib," said Fitzosbert, sternly.

" I know no reason why I should fear to speak to you," returned the African, scornfully. " I owe you no obligation,—and yet you are indebted to me for——"

" For all the misery, the torture, the incessant torture which racks my brain," added the earl. " Oh, Saib, would that we had never met."

" Well, we can quickly end our acquaintance, if you wish it," said the black, with an ironical grin, which rendered his features more hideous than ever ; " but remember, I shall expect to share equally with you that wealth I have been the principal means of getting."

" Would that I could purchase a clear conscience at so cheap a rate," groaned the earl.

" 'Psha !—Enough of this foolery," exclaimed Saib, impatiently. " I cam not here to talk of conscience, but to inform you, that I have made such arrange-ments to remove the objects of your fears as cannot fail to succeed."

" Ah !" cried the earl, eagerly.—" what mean you ?—Tell me, quick !"

Saib, in as few words as possible, informed Fitzosbert of the plans which Will Barnsley and himself had concocted, to which he listened with the greatest atten-tion. A faint smile of satisfaction for a moment or two passed over his features ; but it soon vanished, and was succeeded by the same expression of gloom and intense sorrow which had before overclouded it.

" Of what avail will this be ?" said he. " From circumstances which have already taken place, we shall be suspected of having been the cause of it, and, most undoubtedly, be brought to justice for it."

" Your childish fears will be the means of betraying us," returned Saib ; " but the stratagem shall be put into operation ; I have so far proceeded with it, and I am determined that nothing shall now induce me to abandon it. I would advise you to banish those fears from your mind as soon as possible, or you may repent them when too late."

With these words, Saib stalked out of the room without giving Fitzosbert time to make any reply.

Thus passed away a week, and Tom was a constant guest of ' The Old Com-modore,' and in the society of his beloved Ellen, and indulging in bright antici-pations of the future, was extremely happy. Sometimes they would walk to the place which Rosina had for the present made her retreat, and the two amiable girls in each other's society forgot the difference of their rank, and soon became as much attached to one another as if they were sisters. The settlement of Tom and his sister's affairs, had been placed in the hands of an eminent lawyer, and there was not any reason to doubt but that they would be speedily adjusted to their satisfaction. Tom had not yet quitted the service, and he had determined not to do so, although he expected a higher station than that he had hitherto occupied.

Old Mat still persisted in keeping the purport of his interview with the stranger a secret, and it was noticed that he was frequently absent from home, and no one knew whither he went. The stranger was not seen again at the tavern; but the dame and Ellen had every reason to believe that he was residing somewhere in the neighbourhood, and that it was to him the frequent visits of Mat were paid.

Richard had by this time grown a fine lad, and his mind was as intelligent as his person and features were handsome. There was a certain nobleness and dignity in his general behaviour, which seemed far above his station in life; and there were several who often ventured to premise, that he was not the nephew of old Mat. The voyage he had taken had greatly improved him, and he loved a sailor's life most enthusiastically. Bold, intrepid, vigorous, and enterprising, he possessed all the qualifications for a gallant seaman; and Tom looked upon him with no little pride, and declared that his *protégé* would be an honour to the profession. On board the vessel, he had gained the respect and admiration of all the officers and crew; for he was always ready to oblige any one, and was so cheerful and buoyant, that he kept them all amused. His courageous conduct, by which he saved the vessel and the whole of the ship's company, when the villain Saib made his diabolical attempt to fire the powder magazine, had gained him the gratitude of the officers and all the crew; and he not only received a handsome reward from the Lords of the Admiralty, but a promise of speedy promotion. It was with feelings of delight that Mat watched the expanding virtues of his foundling; and he felt pleased to think he had suffered him to follow the bent of his inclinations, and to enter a service he was so well qualified to adorn. But it could not escape the notice of every one, that lately his affection for the lad appeared, if possible, to increase, and something seemed to raise his spirits in an extraordinary degree. Often the dame caught him watching the lad with more than usual earnestness; and then he would suddenly burst into a joyous laugh, which, when questioned about, he would make no reply to, but hastily leave the house, from which he would, probably, be absent for several hours.

This conduct created much surprise in the mind of the old woman, and she was all anxiety to learn the cause; but Mat, most scrupulously, evaded her questions, generally observing, " that she would know all by and bye." With this reply, the dame was forced to appear contented, though she was far from satisfied; and her thoughts often wandered to the stranger who sought shelter at their house, and whose extraordinary likeness to Richard had so forcibly struck her She could not help thinking that, in some way or the other, they were connected.

Richard and Ellen were very much attached to each other; in fact, had they been related by the ties of consanguinity, they could not have loved each other more. No thought, no wish, had Ellen, which Richard could not read; and, if it were in his power, how readily would he fly to gratify it.

They had been companions from childhood, and never had they been known to have a quarrel. Richard would be the first to resent what he considered to be an insult offered to her by any of their young companions. He stood boldly forth, even then, as the champion of his " pretty coz," as he was accustomed to call her, although Ellen was several years his senior.

Mat and his wife encouraged this attachment, although the former frequently hinted that, probably, at some future period, circumstances might occur to interrupt it.

"Never!" exclaimed Richard, vehemently, one day, when Mat had been making similar observations. "What! cease to love my dear cousin Ellen!—her, who has been so kind to me always;—my companion;—my playmate?—Oh, uncle, I could sooner part with my life, than I could act in such a manner!"

"You are a good lad," observed Mat, "and I know you speak sincerely. Do not suppose, for a moment, that I expect you will ever forget Ellen, or—but, who knows, there are strange things happen sometimes in the course of a person's life;—and, who can tell, but that circumstances may place you in a situation that——"

"What circumstances can ever have the effect to make me forget my dearest friends?" hastily interrupted the lad. "Why do you speak thus, dear uncle?"

Mat appeared to be rather confused.

"Why, you see, Dick," replied he, "you may get on in the world, and get promoted; and then, mayhap, it might not be pleasant for you to acknowledge your old friends, and——"

"Oh! if it is possible that I could ever act with such ingratitude, let me ever remain as I am!" ejaculated Richard, with a fervour which spoke his sincerity. But, you wrong me, dear uncle, by such a supposition: neither time, nor circumstances, can, I am certain, ever alter the sentiments I entertain towards you, my beloved uncle, aunt, and cousin Ellen; nor would I forfeit the love of you all, to be made King of England!"

"Noble boy, noble boy," ejaculated the old man, while a tear of affection forced itself from his eye, and rolled down his forehead and weather-beaten cheek; "damme, you will be made a Lord High Admiral before you die, and that's the truth of it. Dick, how should you like to be a gentleman?"

"A gentleman!" repeated Richard! "oh, I should, indeed, like to have plenty of money, so that I might make those independant that have ever been so good and kind to me."

"Nobly spoken, again," remarked Mat, joyfully. "Mark my words, Dick, you *shall* be a gentleman:—you shall be rich, and——"

"But, why, my dear uncle," said Richard, "are you so sanguine as to my future fortune?—What prospects have I beyond what I may obtain by my own perseverance?"

"What prospects!" reiterated Mat, sharply; "what prospects!—why, ain't you—but, avast, avast, Mat, you are on the wrong tack:—damme, if I know what I'm talking about. But, see, here comes Tom and Ellen; bless her pretty face, she looks as happy as an angel."

Tom and his sweetheart now entered the house, they having been on a visit to Rosina, who kept herself as much secluded as possible, until the law-suit pending with the Earl Fitzosbert was settled. The conversation was, therefore, changed; but Richard had noticed the singularity of old Mat's behaviour, and it made a forcible impression upon him. He was confident there was more in the words than he could at that time understand; and he reflected deeply upon them. But,

why the words of his uncle should continue to haunt his memory, he was at a loss at the same time to conjecture.

He had walked forth from the house, and proceeded along the sea-beach, revolving the above-mentioned circumstance in his mind, when, suddenly, he was aroused by observing a long shadow on the sand, and, looking up, he beheld, standing at a short distance from him, with his arms folded in his mantle, the stranger, who had sought shelter in 'The Old Commodore,' a week or two before. He was immoveable as a statue, and seemed to be gazing upon Richard with an earnest expression of the deepest interest.

For a few seconds Richard paused, and contemplated the stranger with a feeling equally as intense as that which seemed to occupy the bosom of the latter. There was something in the features of the stranger which rivetted the attention of the lad, and caused a sensation in his breast, which, to him, was perfectly unaccountable. It was a sensation of the most unbounded esteem; a feeling that made his young blood glow in his veins; and he could have rushed into the arms of the unknown, and embraced him with all the ardour of filial affection. A deep melancholy seemed settled in the countenance of the stranger; but there was something so mild, so noble, and so amiable in its expression, that it excited immediate respect in the bosom of the beholder.

Determined at length to speak to him, Richard hastened on. The stranger did not move at first, and seemed to be so entirely absorbed by the thoughts that occupied his mind, as to be completely rivetted to the spot; but when Richard had got near him, he suddenly turned round, left the spot with the greatest precipitation, and was quickly out of sight.

No. 11

Richard stood looking in the direction the stranger had taken for some moments, and then made his way towards home, reflecting upon what had taken place. He felt an unaccountable interest in the stranger, and was most anxious to ascertain who he was; but in that he had no prospect of succeeding. Do all he could, he could not erase him from his thoughts the whole of the day; and yet he was at a loss to imagine why he should so particularly engross all his ideas. The expression of deep melancholy which marked his features, had struck the lad most forcibly; and he already sympathised in his misfortunes whatever they might be.

These thoughts haunted his mind long after he had retired to rest; and in his dreams he again beheld the form of the unknown, and saw his fine expressive eyes fixed intently on his countenance. Another time he fancied he was kneeling at his feet, and clasping his knees fervently, while his heart palpitated more powerfully than usual, with the force of the feelings that at that time seemed to have taken possession of his bosom.

Suddenly, he was awakened by a noise in the chamber, and, rubbing his eyes, caught a slight glimpse of what he imagined was some person in the room. He raised himself on his elbow, and looked eagerly around. The moon was riding majestically in the heavens, and her silvery light perfectly illumined the apartment; but Richard could not now behold any object, and, concluding that it had been only fancy, he once more laid himself down, and went to sleep.

Again, however, was he awakened by a similar noise to that which had before aroused him, and, jumping up instantaneously in the bed, he beheld, standing affectionately over him, the tall and handsome figure of the stranger.

For a moment or two after he saw that Richard was awake, and observed him, he stood gazing upon him with a look of the most indescribable tenderness; then, sighing deeply, he raised his hands momentarily, as if invoking a blessing upon his head, and, turning suddenly towards the door, he had quitted the room before Richard had sufficiently recovered from his astonishment to speak.

Completely thunderstruck by what he had seen, Richard jumped from his couch, and went to the door,—but the stranger was gone, and he distinctly heard the outer door closed after him. On going to the casement, and looking out, he saw him hastening away in the direction which led to the high road, and shortly afterwards he was hidden from his view.

Confident that it was no dream, Richard now tried in vain to conjecture the cause of the stranger's mysterious visit to him, and how he had gained admittance to the house. He was inclined to think, however, that he meant no harm, although his motives for acting in so singular a manner were entirely beyond his comprehension.

He knew he should not be able to sleep any more that night, and he, therefore, remained at the window, wrapt in thought, and gazing upon the fantastic shadows which were thrown across the road by the reflection of the moon-beams. Suddenly, however, his attention was drawn to two men, who had just turned a corner of the road, and were advancing in the direction of the house. As well as his sight would permit him to discern, the persons of the men appeared to be familiar to him; and, as they advanced nearer, he was not a little surprised to recognise Will Barnsley and Saib.

Wondering what they could want together at such a strange hour, and apprehending that they intended no good (for Richard had never liked the pirate captain, although he had contrived to insinuate himself into the favour of Tom), he was half inclined to arouse his uncle; but, then, thinking it might cause considerable unnecessary alarm, he abandoned the thought, and resolved to watch them narrowly instead.

They were evidently buried in deep conversation; and from the extravagant gestures of the black, it appeared to be something of importance. Having reached the house, they paused, and Saib looked up with a look of savage meaning, and, addressing himself to his companion, said :—

" In this house is one of the principal objects of my hatred; the bane of my peace; the hated brat, whom I——"

The wind carried away the other part of the sentence, and left the extraordinary curiosity which the tenour of the speech had excited in Richard's bosom ungratified.

" All is still in the house," Richard at last heard the black remark; " the inmates are wrapt in sleep; it would be no difficult matter to force an entrance, and then the deed I have before tried to effect, could be perpetrated without danger. By hell——"

" Hold !" exclaimed Barnsley, " would you spoil everything? What occasion is there for this risk, when all that you can wish can be accomplished in the way I have suggested to you, without the least danger ?—Come away,—come away,— the morning will break soon, and I must aboard ! Fear not ; what I have promised you, I will accomplish ! Grim Barnsley never yet fixed his mind upon the execution of anything, which he afterwards failed in."

" Be it so," said Saib, turning reluctantly away, " I will trust to you."

" You may do so with safety," answered the other ; " the plot is ripening, and soon——"

Another gust of wind which swept around the gable of the house, again rendered the last words of Will Barnsley's speech inaudible; but Richard had gathered quite sufficient from it, to convince him that there was some villanous stratagem in contemplation by the pirate and the African which was directed against himself and his family; and he felt thankful that he had thus providentially become aware of it in time to put them on their guard.

Will Barnsley had been a constant visitor at ' The Old Commodore,' for the last few days, and Richard had taken notice of the particular attention he had paid to Tom and himself; and the former had several times expressed a good opinion of the pirate, and said he was a very good sort of fellow, and just the man he should like to sail under, if he was in the merchant service. When Mat had expressed a contrary opinion, and said, that there was something very coarse and disagreeable about his manners, which was far from taking his fancy, Tom had combatted it strenuously, and said, that although he was rather plain in his manners, it shewed that he was an honest, blunt disposition, and he liked him all the better for it.

Richard was, however, as we have before stated, far from prepossessed in favour of the captain or his crew, who were all dark and savage-looking men, and inspired him with a feeling of dread whenever he beheld them. The lad, too, from certain things which he had noticed, and from words which the men belonging to her had inadvertantly dropped, had strong suspicions that "The Nancy" was not a fair trading vessel, and had ventured to hint the same to Tom; but he would not listen to it for a moment, and reproached Richard for being too ready to suspect such a thing. In fact, the fancy which Tom had imbibed for the society of Will Barnsley, was so great, that he was with him at every opportunity, and nothing could be more favourable to the pirates nefarious designs, than the present position of affairs.

The circumstance which Richard had observed, and the conversation he had overheard between Barnsley and Saib, he had no doubt would alter the opinion of Tom, and render him cautious not to be trepanned into any plot which might be laid against him; at least, so thought Richard, and we shall see whether or not his surmises were verified.

As soon as he heard the inmates of the house stirring about, Richard sought the presence of Mat; and, in the first place, related to him all the particulars of the singular visit which the unknown had paid to him. He, of course, expected to see his uncle evince great surprise, upon being made acquainted with this circumstance; but, to his astonishment, he evinced not the least emotion, and only said that he must have been mistaken, and have been labouring under the delusion of a dream; for, how was it possible that any person could gain access to the house without their knowledge, when he had himself seen that very door and window was properly secured before he had retired to rest?

Richard, however, protested earnestly that he could not possibly have been deceived; in proof of which, he mentioned the circumstance of his having heard the stranger close the outer door, and also watching him from the easement afterwards. But Mat did not seem to like the subject; and still affecting to treat Richard's statement with incredulity, he was about to leave the room, to attend upon his business, when Richard detained him, and related what he had afterwards seen, and the brief dialogue he had overheard between Will Barnsley and Saib. Mat listened to this attentively, but with the same expression of incredulity, and when he had done, he laughed, and said,—

"Avast heaving there, Dick!—avast! You are throwing the hatchet a little bit now, I think, or else your top-lights were rather misty, when you fancied you saw all these things. I tell you, you have been dreaming, lad."

"Indeed, my dear uncle," answered Richard, vexed at the scepticism of his uncle, "I was as wide awake as I am at the present moment. They stood beneath the casement at which I had placed myself; and, as the moon was shining brightly at the time, I could see everything as clearly as if it had been broad daylight. Had it not been for the wind, I should also have overheard every word they said; but what did meet my ear, I should think is quite enough to urge the necessity of our being upon our guard, and to convince us that this Captain Barnsley is a different character to that which he pretends to be."

"'Psha!" exclaimed Mat, as he turned away; "the boy has become crazed to a certainty! What should we fear from such lubbers, if even there was any truth about what you say?—It was all fancy;—nothing but a dream."

With these words, Mat retired from the room, leaving Richard disappointed and chagrined at the result of his communication. Nevertheless, he determined to make Tom acquainted with the circumstance, and, then, if anything did occur, he should not have himself to blame for neglecting to give them timely warning. With Tom, however, he met with even worse success. The honest-hearted sailor, incapable of deceit himself, was not ready to suspect it in others : he, therefore, strongly defended the character of Barnsley, and was of the same opinion as Mat. Richard, therefore, dropped the subject ; but, confident as he was of the reality of everything he had mentioned, he was far from easy, and determined, at all events, to keep a sharp eye upon the conduct of Barnsley, whenever he came to the house in future.

*   *   *   *   *

The malady of Fitzosbert increased : the knowledge of those persons whom he had injured being so near him, and a strange foreboding that the time was not far distant when his iniquities would be brought to light, and shame, ignominy, and disgrace, descend upon his head, continually haunted his imagination, and made him wretched. The plot which Saib had formed, by no means gave him satisfaction ; on the contrary, he never believed that it would succeed : and, if it did, he saw no hope of any abatement of his anguish, or the danger he was in, from such a circumstance. Alas ! what could ever pour the balm of consolation upon a conscience so heavily laden as his was ?—Nothing ! And, yet, there were times when all his natural ferocity would return to him, and he would curse his own weakness, in thus giving way to fear, and he would invoke curses upon the heads of his enemies, and vow the most deadly vengeance against them.

The insolent behaviour of Saib, also gave the earl considerable uneasiness ; and there were times, when he could have rushed upon him, and plunged a knife to his heart, and thus have ridded himself of the only one who was acquainted with all his dreadful secrets.

And, now was the guilty Fitzosbert further tormented by the reports continually being made by the domestics, of strange noises that they heard in the house, at all hours of the night ; and many of them went so far as to declare that it was haunted, and that they had seen a tall figure, enveloped in a dark mantle, stalking through the hall at midnight ; and were nightly so annoyed by dismal groans, as if proceeding from some person in dying agony, that they could not sleep.

Every night these noises were said to increase rather than abate ; and several of the domestics quitted the earl's service, declaring that nothing should induce them to remain in a house, which now seemed to have become the chosen haunt of some evil spirit or spirits. Fitzosbert had become so wretched, that he almost secluded himself in his own room altogether, and seemed to have given himself up entirely to melancholy and soul-harrowing rumination.

On the day succeeding that on which Richard had seen Barnsley and Saib together, the earl had been more than usually melancholy, which was considerably increased by the time which the black had absented himself, he being always fearful of treachery when he did so. He felt uncommonly depressed upon the occasion we have mentioned, and a presentiment of some approaching calamity tormented his mind, which he in vain endeavoured to shake off ; but when night came, and still Saib did not make his appearance, his anxiety and uneasiness became almost insupportable. He arose from the sofa on which he had been reclining, and walked to the window, and looked out; but it was now quite dark, and he was not able to distinguish any other objects than the black shadows of the tall pines in the grounds attached to the mansion.

He returned once more to the sofa, and threw himself upon it;—his mind was tortured, and his brain was feverish. Suddenly, a deep sigh met his ear; and, raising his head, he was horror-struck on beholding a tall figure, such as had been described by the servants, standing with folded arms exactly opposite to him, and with his piercing eyes fixed full upon his countenance.

The earl's blood curdled in his veins;—his heart seemed to be frozen into a lump of ice ;—his limbs shook with violent agitation, and, in a voice of horror, he cried,—

. "Christ save me !—Shade of the murdered Lionel, avaunt! I dare not,— I cannot encounter thy dreadful gaze ! Nay, fix not thy glassy eyes on me !—It was not I who struck the fatal blow !—Horror ! horror ! away !"

" Robert Fitzosbert," said the supposed phantom, solemnly, "the day of retribution is at hand ; repent, and make all the atonement in your power, ere it is too late! Ere long, justice will overtake you, and a terrible punishment will be the certain reward for the many crimes you have perpetrated ! Beware !— repent !"

" Mercy! mercy !" shrieked the horror-struck earl, as he sunk back on the sofa, and, covering his face with his hands, he became insensible.

To what a sense of horror did the wretched Fitzosbert awaken ! The torments of perdition could scarcely be greater than the earthly hell he endured from the pangs inflicted by his self-accusing conscience. That he had seen a phantom, he firmly believed ; and when he recalled to his memory the ghastly looks it had fixed upon him, and the horrible words it had uttered, he shuddered with horror, and was almost afraid to remain in his chamber with no other person present than his medical attendant.

" Hide me ! shield me from his awful gaze !" he would rave. " Fools !—why do you stand there, gazing upon me, and not start forward to protect me from his terrible vengeance ? Ah ! see !—he approaches towards me ! His cheeks, which erst were redolent of the bloom of health, now wear the hue of the charnel-house :—his eyes, the filmy dimness of death ! Oh, horror !—I cannot bear the sight ! Death—death itself, even in its most awful shape, would be preferable to this torture ! He comes nearer !—He raises his long, bony hands to grasp my throat!—I feel his icy touch upon me !—Dread spirit of my murdered brother, mercy ! mercy !"

The doctor looked upon the servants he had called in to his assistance, and shook his head gravely; they followed his example, and shook their heads solemnly at one another, and slowly left the room. Fitzosbert shortly afterwards sunk into a state of torpor, from which the doctor having ordered him not to be disturbed, left the house.

" Ah !" said old Peter, the porter, when he had descended into the servants' hall, where they were assembled, discussing the events of the day, " God pardon me, if I wrong any one by such a supposition, but I always thought that my poor dear master, and his little son, did not come fairly by their end ; for it was very strange, that they should neither of them be again heard of, after the late Earl

Lionel Fitzosbert went, accompanied by his infant son, to settle some affairs in the country; and, then, that ruffian, Saib, who is a wretch, capable of doing anything, soon afterwards returned, having been absent during the time, and my lord and him used to hold such long conferences together, and they both seemed so agitated if the name of Lionel was mentioned, that—that—well, God is just, and if the poor gentleman was murdered, sooner or later, He is sure to visit the assassins with His Almighty vengeance !"

" Well, well," observed another of the domestics, shrugging up his shoulders, and looking volumes, " things are coming round in a most mysterious manner, and the crime, if murder was really committed, will not remain much longer concealed. Only think of the ghost, which it is very evident the earl has seen, and the strange and dreadful noises which we have heard for some nights past !"

" For my part," said a young man, who was more sceptical than any of the others, " I think it's all mere idle fancy,—nothing more. Ghosts, indeed !—a very good story to tell an old woman ;—ha ! ha ! ha !"

" You may laugh, Mr. Wiseacre," said old Peter, petulantly ; " but I tell you what it is,—I am ready to take an oath, that I have not only heard it, but that I have actually seen the ghost !—aye, as many times as I have got fingers and toes !"

" Indeed !" remarked the young man, who had before spoken with an incredulous laugh ; " then, I should imagine you are pretty well acquainted with each other by this time ; and, no doubt, he has let you into a few secrets that are worth knowing. Pray, what sort of a looking fellow is his ghostship ?"

" I do not like to hear people make a jest of such matters," said Peter, solemnly, and looking round him, as though he expected to see the spectre at the moment. " You, perhaps, may be brought to think different, by and by, to what you do now, Master William ; but, what I have seen with my own eyes, and heard with my own ears, I will believe. Why, I tell you, that I open the door to him and let him out every night !"

" Ho ! ho ! ho !—A pretty ghost, truly ;—obliged to have a porter to open the hall-door to him ! Why, I thought such customers made nothing of flying through the key-hole !"

" Never mind what he says, Peter," said the old housekeeper, who had been screwed up pretty close in the chimney-corner, " but, tell us all about it, and how you first saw it ?"

" Why, you must know," began Peter, " that it is about a month ago, since I first saw it. God save me !—I shall never forget it to the hour of my death ! It was a very wet, boisterous night, and I was sitting in the hall-chair, endeavouring to dose off to sleep, as I knew the earl would not be home till a late hour, when, suddenly, I heard, between the pauses of the blast, a heavy groan, as if proceeding from some person in great agony ;—this was followed by the most frightful shrieks and other noises that I had ever heard. Well, you may be certain that I was frightened enough, as any person would have been in a similar situation ; but, at length, when the groans were repeated, my humanity prevailed over my terrors, and I opened the door. I had no sooner done so, than a figure, wrapt in a long dark mantle, swept past me, with noiseless steps ; and, suddenly turning, the rays of the lamp burning in the hall, fell upon his countenance,—and, what was my horror, when I beheld the well-known features of my late master, the Earl Lionel Fitzosbert!—but they were so ghastly pale, and his eyes had such an unearthly expression about them, that it smote my heart with terror as he fixed them upon me."

"God bless us!" ejaculated the other servants simultaneously, and drawing their chairs closer to each other.

"I fell upon my knees," continued Peter, "when the spectre—for, how could it be anything else?—spoke to me, and in a voice, which seemed to proceed from the utmost recesses of a tomb, said, ' Move not;—speak not;—beware!' Then, shaking his figure at me, he hastened up the hall staircase, and was lost to my view. So horror-struck was I at what I had seen, that I was completely petrified to the spot, and I could not move until the ghost again made his appearance, which was in about an hour after, and, as it past me, it fixed upon me such a look as I shall never forget, and went by me, and I saw no more of it that night; but every night since, at the same hour, it has appeared to me in the manner I have described."

"Ha! ha! ha!" laughed the young man, William, as he was called; " well, that is the most probable (?) story I ever heard!"

A deep and awful groan at this moment made every person start, and turn their eyes in the direction from whence it seemed to proceed, when, standing before them, they beheld a tall figure, in a long black mantle, exactly as old Peter had described it.

A simultaneous rush was made towards the door, and it was noticed that William, who had affected to be so incredulous, was the first to scamper out of the place as fast as he could: the others scrambled from the hall as fast as they were able, tumbling over one another in the most ludicrous manner, in their hurry to make their escape; and, as the last one made his exit, a hollow, sepulchral laugh re-echoed through the hall, followed by a noise, resembling the falling of a dozen suits of mail.

We will now leave the wretched Fitzosbert for a while, and return to ' The Old Commodore,' where the usual party were assembled, consisting of Tom, Will Barnsley, several of the crew of the pirate brig, and some other sailors from the different vessels then lying in the Port.

More than a week had elapsed, and Saib and Barnsley, who had been constantly together, had so matured their plot, that they had not the least doubt of meeting with success, and determined to put it into execution on the following day.

Will Barnsley seemed in unusual spirits, and the grog passed briskly round, mirth being the order of the day. The pirate captain acted his part remarkably well; although there were times when the surpassing loveliness of Ellen so excited his admiration, that it was with extreme difficulty he could help betraying his real thoughts and wishes.

There was one, however, whose keen eye watched closely every action of Will Barnsley, and who read everything that was passing in his mind. This was Richard; who, as he beheld the bold glances with which the pirate ever and anon eyed his fair cousin, felt his young blood boil with indignation, and he could hardly restrain the expression of his rage.

"You say right, Tom," observed Barnsley, in reply to something which the former had been saying; "you ought to think yourself one of the happiest fellows in the world to possess the heart of such a lass as your pretty Ellen;—and you should love her——"

"Love her!" interrupted Tom, vehemently:—"love her!—damme, I cannot find words to give expression to the passion I feel for my Ellen! She is my ship, my chart, my life!—By day, by night;—in the calm, and in the storm, her imag was always my beacon-light—the point from which the compass of my soul never varied. Whenever I see her, my heart is as light as a feather, and skips about like a cork in a fair breeze. And, as I mean to remain in the navy, it is my determination not to go afloat again until I am spliced to her."

"It strikes me, that you deceive yourself, my lad," muttered Barnsley, aside. "Well said," he observed, aloud; "I like your spirit;—as for me, the ocean is my only bride, and to her I am wedded, heart and soul. You have never inspected my craft, I believe, Tom?"

"I have not," answered the sailor, "although you have several times invited me on board;—I shall sail alongside of you some of these times, though."

"You will not find a better vessel, for her size, in the whole merchant service, than 'The Nancy,'" said Barnsley. "She stems the waves like a water-sylph, and is as graceful upon its bosom as a fairy. But I don't want to speak so much in favour of her myself;—seeing is believing, you know;—but I would advise you to lose no time, if you feel inclined to inspect her;—we sail on Monday next."

"Splice my topsails!" exclaimed Tom, "you are such a jovial fellow, that I wish I was going to sail with you."

"Perhaps you may have your wish sooner than you expect," again murmured the pirate captain, aside.

"What say you to to-morrow?" asked Tom.

"You couldn't have selected a better time," exclaimed Barnsley, scarcely able to conceal his joy, at the easy manner in which the honest sailor fell into his plot. "I had almost forgotten that; and, yet I came here almost for the express purpose of inviting you to come on board to-morrow. It is the anniversary of my birth, and I always celebrate it on board my ship. We shall have a comfortable party; and you need not fear to bring your pretty Ellen with you, for there will be plenty of respectable females aboard. What say you, will you persuade your sweetheart to honour the old captain with her company?"

"Aye, aye, to be sure I will, captain," said Tom; "and I know she will be glad to sail with me, wherever I may think proper to cruise.—We will sure to be aboard."

"All right," said Barnsley, with a smile, which Tom took to be one of welcome. "I shall expect you at an early hour: but, do not neglect to bring your sweetheart along with you, or it will be a great disappointment to us all. Here's Master Richard, too, will you not make one of the party, my lad?"

"I have business to transact in another place," replied Richard, with an air of as much carelessness as the nature of his thoughts would allow him to assume, "and cannot avail myself of your invitation, sir."

"Avast, there! Dick," ejaculated Tom; "I must not hear of any excuses from you;—you must put off your business till the next day; for I am resolved that you shall go; and I know you would not like to be away from any place which was attended by your cousin Ellen. You may enter his name, captain—I will answer for his coming."

Richard made no further objection, for he saw it would be useless; and he hoped that he should be able to persuade Tom to abandon all idea of fulfilling his promise. He now saw through the whole of the villanous design in a moment; and he trembled lest Tom should remain obstinate, and persist in going on board the pirate ship,—for such he felt assured 'The Nancy' in reality was; for that it was the captain's plan to detain them when he got them aboard; and to this he imagined that he was not only instigated by the miscreant Saib, but also from a desire which he had to get the beauteous Ellen in his power. He marked well the savage look of exultation which passed over the features of Barnsley when he had elicited the assent of Tom, and he also noticed the change which his countenance evinced, when he (Richard) endeavoured to excuse himself from being one of the party; which were convincing proofs that his surmises were correct; and he was determined that there should be no exertion wanting on his part to endeavour to frustrate the villain's designs.

"Then you will not fail to be there, Tom?" demanded Barnsley, as he finished the contents of a glass, and arose to depart.

"I have said so, captain," returned Tom, "and I never break my word."

"And the pretty Ellen?"

"She shall be my companion."

" At what time may I expect you ?" demanded the pirate.

" Oh, I shall be on board early," replied Tom : " where there is merry-making, Tom Clewline is always ready at the first sound of the boatswain's whistle.—Good night."

" Good night, my lad," said Barnsley, pulling up the collar of his P jacket, and unable to repress the feeling of gratification which filled his bosom at the thoughts of his success.—" Come, my men !"

With these words, the pirate captain and his companions arose, and left the house, and Tom, Richard, and two or three other sailors, were all that were left behind. These, one by one, having finished their grog, retired also, and Tom, having kissed the cheek of Ellen, and heartily shook the hands of old Mat and the dame, prepared to leave the house.

" As it is a fine night, and I want a walk," said Richard, " I will walk a little way with you, Tom, if it is agreeable."

" Agreeable !" repeated Tom ; " aye, to be sure, it is ; so, just tow yourself alongside of me, and we will weigh anchor directly, for my sister is all alone, and will get as dull as a sailor without flip, if I do not soon rejoin her."

When Tom and the others had got out of sight and hearing, the pirate captain indulged in a hearty burst of laughter, to think how well his nefarious plans had so far succeeded.

" Fool !" he exclaimed, exultingly, " I did not think him half such a swab, as to fall so readily into the trap laid for him.—Ha ! ha ! ha !—how enraged and disappointed he will be when he finds out what sort of craft ' The Nancy' is, and the characters of the men he has to deal with. This is the best job I have had for a long while,—and the girl even is worth all the prizes I have taken for the last two years !—Well, she shall find the pirate captain not a bad companion,—that is, if she does not attempt to cross me."

" She is, indeed, a fair craft, captain," said the lieutenant of the pirate, " and well worthy to sail alongside of you : " as for Tom, we shall find him a very useful chap,—that is, if he does not show his teeth upon this subject."

" If he does he's a fool, that's all I've got to say upon the subject," said Barnsley; " for, if a rope's end won't bring him to his senses, I'll warrant me that a hempen cravat will quiet him."

" Aye, aye," answered the other, " but there's that boy, Richard."

" Ah ! I do believe the young shark partly smells our plot," observed Barnsley; " I noticed his manner closely, and I could not help observing the manner in which he tried to excuse himself from coming aboard to-morrow."

" Should he blab his suspicions to Tom," said the lieutenant, " he might persuade him not to come according to his promise."

" 'Psha !" cried Barnsley. " the sailor will not be so easily persuaded by a boy, —don't you believe it."

" There's something particular connected with that brat," said the lieutenant, " or else Saib would not be so anxious to have him removed."

" You're right," returned Barnsley ; " I am of the same opinion as you are yourself ; and, if all that I have heard is true, the Earl Fitzosbert has very good cause to dread him. I will make something of him by and by, or my name's not Will Barnsley."

With these words, Barnsley and his companions stepped into the boats, and were quickly rowed alongside the pirate brig. When they got on board, Barnsley found that Saib was waiting to see him, and was all anxiety to know how he had proceeded.

" Well, captain, what success ?" demanded the black, eagerly.

" Why, as well as we could desire," returned the pirate.

" Ah !" exclaimed the African, while a grim smile passed over his sable countenance ; " and have they fallen into our plot ?"

" They have ; and to-morrow they will be on board my craft."

" By hell ! this is glorious !" exclaimed Saib, in accents of triumph. " Barnsley, you have managed this business so far admirably."

" Will Barnsley seldom fails in what he undertakes to perfom," replied the pirate.

" But the brat, Richard," said the black, " what of him ?"

" He will be one of the party," was the answerr.

" Good !—By my soul, Barnsley, if you complete this business with the same skill as you have begun it, you deserve an addition to the reward which I have promised you."

" And, trust me, Saib, I will have it."

" Ah !" cried the black, looking suspiciously upon the pirate captain, " what mean you ?"

" Oh, I dare say you understand me," remarked Barnsley, smiling significantly and sarcastically upon Saib;—" this boy is a great eye-sore to you and the Earl Fitzosbert ;—of course, it would not be very pleasant to either of you to let the world know this ?"

Saib frowned, and, walking to another part of the deck, muttered to himself,—

" I have divulged too much ; Barnsley already knows the advantage he has gained over me and the earl, and will, no doubt, avail himself of the opportunity I have thus thrown into his hands. Fool that I have been ;—I have had to pay already dearly enough for it, and it will cost me much more, ere I can accomplish my wishes. Curses light upon the ill-luck which has hitherto prevented me from putting into execution my schemes against that hated boy !"

Turning to the pirate captain, Saib said,—

" But, of course, Barnsley, admitting that you were certain of what you now only suspect, you would not be the one that would publish the same to the world ?"

" That depends upon circumstances."

" You would never so deceive your friend ?"

" Friend !—'Psha ! I have no friends.—I seek none.—My maxim is to make as much as I can, and study no one but myself. That is the motive from which most persons act, although they may pretend to the contrary. You act upon that principle in your engagement with me, Saib, and, of course, I must make you pay for it. How far my services, or my silence may be considered valuable, rests entirely with yourself, and——"

" Come, come, enough of this, Will," interrupted the African ; " you were not wont to talk thus."

" Perhaps not ; but experience makes fools wise, they say," replied the pirate ; " that is the style I now choose."

" Well, I dare say we shall not quarrel."

" I dare say not."

" That boy might be easily tossed overboard by accident."

" Exactly ; and he might as well be sold as a slave, and then he would bring some profit for the trouble he may put me to."

" It would be better that he were given as food for the sharks, and then there would be an end of him."

" No doubt *you* think so !" said the pirate, significantly.

Saib scowled, and traversed the deck with uneasy steps: he now repented, or half repented having confided so much to Barnsley, and, above all, he regretted that he had made any arrangement with him about taking Richard at all.

" Well, well," at length he said, after a few minutes' reflection, " I think, after all, it will be as well to leave the lad out altogether."

" Here you and I differ," answered Barnsley, with another significant smile, which was anything but pleasant to the African ; " I have no doubt I shall turn him to some account before I have done with him."

" Not if I can help it," muttered Saib to himself : " I must contrive, somehow or the other, to prevent the boy from falling into your power, and I dare say I shall be able to dispose of him myself some time or the other. — Well," he added, aloud to Barnsley, " I shall leave everything to you ; and, of course, you will not act otherwise than right?"

" Oh, of course not ;—I am a very *honourable* sort of fellow,—ha ! ha ! ha !"

" You seem in a merry mood, Barnsley."

" Aye, aye,—what's the use of being sad,—especially when a man has got the prospect of so much additional happiness ?"

" What mean you ?"

" Why, the person of the pretty Ellen," replied the pirate ; " is she not a prize, think you, sufficient to urge a man to anything to obtain possession of her ?"

" You say right, Will," answered Saib, " and, therefore, ought you to feel grateful to me for having put you in the way to obtain possession of her."

" Avast, there, my sable land-lubber," said the pirate, " I should have had her whether or not, for she had taken my fancy ; and, previous to your making to me the proposition that you have done, I had fully made up my mind to have her in my power, if it cost me my life even in the attempt ; — and you know, Saib, that I am not one who easily gives up anything upon which I have fixed my mind."

" But, methinks, the eyes of her parents and her lover would prove too keen for you. They keep too strict a watch over her."

" They might keep watch over her," said Will, " as if she was a barrel of gunpowder, expected to go off with the first spark ; but they would have been sure to have found me too cunning for them. But, come, there's enough of this ;—by this time, or before, to-morrow, they will all of them be in my power."

" I hope so."

" And, what is there to fear ?"

" Did they seem to catch the bait easily ?"

" Why, as for that matter, Tom hath taken such a fancy to me,—my usual *insinuating* manners have so got over him, that he thinks me the best fellow in the the world, and was ready enough to accept of my invitation; but the boy, Richard,——"

" Ah! what of him?"

" Why, he did not seem to fancy it, and tried to excuse himself from being one of the party," replied Barnsley.

" The shrewd brat!" cried Saib, in a tone of vexation, " he guesses the whole plot!"

" 'Psha!—impossible! But, come, enough of this. Fear not, but all will be well, and succeed as well as we can wish."

" I hope so."

" You'll take a glass of grog before you depart?" demanded Barnsley.

Saib nodded assent, and the pirate captain led the way to the forecastle, where the pirates had already assembled, and were carousing gaily, and Barnsley and Saib having joined them, riotous mirth soon prevailed. The glasses went freely round, and deep were the potations which the pirates quaffed, and at length most of them having became nearly inebriated, burst forth into the following wild chorus, which they sang with more noise than harmony :—

> Hurrah! for the pirates' merry, merry life,
>   No troubles cross their mind;
> Their pastime is the battle strife,
>   Their music the roaring wind.
> On the billows their gallant vessel rides,
>   Hurling defiance around ;
> The tempest shock their barque derides,—
>   For plunder they are bound.
>   Then, burrah! hurrah! hurrah!
>   For the pirates' merry, merry life!
>
> Hurrah! for the pirates' coal-black flag,
>   The terror of the seas ;
> Which floats on high, to the open sky,
>   As free as the whistling breeze.
> The mariner, though e'er so bold,
>   To cheer him tries in vain,
> When he sees the pirates' coal-black flag,
> Which floats o'er the raging main.
>   Then, hurrah! hurrah! hurrah!
>   For the pirates' merry, merry life!
>
> The pirates' is a jovial life,
>   No laws—no chains owns he ;
> His gallant ship is his castle bold,
>   And his home the dark blue sea.
> His prey in sight—prepare for fight,
>   The foemen strive in vain ;
> All must yield to the pirates' coal-black flag,
>   Which floats o'er the raging main.
>   Then, hurrah! hurrah! hurrah!
>   For the pirates' merry, merry life!

Oh ! how dreadful is the pirates' strife,
　　For quarter vain's the cry;
They who dare to meet his dauntless sword,
　　Must conquer, or must die !
Or, the hapless wretch who survives the flag,
　　The chain of the slave must drag :
Death, chains, and despair, are the emblems we bear,
　　Then, beware of the coal-black flag !
　　　　　Death, chains, and despair, are the emblems we bear,
　　　　　Then, beware of the coal-black flag !

After about an hour longer passed in this manner, Saib arose to quit the vessel, having informed Barnsley that he should not fail to be there on the following day to receive those he so mortally detested, in a manner, which his revengeful feelings dictated.

In the meantime, Richard, who we left in company with Tom, intending to accompany him a short distance on the way home, did not fail to explain to him his suspicions as to the real character of Barnsley, and the treachery that was intended them, and endeavoured to persuade him from going the following day on board the pirates' brig, according to the promise he had made Will Barnsley; but Tom only laughed at his fears ; and finding that all the arguments he could make use of, would not be of any avail, he gave up the attempt, and bidding Tom good night, separated from him, and made his way back towards ' The Old Commodore.'

Richard, however, found it impossible to divest his mind of the suspicions it had imbibed, and he walked on at a slow pace, through the fields, ruminating upon the subject, and darkness had completely enveloped the earth by the time he left Tom. It was a fine night, and, therefore, he did not hurry himself, the air being refreshing. He had just emerged upon one of the green lanes, when his arm was suddenly arrested violently by some person close by, and, looking round, what was his terror and astonishment to behold the fierce eyes of Saib fixed with revengeful fury upon him.

"Ah !" exclaimed the wretch, in a tone of exultation, which was perfectly fiendish, " the opportunity I have so long, so ardently wished for has at length arrived. I swore that you should not escape my clutches, and now I have you in my power, your doom is sealed. Hated brat—bane of my peace ;—the imp who foiled me in my deep laid scheme of vengeance, which would have immolated me and all my foes—this night—this hour, you die !"

" Oh, Saib," ejaculated Richard, trembling with terror beneath the ferocity of his glance, and vainly trying to release himself from the fellow's powerful grasp, " why should you seek in the first instance to take my life ?—I never offended you ; I could not have given you cause for anger, and cannot account for the hatred and revenge you have ever exhibited towards me. I implore you to release me, and suffer me to proceed about my business, and I promise you that no one shall be informed of the attack you have just made upon me."

" Fool !—idiot !" cried Saib, " think you the wolf will so easily resign his prey ?—Ha ! ha ! ha ! You plead in vain ;—indeed, your anguish but serves to add to my delight. This spot you shall never more quit alive. There is no one near—no one now to rescue you, and give me over to punishment! Thus, then, do I perform the bloody deed for which I have long prayed. Earl Fitzosbert, your fears will now be at an end.—Die! hated offspring of——"

" Die yourself, you damned black swab!" exclaimed the well-known voice of Tom, just as Saib had dashed the lad to the earth, and was about to plunge a knife in his breast.

After Tom had parted from Richard, some misgivings crossed his mind, and notwithstanding the anxiety he knew his sister would feel at his long absence, he turned back, thinking to overtake him again, and resolved to be his companion back to the inn. It will be seen that he came up at the critical moment when Richard's life was about to fall a sacrifice to the diabolical vengeance of the African.

The report of a pistol immediately followed the words of Gallant Tom, and then a cry of agony escaped the black, as he clapped his hand to his arm, and staggered back a few paces, crying, in a voice rendered hoarse with rage and pain,—

" By the infernal host I'm shot! What foul fiend hath done this? Ah! the sailor—the—the—oh, curses light upon his head!"

" Another word like that, you cowardly shark," observed Tom, "and, damme, if I don't blow your brains out directly. However, this shall be the last time you shall have a chance of gratifying your bloodthirsty disposition.— If there is any justice to be obtained in the country, you shall be punished for this. But, as I don't wish you to escape the retribution you deserve, I will bind up your wound, which appears to be an awkward one, and securing you to this tree, leave you here until I can get the officers of the law to lay their grappling irons upon you."

" May the bitterest malediction of the black man descend upon your head!" vociferated Saib, groaning with rage and pain, while Tom, in spite of his kicking and biting at him, persisted in binding up the wound in his arm with a handkerchief, and having fastened him to a tree, so that it would be impossible for him to release himself,—in that far from agreeable situation he left him, hurried Richard away from the spot, and made his way to town.

In less than half an hour, Tom returned to the place where he left the black, accompanied by a couple of officers, but was astonished to find that Saib was not there. He was extremely vexed at this circumstance, for he had hoped to put an end to all further annoyance from the African, but he had again escaped him. However, it was hoped that it would not be long before he was apprehended, and Tom immediately despatched the officers to the mansion of the Earl Fitzosbert, to see whether he was there; but the earl assured them that he had seen nothing of his myrmidon since the day before, and appeared to be extremely agitatated when the officers briefly informed him of the circumstance that had taken place.

" Bungling fool!" ejaculated the earl when left to himself, " he is always foiled in his rash and badly planned attempts. He will bring destruction on us both. Ah! now do I more than ever see good reason for my being anxious that the plot laid by the pirate captain and Saib, to entrap Tom and the boy, should succeed. They must be got out of the way, or when Saib is taken, which he undoubtedly

will be, their evidence may be the means of elucidating certain circumstances that will at once reveal the dark and nefarious deeds of which we have been guilty. Oh ! what a weight of care, of continual fear and uneasiness, does guilt bring with it !"

He traversed his room for several minutes in a state of great agitation, and he then summoned one of his most confidential servants, and, late as it was, desired him to make all the inquiry he possibly could, to ascertain what had become of Saib, and not to forget to endeavour to see Captain Barnsley, and learn from him whether he knows anything of him.

The man returned in about a couple of hours with the information that Saib was on board the pirate brig, and was not so severely wounded as had been imagined, but that he thought it would be advisable for him to remain where he was for the present, until after the completion of the plot.

It appeared, that soon after Tom and Richard had left him bound to the trunk of the tree as we have described, some of the crew of the pirate ship happened to be passing that way, when they were attracted to the spot by the groans and curses of the black, and immediately released him, and conveyed him to the vessel ; and thus the earl's fears were, in a great measure, quieted.

This event increased the surprise of Richard, and added much to his apprehensions, more especially when he heard of the escape of Saib, for which he was perfectly unable to account. He recollected the remarkable words which Saib had made use of in allusion to himself and the Earl Fitzosbert, and when he added to that there was some mystery connected with him, in which the earl was concerned, and which time would, probably, unravel.

Richard slept but little that night, and when he did, strange visions haunted his imagination, and rendered sleep more fatiguing than his waking moments. The different remarkable events that had occurred to him, all crowded upon his fancy at once, and conjured up a variety of singular ideas, which formed themselves into dreams of an equally perplexing and extraordinary description. Sometimes the frightful form of Saib appeared to him, looking upon him with that diabolical expression of revenge, which had ever marked him in the attempts he had made upon his life; and then the mysterious words he had uttered in allusion to the Earl Fitzosbert, recurred to his memory, and added to the ambiguity of the vision. Then the scene would become changed, and he would fancy himself again in the presence of the stranger, who had sought a shelter at the 'Old Commodore,' and had behaved himself in such a strange manner, more especially towards him, in whose fate he appeared not only to take a lively and unaccountable interest, but to have some good reason for so doing. He imagined that he gazed upon him with looks of the utmost affection, and raising his hands above his head, pronounced a benediction upon him. Suddenly, the scene again became changed, and he fancied in his dream, that himself, Tom, and Ellen, were on board the pirate vessel, and were held prisoners by the ferocious-looking crew, while Barnsley, the captain, stood by, confessed in his own true colours, and mocked, and scoffed, and exulted in their reproaches. Richard was heartily glad when he awoke and found it was morning, and he, therefore, arose, and descended into the breakfast-room, where he found the little family already assembled, and awaiting his appearance.

"Why, Dick,—boy," said Mat, after eyeing him for a moment, "you look as queer and as melancholy as if you had been put upon six-water grog.—What's the matter with you?"

"I have not slept well," replied Richard; "and what little sleep I have had, has been disturbed by frightful dreams."

"Dreams!" repeated old Mat; "oh, there's nothing in them: why, if what I have dreamt at different times had come true, I should at this time have been as rich as an emperor. But you have not greeted Ellen this morning; and see, she looks as pretty as a little angel: for she has rigged herself in her best, and I'll warrant there is not a trimmer or a better-looking craft going."

Richard turned to Ellen, and saluted her in his usual affectionate manner; but there was an air of sadness about him, which no effort that he could make, could overcome, and which did not escape the observation of Mat and the others.

"Well, splice me, Dick," said Mat, "I cannot, for the life of me, make out what can be the matter with you; you look as dull as a collier, and you should be merry, you know, to day, as this invitation of Captain Barnsley's——"

"The truth is," answered Richard, interrupting the old man, "I do not like that Captain Barnsley, nor the invitation he has given us; and I would fain dissuade Tom and Ellen from going on board his ship to day."

"Hollo! what's in the wind, now?" cried Mat. "What are your reasons for disliking Barnsley?"

" What think you, he is, then ?"

" A pirate !"

" A pirate !" reiterated Mat, and the dame and Ellen turned ghastly pale, and trembled very much : " come, come, Dick, these are strong assertions, and you ought to have good cause for suspicion before you venture to make them. But, 'psha ! its all stuff : you wrong Will Barnsley ; I have known him at this part for many a day, and always considered him a good, jovial sort of fellow, only a little coarse and abrupt in his manners at times ; but that is nothing at all to wonder at, when a man has had to buffet about on the ocean of life."

" I should be very sorry to suspect him wrongfully," returned Richard, " but I cannot divest my mind of the impression. I have watched him very narrowly, and have frequently seen things in his behaviour, and heard expressions fall from his lips, that were sufficient to give rise to the suspicions I have entertained.

" Oh, father," observed Ellen, " something tells me that Richard's remarks ought not to be treated lightly ;—I would much rather not go on board to day, I——"

" Nonsense !" interrupted Mat, " you are both gone crazy I think ; I do not hold with this trying, and condemning a man without judge or jury ; and, for my part, consider that there is not the least cause for any apprehension of the sort. But what says Tom about the matter ?"

" Why, he treats it the same as you do, sir, " replied Richard ; " I have tried to persuade him, but all to no purpose."

" Well, then, that settles the business at once," said Mat, " and I feel confident that your fears are groundless, Dick. Deceive Tom, and there is only another to do. Come, come, Ellen, do not alarm yourself, you will have a cheerful day of it, I'll be bound ; besides, if you and Richard were both now to decline, you would not only offend Captain Barnsley, who is a good customer to me whenever he is ashore, but Tom, also, and make us all look like fools into the bargain. Why I did not believe you could have feared, Richard——"

" Feared, sir !" interrupted the lad, warmly, " pardon me, but that is a word, I trust, that has never yet formed a portion of my vocabulary ; I fear not for myself, but those I love much better ;—for Ellen, for Tom,—for——"

At this moment, Tom entered the room.

" Oh, here is Tom," said Mat, " just come in time to speak for himself. Here's Richard, just been spinning a yarn enough to give us all the blues. He entertains suspicions that Barnsley is a pirate, and that this invitation will turn out to be no good, and had better be avoided."

" Bah !" cried Tom, impatiently, " you musn't mind what Dick says on this occasion ; for he has got some strange crotchets into his upper-works, and it seems as if nothing would drive it out, either. Now my lass,—my dearest Ellen, I see you are ready and all as tant and as trim as—but, damme, you are looking pale, and you tremble ;—I suppose Dick's fears have been catching ;—but do not give way to them, while you place your trust in the great Commander aloft, and your lover is by your side, you have nothing to dread."

" I know it, Tom," said Ellen, with a sweet smile, " and will, therefore banish the suspicions that, I confess, had taken possession of my mind, from the observations of my cousin, and which, of course, were only meant for the best, and made from the most affectionate motives,"

" To be sure they were," said the honest sailor, "and we are all liable to mistakes, you know. But, will you accompany us, Dick ?"

" Will I ?—certainly," replied the lad! "and Heaven grant that my surmises may not be confirmed ! but I am extremely doubtful whether you ought to treat the matter so lightly."

" Well, well, we shall see," said Tom ; " at any rate ; should your suspicions prove to be correct, Barnsley would get none of the best of it ; for, am I not a king's man ;—and should he detain me, he would very quickly be brought to his senses."

"You're right, Tom," said Mat, " and so there's an end to the matter I hope, I wish you a merry day of it, and shall expect you to return before late at night."

" Oh, yes, Mat, (or father I shall call you now, for you know I shall soon have a just right to call you so), never fear, I will convey my Ellen safe into port again before the moon rises."

With these words, they shook hands, and separated.

But, notwithstanding Mat had affected to despise the observations and suspicion of Richard, and endeavoured to do so sincerely he was far from being successful. He could not help feeling very uneasy at times, and fearful of evincing the same before his wife, he left her presence upon every opportunity. He several time repeated having so readily given his consent to Ellen's going on board, more especially as he, after they had departed for some time, recollected having seen Barnsley and the African, who had proved himself to be such an implacable foe, in earnest conversation together, and he was at most times, inclined to act upon the principal of, "judge of a man by the company he keeps." yet, on the other hand, as he told Richard, he had known Barnsley for several years, his house his principal place of resort, and never had he seen or heard anything from him, to cause the least suspicion, and, therefore, he had no right, he imagined, to judge of him so harshly, as he and Saib might have business to transact of a nature quite foreign to anything wrong.

Notwithstanding these conflicting thoughts, the day passed away in anything but a comfortable manner with Mat and his wife ; the latter, in spite of his precautions, having caught the infection. Once or twice during the day, he had walked forth to the beach, to see whether the Nancy was still at anchor, and when he beheld her there, his mind become more at rest ; although he was frequently half inclined to take a boat and row alongside the vessel, to see if all was right; but, then, the idea that he should, probably, be only laughed at for his groundless fears, he abandoned the design and returned home.

As evening approached, Mat, and the dame likewise, became still more uneasy, and as twilight was rapidly declining into the more sombre shades of night, unable to endure the state of agonizing suspense which racked his bosom, he hastened once more to the sea-beach with the full determination to row to the ' Nancy,' and ascertain the reason they did not return home. He was not long in arriving at the spot from whence he could command a full view of the ship, and the moon shining brightly in the heavens, he was enabled to see everything as clearly as if it was in the broad daylight. He eagerly cast his eyes across the ocean,—but, judge of his horror and astonishment when he could not discover any signs of the ' Nancy. At first, he could scarcely believe the evidence of his senses ; but when he was aroused to a full sense of the truth, his emotion was so great, that for several minutes he was totally incapable of moving. When, however, he had somewhat recovered, he inquired of all the persons whom he met near the spot, and particularly the coast-guard, how long it was since the ' Nancy' had weighed her anchor, and whether they had seen or knew anything of Tom, Richard, and Ellen. These questions first directed the attention of the persons spoken to, to the subject of the sudden disappearance of the ship, and when Mat repeated his tale, and the manner in which Tom and Ellen, and Richard had been decoyed on board, it was immediately concluded by every body present that it was a pirate, and immediate steps were taken to go in pursuit of her.

In the meantime, notwithstanding the dismal forebodings of Richard, the gaiety of Tom served almost entirely to dissipate the fears of Ellen ; and by the time they reached the boat which was to carry them to the ship, she was nearly restored to her usual spirits.

Richard, ere they stepped into the boat, in which they found two of the crew of the ' Nancy' awaiting their arrival, cast a doubtful glance towards the vessel, and once more endeavoured to urge his suspicions, and persuade him to pause ; but Tom, again, only laughed at his fears, and desired, if such were his ideas, that he, at any rate, would not run the risk, then he could not blame him. Richard, however, ashamed to be thought afraid to encounter danger, and likewise unable to bear the thought of quitting his cousin Ellen, proudly rejected such a proposition, and having stepped into the boat, they were quickly rowed alongside the ' Nancy, and went upon deck. Scarcely had they stepped upon deck, when they found themselves surrounded by a number of fierce-looking fellows, who exchanged glances with one another, and eyed the beauteous Ellen with looks of boldness that involuntarily made her shudder, and she clung closer to the arm of her lover.

" What's the matter, lass ?" said Tom ; " how you tremble. I wish Dick had been at the devil before he filled your mind with these qualms. To be sure, these are not the best-looking chaps I have seen in the course of my cruise through life, and do not appear by any means calculated to make particular agreeable guests at a merry-making."

At this moment, there was a loud burst of coarse and uproarious laughter, mixed with oaths, which seemed to proceed from the gun-deck, and which made Tom start with amazement, and chilled Ellen with terror.

" They are rather jolly, certainly," said Tom, " but I can't say that's the sort of mirth which I consider exactly suited to a female."

" Oh, Tom," ejaculated Ellen, clinging closer to him, " I wish we had taken Richard's advice ; my heart misgives me."

" And not without good cause, I fear," said Richard aside to his companions ! " trust me, this is no honest vessel !"

" Eh—what—damme, if I thought," faultered Tom,—" but no, no, I will not believe it !—messmates, where's the captain ?"

" This way, my lad," said one of the men, pointing to the door of a cabin, " this way ;—" he desired us to shew you to him."

Ellen shrunk back as Tom sought to lead her towards the place, to which the man pirated, and observed,—

"Oh, Tom,—I cannot,—I—I——"

"Nonsense, my love," interrupted Tom, encouragingly, "we shall see Barnsley, and then all will be right. Come, come."

Before Ellen could make any reply the man had opened the door of the cabin, and Barnsley advanced to meet them, his features expressive of such strong feelings of exultation, occasioned by the success of his schemes, that it could not escape the observation of Tom and his companions.

"Welcome, Tom, on board the ' Nancy,' and you, fair lady, I greet you with pleasure. I ought to feel honoured by your punctuality; but I dare say I shall have an opportunity of marking my sense of it before we separate."

"Aye, aye, captain," said Tom, answering for Ellen, "but where are our guests, of course you have some more females aboard!"

The pirate captain, upon whose features was an ironical smile, was about to reply, when the same rude voices they had previously heard burst upon their ears, bawling in loud tones the following verse of the pirates' chorus :—

> " The pirates' is a jovial life,
>   No laws—no chains owns he ;
> His gallant ship is his castle bold,
>   And his home the dark blue sea.
> His prey in sight—prepare for fight,
>   The foemen strive in vain ;
> All must yield to the pirates' coal-black flag,
>   Which floats o'er the raging main.
>   Then, hurrah ! hurrah ! hurrah !
>   For the pirates' merry, merry life!

"Eh !—no—damme, I begin to suspect," cried Tom.

"Suspect what ?" demanded Barnsley, with an ironical laugh.

"Why, that you have played us false," replied Tom ; "but, come, come—aye, shiver me, you laugh, do you, you swab ?—Suffer us to depart directly ; I do not like the appearance of your craft, or the crew by which it is manned. I am quite a-ground at finding a merchant vessel so strongly gunned, while her fitting-out, and strong build, would do honour to the first architect of a line-of-battle-ship."

"Ha ! ha ! ha !" laughed the pirate ; " I thought our build would astonish you. The ' Nancy' is no cockleshell,—eh ? And, I promise you, that a more swift cruiser never floated over the water, as you yourself will acknowledge before our return from the coast of Guinea !"

"Ah ! we are betrayed !" cried Tom ; and, Ellen, with a loud scream, fainted in his arms.

"What ho, there !" shouted the pirate captain; "slip the cable, and weigh anchor directly."

"Weigh anchor !" ejaculated Tom, completely aghast, and yet scarcely able to come to the conclusion that he heard aright ; " why—why, you damned——but, you are only jesting, captain !"

"Jesting or not," answered Barnsley, " I must warn you that I do not suffer any lubber on board the ' Nancy' to dispute my orders."

"Hillio !" cried Tom, still doubtful whether or not to be serious; "what wind is blowing now?—Here's a veer about. Ha! your words are too true;—the vessel has set sail !—you—you—you are——"

"Behold;" exclaimed the pirate, pulling the black flag, their well known and terrible ensign, on a staff, from the locker.

"Ah !—all the suspicions of Dick are confirmed," cried Tom.—"You are a pirate !"

"A free-trader," is a better word, "replied Barnsley, with sarcastic coolness, *fair*-trader when ashore *free*-trader at sea. I have shown you our ensign; it is a colour which you cannot mistake;—that which has ever been true to his craft: respect it, therefore, and remember that you are in my power, and if you refuse to obey my commands, you may stand a very good chance of being spliced to yonder yard-arm."

"Your commands !—you—you—why, I am a king's man !"

"So much the luckier :—you understand discipline the better;—why should the king have all the best hands ?"

"You cannot be in earnest?"

"Well, call it by what name you please; you have already been witness to the nature of my jokes !"

"And—and, my Ellen ?"

"Will make me an excellent wife, and you can be present at the wedding !"

"Why, you infernal scoundrel!" cried Tom, almost choaked with indignation.

"Avast ! or I will order my crew to gag you with a wet nipper !" said the pirate; "you and this boy will enter your names as two of the crew of the "Nancy."

"Never !"

"Ah ! do you defy me ?"

"I do ! What ! have I been playing at ducks-and-drakes with death so long, in the defence of my king and country, who demand my service ?—when I desert my colours, then brand me for a traitor !"

"Ha ! ha ! ha !" laughed the pirate, sneeringly, "we shall see that. But, come; I will ease you of your fair and insensible burthen, the girl——"

"Stand off—dare not, at your peril, to approach me, or to attempt to lay a finger upon this poor girl, and may I never go aloft, if I don't strike you a corpse at my feet !"

"Rash fool !" answered the captain, "in a moment I could prevent the possibility of your putting your vain threat into execution, by scattering your brains upon the deck. But I spare your life, because I think I shall be able to make you of more service to me.—Within, there seize your prisoners; but at your peril, harm not the girl;—she is the affianced bride of your captain !"

"Liar !" vociferated Tom, half maddened with rage, as several of the pirates rushed upon him, forced his lover from his arms, and secured him and Richard; "Barnsley, by all your hopes of mercy from that Almighty Judge in whose presence we must all some time or the other appear !—I warn you not to attempt to

" Take my life," cried Richard, in tones of distraction, " but, spare, oh, spare my cousin,—my adored Ellen."

" Bear her to my cabin," ordered the pirate, with a look of diabolical exultation at the agony evinced by Tom and his companion. " You see," he continued, in a sarcastic tone, " that the pirate's power is not so contemptible as you at first seemed to think it."

" But you cannot,—you will not injure her ?"

" Oh, no; I tell you, again, I have selected her for my bride."

" Villain !"

" You may spare your ephithets ; they are only a waste of breath, and, at another time,—only just now I am inclined to be merciful,—they might get you promoted to the yard-arm. I have, however, an old acquaintance of yours on board, whom, perhaps, you may be happy to see."

Thus speaking, the pirate captain made a sign towards the door which opened into an inner cabin, and immediately upon the signal being given, Saib came forward, and with fiendish looks of triumph, gazed upon his victims.

" Tom Clewline," cried the African, " I told you that the black man would never rest until he had obtained revenge against those who had wronged him. That promise I have now fulfilled. It is now my turn to triumph and exult in your misery. You are now one of the crew of the pirate brig, and must obey the commands of your captain, or a rope's end will teach you better manners.— Ha! ha! ha!—in vain you writhe and foam with the power of your rage ; you exhaust yourself in vain. Your sister, too, as you have called her, Rosina Burlington, ere many days shall be the slave to the passions of the hated black, whom you ever effected so to despise !"

In vain Tom struggled to release himself from the clutches of the fellows who held him, while his cheeks glowed with indignation, excited by the taunts and revilings of Saib.

" You infernal black swab !" he exclaimed, " if these lubbers would only take their grappling irons off me, I would pour such a broadside into you that—I say, Barnsley, damme, if I don't forgive you for all you have done to me, if you will just order me to be released, so that I may have satisfaction on the black lubber !"

" Away with him below," commanded the pirate, " I shall have some business with him by and by."

" What," cried Tom, once more struggling vehemently, " place a true British sailor under hatches ?—Why, you pitiful swab ! you deserve to be flogged round the fleet with a double rope's end, and then to be soused into a tar bucket."

" Away with him, I say ;" cried Barnsley.

" Nay, but for a moment, captain," said Saib, " his rage, his fruitless passion is food to my soul. And, you boy, yon hateful brat, who so often hath eluded my power,—now I have him secure, and in a moment my knife could pierce his heart !"

" Avast ! avast !" exclaimed Barnsley, " not so fast ; the boy is now in my power, and I must be left to dispose of him as I think proper. It is time you were away, unless you think proper to take a voyage with us.—Boat ahoy,

release himself, as he saw the look of derision and exultation which the African fixed upon him; " and I to be thus taunted by that figure-head of the devil ?"

" Ha! ha! ha!" laughed Saib, folding his arms across his chest, and his large, fierce eyes fixed upon the countenance of Tom with the expression of a demon. He stood gazing at him until he was, with Richard, forced below; then sprang into the boat which was lowered for him, and was rowed ashore.

We need not seek to describe the sufferings of Tom when he found himself in this situation. A thousand times he blamed his own mad folly in being so easily made the dupe of the pirate captain, and in not paying any serious attention to the suspicions of Richard, which had now turned out to be so well founded. But it was not for himself that he cared so much, but for Ellen, who in the power of so desperate a villain as Barnsley, he felt certain need expect but little mercy. His sister, too;—alas! what would be her anguish when she heard what had become of him ?—And, what would she do, deprived as she was, of his protection at that particular juncture ?—Should the miscreant Saib discover the place where she resided, there was no doubt but that he would run every risk to put the threats he had made use of into execution, and the fate which would thus attend Rosina would be too dreadful to think upon. His only hope of a rescue from their present alarming situation, was by the pirate brig being overtaken by the vessel which would no doubt be sent in pursuit of her, when it was known that she had a king's man on board of her, and her real character was discovered; but then the brig was such a fast sailer, that she might almost bid defiance to the Governm ters, and thus there was too good reason to despair again.

No. 14

It would be impossible to describe the anguish he endured all that night, correctly, and especially as hour after hour elapsed, and the pirate pursued her course without any signs of being molested ; and he could not but believe that she had by far outstripped any vessel that might have been sent in pursuit, or otherwise such pursuit had not taken place at all. He traversed the place of his confinement, with hasty and uneven steps, and pictured to himself the sufferings which Ellen was in all probability at that time undergoing ; and his agitation became so violent that he could scarcely contain himself. Before the morning, however, he became more calm, and began to reflect with his accustomed coolness and reason upon what was best to be done under the dangerous circumstances in which they were placed. To heap reproaches and invectives upon the head of the pirate captain, would only exasperate him to further outrage, and, probably, incite him to put his diabolical threats against Ellen into immediate execution. Resistance to the power of such a number of ruffians would be madness.—No, he must endeavour to fight another game. He must pretend to submit to his lot ; to appear to yield to Barnsley's wishes, and by becoming one of the crew, the dangers he dreaded might be averted until such time as something should occur to rescue them.

"It will only be a matter of form," reflected Tom ; "and if I enter my name as one of the crew of this piratical craft, I shall have my liberty in the ship, and, mayhap, be able to prevent any attempt that might be made against my Ellen. Poor girl!—Little did I ever expect that she would be placed in such a predicament!"

The next morning Barnsley ordered Tom to be brought into his cabin, and Richard was soon afterwards placed beside him.

"You see, Tom," said Barnsley, "that I have you now securely in my power, and we are far beyond pursuit ; therefore, any resistance to me would be complete madness. What say you,—will you purchase your liberty in the ship, by entering your name as one of the crew?"

"But, Ellen, you will not harm her?" asked Tom, eagerly.

"That all depends upon your answer,"

"And, will you not suffer me to see her?"

"I don't know what I may do by and by," returned the pirate ; "it's according how you behave ; but, at present, I can make no such promise."

"You will give me your word, then, that if I consent to become one of your crew, you will not injure her?"

"I will. And now, what say you?—Quick ! I do not like long palaverings."

"Why, you see, Barnsley," said Tom, in a well-assumed tone, "you have no right to lay an embargo on our departure ; but, as I see it would be folly for me to oppose you, and as I can't abear the thoughts of being kept under hatches, why, I suppose, I must consent."

Richard started when he heard the answer of Tom, and fixed upon him a look of astonishment and incredulity ; but a significant glance from Tom quickly made him understand, and he became satisfied with the plan, and the object he could see he had in view.

"You agree, then?" demanded the pirate.

"Upon those conditions, I do," replied Tom.

" And the boy,—will he follow your example?"

" Of what use would it be to remain obstinate?" said Richard, calmly.

" Enough," said the pirate captain; " but, remember, any treachery will be followed by immediate death, and that by the most lingering torments. You will be constantly watched, and any designs which you might contemplate, would be sure to be thwarted."

With these words he bade them, with the men who still held them in custody, follow him upon deck, and having, in the presence of the whole of the pirate crew, seen them enter their names in the book, he commanded them to take the oath of obedience to the rules.

" Avast heaving, there!" exclaimed Tom; " I know you chaps pay devilish little respect to an oath; and if the word of a British seaman is not sufficient, you shall have nothing else from me."

" Nor from me," said Richard, boldly.

" Humph!" cried Barnsley, " these are rather bold words; but, no matter, I will take your word; there will be plenty on the look out for you, so you had better mind how you act. Away to your duty; you will find the life of a free-trader a most jovial one, and will have no cause to regret the circumstance which brought you on board my craft.

As the pirate captain thus spoke, he started from the deck, and entered the cabin in which Ellen had been placed under the care of a female who was on board.

We will pass over the night of horror which Ellen had passed; the reader may better conceive it, than we could pourtray it. When she beheld the pirate enter, her blood chilled with horror, and she clung to the woman who had attended upon her, with an expression of the utmost dread.

" Oh! no, no, no," ejaculated Ellen in tones of distraction; " for pity's sake do not leave me alone with this man."

" Begone!" said the pirate captain, in sterner accents. The woman, apparently, reluctantly obeyed; and Barnsley advancing to Ellen, and forcibly taking her hand, said,—

" Now, my pretty lass, you must conquer this timidity as soon as possible, and look upon me as your future husband."

" You!—you!—" screamed Ellen in a voice of disgust and abhorrence; " villain!—where is my lover?—where is Tom!"

" Better language would more become those pretty lips," returned Barnsley; " but, if it will be any satisfaction to you, Tom has gone ashore, and resigned you to me."

" Left me!—impossible!" cried Ellen. " Resigned me to you?—wretch! you would deceive me!—I'll not believe it!—we have loved each other for years;—'tis not in Tom's nature to thus requite a poor girl who confided her whole heart to his keeping. Tom! Tom!—why doesn't he answer?—He——Oh, man, man, what means that fierce, exulting smile!—You have killed him!—you have killed him! He is dead!—dead!"

" Why trouble your head about him?" said Barnsley, " isn't the captain of the craft preferable to him, who, if he were on board, would only be one of the crew?!!

"I am one of the crew of this vessel !" ejaculated Ellen "I am lost !—What will become of me ?"

"I'll take care of you," replied the pirate; "my fortune, shall be your fortune. Ellen, listen to me."

"Is there no one that will help me ?" cried Ellen, as Barnsley forcibly threw his arms round her waist, and pressed her towards him. "Am I so utterly forgotten by all !— so worthless in the eye of heaven, that I must sink thus degraded ?—mercy ! mercy !"

"Ellen," articulated Barnsley.

"Release me !—release me, monster !" exclaimed Ellen, forcibly breaking away from him, and running to the foot of the ladder;—"Help ! help !—Tom, where are you ?—save me !"

At that moment Tom appeared at the top of the ladder, and calling upon the name of his lover.

"Ha ! ha! ha !" cried Ellen frantically, as her eyes rested upon him, "'tis he ! —'tis he !"

With these words her feelings overpowered her, and she sunk upon the floor ; in an instant Tom sprang down the ladder, and stepping between her and the pirate captain, stood in an attitude of defence.

"Ah !" cried the latter, gazing with some surprise at the sailor, "have you then so soon broken through your pledge ?—what do you here ?"

"You infernal villain !" exclaimed Tom, in a tone of fierce and ungovernable indignation, "and, is that the way you keep your word ?—I fly to the protection of this poor girl, and, damme, if you shall lay your grappling irons upon her, while I have a spark of life remaining !"

"Shall not !" repeated Barnsley; "this is the language of mutiny. Have a care, or I shall order you into irons ; and you know what I promised you for disobedience. Above to your duty, sir, and leave that girl to me !"

"If ever there was a villain unhanged," said Tom, coolly, and drawing a knife from his waistcoat pocket,—"if ever there was a villain unhanged, who most deserved to die, Barnsley, you are that villain !—But, beware ! I am a desperate, determined man ! One step to touch her, and this knife shall drench these timbers with your treacherous blood !"

Tom raised the insensible form of Ellen in his arms, and stood with an air of determination to put his threat into execution. Barnsley was so surprised at the boldness of the sailor, that he stood for a second or two unable either to move or to utter a sentence. But at length he suddenly seemed to recollect himself, he blew his whistle, and immediately a number of the crew rushed down the ladder into the cabin.

"What ho ! there, my men ?" cried the pirate, "quick ! or murder will be done upon your captain ! seize yon mutineer !"

"Men," exclaimed Tom, resolutely, and brandishing the knife, "stand off ! or I'll stave every rib in your hulls !"

The pirate stood back for a few minutes, until again urged on by Barnsley, when they rushed upon him altogether, and tearing Ellen, (who had now recovered) from his arms, wrested the knife from him, and seized him with the greatest fury.

"Mutiny ! mutiny !" vociferated Barnsley, in savage accents :—"you shall swing for this ! Death to the mutineer !"

"Death to the mutineer !" shouted the crew;

"A word and a blow, is our law," said Barnsley; "up with him, to the yard-arm !"

Ellen disengaged herself from the hands of those who held her, and rushing frantically to the pirate captain, threw herself on her knees at his feet, and in tones of the most poignant anguish, she cried,—

"Oh ! hear me, I beseech you !—I will consent to remain—be your servant—your slave !—only spare him—his life—his——"

"Is the yard-rope rove, I say ?" demanded the pirate captain.

"Aye, aye, captain," replied one of the crew, from the top of the ladder.

"You swing in less than ten minutes," observed Barnsley.

"Ellen !" said Tom, in a voice of the deepest emotion.

She rushed to him, and threw herself in his arms.

"I deserve it," he continued; "'tis the reward of my own mad folly, and I deserve it : but you will live to curse my memory when I am no more !"

"I curse you, Tom !" sobbed Ellen; "never, Tom,—never !"

"Ellen," said Tom, his voice almost choked with emotion, "I have loved you through fair weather and through foul, sweet girl ! When you go back—for he who forsakes me, cannot abandon you, so innocent—tell——"

"Cease this folly !" cried the pirate, impatiently;—"to the yard-arm—away with him "

Ellen had once more become insensible, and Tom, having kissed her distractedly, said,—

"Take her from me, now, while she is in a dead calm. Heaven bless you, my poor girl ! We shall meet aloft :—as for you, Barnsley, this will be a leak to sink your soul in that hour when we come to pass our accounts; and she will stand there between us, as your accusing angel, for the murder you do this day."

Barnsley turned upon him a look of scorn, as the men, having borne Ellen away, were preparing to lead him to execution. At this juncture, the report of distant guns was heard, and directly afterwards, one of the men cried out from the top of the ladder,—

"Sail coming up with us, on the larboard quarter !"

"Ah ! a sail !" exclaimed Barnsley; "can you make her out ?"

"She is a British frigate !"

"Ah !" cried Tom, aside, "probably sent in pursuit of the pirate; my death, then, will be avenged, and she rescued."

"Silence ! sir," cried Barnsley, who had overheard what he said; "you are out of your reckoning for the last time ;—on stunsails alow and aloft, and my life on it we'll outsail the devil !—On,—on. Bear the mutineer to his death."

The pirates hurried Tom away, and then the same man who had given notice of the appearance of the vessel, ejaculated,—

"She nears us, sir ;—they're close aboard."

As he spoke, loud shouts from without confirmed the truth of his assertions, and the sailor hastily quitted the top of the ladder. The shouts increased, and Barnsley, addressing himself to the men who were around him, said,—

"Up, men ! and if they attempt our decks, fire upon them.—Man for man—life for life !"

He led the way, sword in hand, and the men followed him upon deck. The engagement was terrific, and was for some time doubtful on both sides. Tom had been hurried below, and as he heard the loud shouts of those engaged in the deadly strife, his blood boiled to be in the battle, while his bosom was the abode of the most indescribable anxiety, when he thought upon the danger to which Ellen was thus exposed. At length the crew of the British frigate boarded the pirate, and then the carnage became terrific.

"Surrender! pirate," cried the captain of the frigate, when he encountered Barnsley, "surrender, or——"

"Surrender!—never!" returned the other, resolutely.

"Resistance is in vain," remarked the captain of the frigate; "you are charged with the violent detention of one of our men; which charge, his having just been seen upon this deck, fully confirms. You are also charged with detaining on board one Ellen Saunderson, and Richard, her cousin, also belonging to the king's service; and what is more, you now stand arrested on the king's evidence of your own lieutenant, William Hatten, for many acts of desperate piracy, committed on the high seas."

"All of which is true," returned Barnsley, with the most consummate coolness; "but you must not imagine that I am going to yield so easily.—At the swabs again, my lads! Let us conquer or die!"

Encouraged by the words of their captain, the pirates rushed on their assailants with the most irresistible fury and impetuosity, and the slaughter that ensued on both sides was truly terrific. The pirates fought with the most desperate bravery, and the others were forced to give way; many of them being driven overboard, amid the demoniac shouts of the pirates; the others made to the frigate as fast as they could, and had scarcely done so, when it was discovered to be on fire, and in a few minutes it was completely enveloped in flames. The yells and shouts of triumph that rent the air from the wretches on board the pirate vessel were truly awful to hear; and as many of the crew of the ill-fated frigate committed themselves to the mercy of the waves, they took a savage delight in firing upon them. In less than half an hour, the frigate was burned to the water's edge, and every soul on board perished. The pirate brig had by that time got far away from the scene of the late horrors.

We will now request the reader to follow us on shore, where the grief and distraction of Mat, his wife, and Rosina, at the disappearance of Ellen, Tom, and Richard, was powerful beyond all conception. But the suspicions which Richard had given utterance to, and many other circumstances, which had come under his own personal observation, served to convince Mat that Barnsley was really what the lad stated he thought he was, and that he had had this design in contemplation for some time. The first thing he did, therefore, was to make the circumstance known at the proper place, and the frigate was despatched in pursuit. A week elapsed and nothing was heard of the frigate, and during this time, Mat and the others—Rosina particularly—felt their suspense and agony increase to an almost insupportable degree. Upon more nature reflection, and the circumstance of his having frequently seen Barnsley and Saib conversing together, Mat could not help thinking that there was more in this circumstance than he had at first thought, and that the latter was at the bottom of the whole plot. So confident was he of it, that he at last determined to visit the mansion of the Earl Fitzosbert, and demand the truth, although Rosina would fain have dissuaded him from it, for, knowing the power of the earl, she dreaded that it would be attended with some painful result. Mat, however, persisted in going, and the reception he met with may be readily imagined. The earl firmly and haughtily denied all knowledge of the affair; and when questioned about Saib, declared that he did not know what had become of him, although at that time he was concealed in his house. Mat returned home in a state of the greatest anguish, which was much increased, when, the following day the news reached them the fate of which the frigate had met with, and the escape of the pirate; and Rosina was reduced to a state bordering upon frenzy.

In the meantime, the earl and Saib exulted in the success which had attended their designs, and the former felt more at ease than he had done for many years, and highly applauded the ingenuity and perseverance of his faithful creature. He also expressed his earnest wishes that Saib might be able to get Rosina in his power, and promised to assist him all that lay in his power, to effect that object.

Several weeks now elapsed since these occurrences had taken place, during which, nothing very particular happened. At this period it was publicly known, and had been for several days, that the Earl Fitzosbert intended to get up some extraordinary festivities, to celebrate the anniversary of his birth, the principal of which was to be a masked tête, to which he had invited all the nobility and gentry in the neighbourhood.

At length the important day arrived, and never had there been known to be such a scene of mirth and festivity in the mansion of the earl; he having also thrown off his forbidding manners, and appearing to enter into all the festivities with much spirit. The masquerade was got up with much taste, and was well attended; the variety of masks, and the fancy dresses, presented a pleasing and effective sight, and every one seemed to join in the gaieties of the evening with alacrity. In the midst of all this happiness, however, the earl could not help noticing the singular conduct of a black domino, and whose figure struck him as bearing a great resemblance to the one he had on a former occasion seen, and which had caused him so much alarm. This black domino watched him about wherever he went; he could not turn but he was at his elbow; and whenever he went to address him, he was speedily gone and lost among the revellers.

He could not account for it, but a singular trembling came over him, as he gazed upon this mysterious individual, who so narrowly seemed to scrutinize his motions. His figure was tall and commanding, and he moved with a noble and majestic air.

Several hours passed in this manner, and still the black domino seemed to dodge him about. At length the earl, being somewhat apart from the rest of the company, did not see him, so he thought he had retired, and paused to reflect upon who he was, and his unaccountable behaviour. While he thus stood, he was startled by hearing his name pronounced in a solemn voice, from behind him, and turning round, he beheld the tall figure of the black domino standing before him.

"Can Robert Fitzosbert," said the back domino, in a voice which made the earl tremble with horror, "yield to mirth while the blood of his murdered brother and his offspring is upon his head?"

The earl was completely petrified by the words of the black domino, and gazing upon him vacantly, he in vain tried for some time to speak. The stranger stood unmoved, and Fitzosbert could perceive through his mask, that he was gazing upon him with an earnestness, which seemed as if it would penetrate to his soul. A strange sensation fell upon the heart of the earl, and thrilled through all his veins, as he contemplated this mysterious man; there was something in the tones of his voice, and in the expression of his eyes, which was familiar to him, and caused him to shudder with horror.

"Fitzosbert," ejaculated the black domino, in the same solemn manner as before, "the blood of the murdered calls for vengeance; and the time is coming when retribution shall overtake the assassin.—Tremble!"

"Insolent intruder!" cried the earl fiercely, as he regained, in some measure, his self possession—"insolent intruder, who are you, that presumest to address me thus?—For what purpose come you hither?"

A hollow, derisive laugh was the only answer given to these interrogatories, and, in a moment raising his mask, the eyes of the earl fell upon the lineaments of a countenance, the contemplation of which seemed to freeze the blood in his veins with horror. His eye-lids became distended,—his face ghastly pale,—and his limbs trembled as he gazed upon the phantom before him (for such he thought it was) with speechless terror. The black domino seemed to behold his emotion with satisfaction, then repeating the word "*Tremble*," he glided with the rapidity of thought, among the joyous revellers, and was hidden from the sight.

For a few minutes the earl remained in the same position as when the black domino had left him, and continued with his eyes fixed, as if he was still standing before him, then suddenly starting, in a voice which made the spacious saloon re-echo again, and reached the ears of all the guests, he exclaimed,—

"Where is he?—Whither has he gone, with his ghastly features, and his blood-stained form?—Horror!—Shall the spirits of the dead rise up in judgment against me?—Yes, they will:—but now I saw him:—he stood before me,—his filmy eyes were fixed on me with terrible solemnity—his sepulchral voice breathed curses upon my head! It spoke of retribution; but where is he now?—Was I deceived?—Oh, no, it was no delusion. But it was not I who——"

"Psha! my lord, are you mad?" said Saib, who at that moment came up, but was unacquainted with what had taken place, although the agitation evinced by the earl much alarmed him; "see you not the gazing listeners around?" he added, in an under tone. By hell! your folly will bring us to destruction."

The earl gazed wildly upon the black, without seeming to comprehend the meaning of what he said, and then exclaimed, in frantic accents:—

"Ah! it was you that struck the fatal blow. Even now your hands are reeking with the blood——"

"Idiot!" exclaimed Saib, in a hoarse voice, as he forcibly dragged the earl away, and hurried him into his own apartment, where he was immediately put to bed, and his ravings became terrific.

The festivities abruptly ceased, and the astonished guests stood paralyzed by what they had heard, and gazed upon each other with looks of mysterious meaning. Gradually they dispersed; the music ceased—the lights were extinguished, and silence reigned in that mansion where lately nought was heard save the sounds of exuberant mirth.

The earl continued in a delirious state the whole of the night, and Saib was so alarmed that he never quitted his chamber, and would not suffer any one else than himself and the medical man to enter it. From what he could elicit by the words of Fitzosbert, the black man felt convinced that he must have heard or seen something to cause him to be so much alarmed, and his fears and anxiety were great, lest the earl should utter something which might lead to a disclosure of the dark deeds of other days. Towards morning, however, the earl became more calm, but still remained in a state of insensibility.

This incident caused Saib many hours of painful and perplexing thought; but he could not by any means unravel the mystery. And now his astonishment was increased by the reports that were continually being made by the servants, who again persisted that the house had lately been haunted by an evil spirit, and the mania was spreading all over the household, so that it assumed anything but a pleasing aspect. They reported that they heard strange noises in the house, at all hours of the night, and many of them went so far as to declare that they had seen the spectre, stalking through the different chambers at midnight, and that it gave utterance to such melancholy groans, it was quite awful to hear them.

These statements very much disturbed Saib, whose conscience now conjured up a thousand terrors; and he was soon convinced that the servants spoke the truth; for, regularly at the hour of midnight, the same sounds they had spoken of, met his ears, and prevented him from obtaining any rest. Once, too, he was almost certain he beheld a shadowy form in his chamber and these circumstances combiued, and the dread of their crimes being brought to light, and himself to condign punishment, rendered the villain truly miserable.

How truly has the immortal bard said,—

" Conscience doth make cowards of us all;"

and never was it more powerfully exemplified than in the case of Saib and his master. Frequently, when the earl spoke of the circumstances that had so alarmed him, when he had again become insensible, Saib would affect to discredit it, and tried to persuade him that he was labouring under a delusion ; but it was easy to be observed, in spite of his assumption of firmness and incredulity, that his terrors were equal to those of the wretched earl.

" Why should we fear ?" he remarked upon one occasion to his master ; " have not those from whom alone we had cause to apprehend danger, been removed ?— Yes ; the plot was a good one, and Will Barnsley performed his task excellently, and well deserved the reward he received."

" But, my brother, Lionel!—what of him ?" ejaculated the earl. " Oh, Saib, how I shudder when I think upon him."

" Psha! these coward fears are groundless, my lord," returned the African ; although his manner was agitated, and but ill accorded with the air of confidence he assumed ; " his bones have long been mouldering in—"

A deep groan interrupted him, and made them both start ; but what was their horror to behold, standing in the distant part of the chamber, the same dark and mysterious form, which had twice before so awfully alarmed the guilty Fitzosbert.

The countenance of the supposed phantom was fully revealed to them, and its ghastly complexion ; the supernatural expression of the eyes, and the well known features, smote the hearts of Saib and Fitzosbert with horror, and enchained all their faculties.

" Spirit or demon !" at length cried the black, " I will ascertain the truth of this."

With these words, Saib rushed towards the spot where the form stood, but, before he could reach it, a hollow sepulchral laugh resounded through the apartment, and the mysterious figure had vanished.

Saib passed by the door which opened into the adjoining apartment, and through which he imagined the awful visitant had vanished, but he could see nothing of it, and to the inquiries which he made of the servants, he received the most positive assurances that they had admitted no person to the house answering the description which Saib gave of the form, and that none of them had seen it. They all shrugged up their shoulders when they heard his brief recital delivered in the interrogatories he put to them ; and, although they said nothing, the significant glances they exchanged with one another, spoke volumes.

As the African returned to the room in which he had left his terrified master, he muttered to himself,—

" By hell! this is strange ;—and can, then, the dead rise up in judgment against us ?—But there is something more in this than I can at present fathom. Psha ;—I am getting as weak and fearful as Fitzosbert."

On his return to the room, he found the earl in a most wretched state, and conveyed him immediately to his chamber.

" Would that death would do its work with him :" soliloquised Saib, as he retired from the couch of the earl, " then should I fear but little.—In his frenzy he will disclose all ; and destruction to us both will be the result."

Thus passed away a week ; the noises in the house became still more frequent and violent than ever, and several of the servants left the earl's service, declaring that nothing should induce them to remain in a house which now seemed to have become the chosen haunt of an evil spirit. The earl no longer kept his bed, but he almost entirely secluded himself in his own room, and seemed to have given himself up entirely to melancholy and soul-harrowing reflection. He would have quitted the house, and retired for a while to another part of the country,—but the medical men declared that he was yet in such a weak state, that if he attempted the fatigue of travelling, it might be attended with the most fatal consequences. As for Saib, he was seldom at home, and invariably, since the mysterious event, had slept out.

One evening he was returning from the mansion of the earl to the place at which he was at present lodging, and having to pass by the ' Old Commodore,' curiosity, or some unaccountable impulse induced him to peep through the casement into the parlour ; judge his astonishment and delight, then, when the first object upon which his eyes rested was Rosina !

She was seated in the company of Mat and his wife, and although the most poignant anguish was depicted in the countenances of them all, the African thought he had never before seen her look so handsome as she did on that occasion. Scarcely could the miscreant keep his rapture within the bounds of prudence, and as his eyes gloated upon the form of that poor girl whom he had marked for his victim, he could scarcely suppress a laugh of demoniacal exultation. Here, then, she was all but in his clutches ; but should he attempt to seize upon her then ?—No ; it would be rash to do so, and would be sure to be frustrated ; for there were, doubtless, persons in the tavern, who would lend their assistance to Mat, and she would be easily rescued from him, and himself brought to punishment for the outrage he had not only committed upon her, but Richard ; and although all evidence of the latter offence was safely removed, he would be placed in a dilemma which would be far from pleasant or desirable. He, therefore, at last came to the resolution to await near the house, until she should take her departure, when he might watch whither she went, and at some future period, devise a plan by which he might with safety seize her, and bearing her to some place of security, have her entirely in his power, and enforce her to submit to his will.

In about an hour Rosina arose, and putting on her cloak, it was evident that she was about to depart, and shortly afterwards she quitted the tavern, accompanied by Mat. With the utmost difficulty did Saib keep from revealing himself to the poor girl and forcing her away from her companion ; but he did resist the temptation, and followed them at a distance, contriving to keep them constantly in sight, and concealing himself from their observation. In this manner he followed them to within a short distance of the house in which Rosina at present resided, and after bidding Mat good night, he saw her enter, and the latter began to retrace his footsteps to the tavern.

Saib suffered him to pass on, and then walked closer up to the house, and went round it, gazing up at every window, with looks of the most unbounded satisfaction and exultation. At length, fearful that he might be observed, and thus his designs be frustrated, he turned away from the spot, and hastened towards the house where he himself lodged.

"She's mine! she's mine!" the African exclaimed, as he walked away from the place, and his heart bounded with a feeling of triumph; "the proud,—the haughty beauty is now securely mine, and no power shall this time rescue her from me!—She has no one near to fly to her aid, no one that can save her, and my triumph is complete!—Ha! ha! ha!"

Thus exulting in his diabolical designs, Saib entered the house, and retired to his chamber; where he became quickly immersed in thought, and endeavoured to concoct a scheme by which he might put his plans with more certainty into execution.

While these events were going on on shore, the sufferings of those at sea, as may be conceived, without much difficulty, were most poignant. After the engagement, and the disastrous fate of the frigate, Will Barnsley ordered Tom once more to be brought before him, and having now made up his mind to die, he endeavoured to meet the untimely fate, to which he imagined he was being led, with becoming fortitude. But to reflect that his Ellen would be left in the power of the pirate captain, and forced to a compliance with his desires, was almost more than he could endure, and the honest tar's heart swelled to nearly bursting.

When he came before the pirate, he found him surrounded by several of the crew, and among others, manacled like himself, was Will Barnsley's lieutenant who had betrayed him.

"Now, Sirrah!" he cried, addressing himself to Tom, "you have seen I should think, the folly of endeavouring to disobey my commands; your life is forfeited; but as you are a good seaman, I believe, I will grant it you, on your promising that you will not so offend again. What say you,—will you give the required promise?"

"While you ask me not that which honour and honesty would not revolt against, I will endeavour to conform to your rules;" answered Tom.

"Honour!—honesty!" reiterated the pirate captain with a sneer, "bah! what have we to do with such terms here? Will you promise to obey?"

"If you will promise me not to harm my Ellen," returned Tom, "I will give my consent; but not without, for damme, though I may be slung to the yard-arm the next moment, if I see any one, be he man or devil, lay a finger upon that poor girl, I will level him with the deck in an instant!"

"You talk very boldly, methinks, young fellow," said Will Barnsley.

"A true British sailor does not understand any other language," answered Tom, "especially when talking to a damned——"

"Ha! dare you?" cried Barnsley, fiercely.

"Well, well," answered Tom, with the utmost coolness, "I suppose it is as well to belay such lingo, and, therefore, I will not give utterance to what I was going to say. It rests entirely with yourself as to how I shall behave."

"Well, I am disposed to try you," said Barnsley, "but, beware; the least signs of mutiny, and you swing in a moment, as for injuring your Ellen, as you call her, my intentions are quite different, as it is my design to make her my wife!"

"Your wife!" exclaimed Tom, in a voice of indignation.

"Aye," answered the pirate captain, "and so you will see in a short time.

But enough of this for the present. I would shew you how I punish a traitor !— This is the fellow who betrayed us, and this is his reward !—Lash the rascal to the gun, and cut the flesh from his bones !"

In a moment the unfortunate wretch was stripped, and secured to the gun, and then two of the pirates, by the orders of the captain, came forward, and prepared to flog him with a couple of rope-ends, bound round with fine wire.

"Have you anything to say in mitigation of your punishment, traitor?" demanded Barnsley, in a stern voice.

"Nothing," replied the unfortunate man, firmly, "only that I regret that the frigate was unsuccessful, and that it did not blow ye all to perdition."

"Commence your work, my men," said the pirate captain, "and see that you give it him soundly, or look to your own backs !"

The pirates commenced their frightful work, tearing the flesh away from the back of the sufferer, with the heavy blows they inflicted, and seeming to exult in the excruciating agonies they were inflicting, while Barnsley stood by and looked on, seeming to view the writhings and contortions of the unhappy wretch, with the utmost satisfaction. Soon the deck was floating with the blood of the poor fellow, who bore the punishment with the most astonishing fortitude, and but rarely uttered a groan, and then only when the torture being inflicted by the inhuman wretches, became too terrible for human nature to support. Tom's heart was smote with horror and disgust, and he would have hastened from the revolting scene, had he not been forcibly withheld, by the orders of Barnsley, who was determined that he should witness the whole of the horrible punishment.

At length, when the unfortunate man had received upwards of a thousand lashes, and the flesh was literally cut from his bones, Will Barnsley ordered him to be unfastened from the gun. Tom imagined that here his punishment would cease, but he was soon undeceived. The monster, Barnsley's vengeance was not yet satiated, and he ordered his victim's tongue to be cut out, and burnt before his face; the poor fellow having become totally insensible from the barbarous punishment he had undergone. While in this condition, Barnsley commanded him to be hung by the heels to the yard arm, and in that state the ill-fated man was left to expire.

"Thus do I punish those who would betray me, or disobey my orders;" exclaimed the pirate captain, "and therefore, you may see what you have to expect, should you infringe upon our laws !"

"Monster !" was upon the lips of Tom, but he stifled the expression, knowing what would be the consequences attending it; and that the pirate might be excited to some act of brutality against Ellen.

"There, away to your duty," commanded Barnsley, "and, beware !"

Tom was released from his fetters, and walked away. Had it not been for the sake of Ellen, he would quickly have put an end to the state of misery in which he was involved, by leaping overboard, and preferring a watery grave to any association with such wretches; but hope, also, had not entirely forsook him; and he, therefore, endeavoured to keep up his spirits as well as possible,—an effort which he accomplished much more effectually than could have been anticipated.

He had not seen his lover since the day on which he had been sentenced to die by the pirate captain, for Barnsley kept her closely confined to the cabin in which he had placed her, and where he ordered her to receive every possible attention, and anything she might wish for. Tom's anxiety concerning her we need not seek to pourtray, as the reader may easily form an idea of it; and many a wretched hour did he pass, constrained as he was, in order that he might not betray his real thoughts to the wretches with whom he had so unfortunately become connected, to appear contented with his lot, and to enter into their ways without any repugnance. But, still the courage of the true British sailor surmounted all these difficulties; and Tom, placing his firm reliance in the protection of Omnipotence, did not despair that a time would soon arrive when they should be released from their present miserable situation, and that they would escape unscathed and free.

Richard, perhaps, suffered more than either of them, not from any lack of courage, but such was his attachment to Ellen and Tom, that he felt more for them than he did for himself, and was fearful that the former would fall a victim to the cruelty and wicked designs of the pirate captain. It was not likely that she would long be able to resist the villain Barnsley, or that he would long delay the gratification of his nefarious desires, and the poor lad shuddered with horror as these too probable thoughts occurred to him, knowing that the peace of both Ellen and her parents would be for ever broken, and that nothing, after such a blow, would ever be able to restore them to happiness.

To be compelled to appear friendly, and to associate with such heartless and guilty wretches as the crew of the pirate vessel were, was another and a principal source of the most indescribable misery to the noble-minded youth; their coarse language, bitter oaths, and ribald jests were sufficient to fill his mind, also, with the greatest disgust; and there were moments when he thought that death would be far preferable to the life in which cruel fortune had thus placed him; and at such times, young as he was, as he gazed upon the blue waters of the expansive ocean, he was half inclined to plunge into its bosom, and at once escape from it. He could not but continue to reproach the headstrong folly of Tom in not listening to his suspicions; and he also regretted that he had not persisted in remaining on shore, when the information he might have given, would, in all probability have frustrated the designs of Barnsley, before he had had an opportunity of escaping. As day after day passed away, and he saw no alteration in their condition, or any prospect of their being released, his anguish increased until it became almost insupportable. What would be the dreadful anxiety, and intense grief of poor old Mat and his wife? The heart might conceive it, but language could not properly depict it.

Tom, notwithstanding, as we have before observed, he put the best face he could upon the matter, felt as deeply the misery and danger of their situation as any person placed under similar circumstances could possibly have done; but by giving way entirely to the power of his feelings, he could not, he was well aware, amend their lot, and, on the contrary, he considered, and that very justly, too, that by so doing he would be the more likely to increase their misery, and expedite the fate of Ellen, which otherwise might be retarded, until it was ultimately completely avoided. All schemes did he try to gain an interview, nay, even but a sight of the ill-starred girl, but in vain; neither could he elicit anything from Barnsley's behaviour, or the words he would occasionally let drop, that could assist him in forming any conjecture as to what extent he had actually proceeded, as regarded his loathsome advances and importunities towards Ellen.

In the meantime, the poor girl was enduring the most poignant anguish that can well be imagined, not only on her own account, but in consequence of her uncertainty as to the fate of her lover, for Barnsley never would give her any satisfactory answer to the questions she so often put to him upon that subject, and in fact endeavoured to evade it as much as possible. There were times, when the dark hints which she imagined the pirate captain threw out, almost persuaded her that Tom had fallen by the hands of the pirates, and then her horror and misery would reach a pitch which was truly pitiable. In such moments Barnsley always took especial care to leave her, and his object seemed to be to keep her in a state of uncertainty and suspense, so that he might make her the more readily subservient to his wishes. Yet was the villain's forbearance most remarkable: although he urged his suit with all the energy he was capable, there was a sort of respectful demeanour towards her, which could be accounted for in no other way than that her charms had inspired him with other sentiments than those of insatiate lust and desire. Sometimes, when he seemed inclined to be bolder than others, the beauty and dignity (the dignity of virtue) which Ellen would assume towards him, awed him into forbearance, and he would quit her presence abruptly, and not annoy her again for some time. Frequently, as the rude mirth, and coarse language which the ruffians were in the habit of making use of reached her ears, she shuddered with horror and disgust, and pictured to herself, if even her beloved Tom still lived, what must be his disgust, his misery, in being compelled to mingle with such wretches. Often, too, she could not help surmising that, if even he had not fallen by the hands of the pirates, he had, in all probability, rushed upon death of his own accord, rather than be in any way connected with such desperate and blood-thirsty wretches; and yet, again, she reflected, that he would not do so, while she was in the power of the villain Barnsley, and her fate was so uncertain. With Richard, she could not but blame Tom for not having listened to the advice which the former had given him, and which had not only been most reasonable, but very probable, and which, had he availed himself of it, would have been the means of saving them all three from the terrible fate with which they were now threatened. But the sufferings of her dear parents,—that racked her mind more than everything else, and she could not reflect upon it with any degree of patience,—which would be increased, she was aware, ten-fold, when it should become known to them that the vessel which had been sent in pursuit of the pirate had been destroyed, and that, therefore, all hope might be considered to be at an end. Yet, ever and anon, a latent thought would spring up in the bosom of Ellen, which prevented her from giving way to the utter despair, which otherwise would have filled her breast; and it was that which enabled her to maintain her fortitude in a manner that both surprised and abashed the pirate captain.

In this manner, several days elapsed without any material change taking place, or anything of sufficient importance occurring to render it worthy of mention in these pages. Barnsley, however, it was very evident, was daily becoming more impatient, he had, in fact, intimated to Ellen that he should only give her three days longer to consider of his proposals, when, if she still persisted in rejecting them, he should use force. The state of mind this produced in the poor girl, may be very easily imagined ; and, in fact, there were moments when she was completely distracted.

Two days out of the three passed quickly away, and the morning of the third dawned, and a most terrible morning it was. The thunder rolled fiercely through the high vault of Heaven ; the lightning blazed with fearful violence ; the wind blew a perfect hurricane ; the waves rolled mountains high, and the brig was tossed about like a straw. In this manner it continued with unabated fury throughout the day, and at night it seemed rather to have increased than abated.

Barnsley, notwithstanding the raging of the tempest, and the imminent danger in which they were placed,—it not being expected that the vessel could live one moment from another,—had been with Ellen, and had once more urged his hateful suit, in more urgent terms than before, when, suddenly, the ship lurched frightfully,—a terrific crash was heard, and several voices, in tones of horror and despair, shouted that she had sprung a leak, and Barnsley rushed hastily from the cabin, leaving the door open behind him. Great as were the terrors of Ellen, they did not so far overcome her strength as to prevent her from immediately leaving the cabin, and hastening upon deck, where the consternation was frightful to behold ; the miscreants, desperate as they were at other times, were now pale and trembling at the prospect of death, and every one was using such precautions as the time would permit, to rescue themselves from the danger by which they were surrounded. The ship was rapidly filling, and completely frantic with despair, Ellen screamed aloud, just as her eyes fell upon Tom and Richard, who were looking around them with frenzied eyes, as if in search of some particular object. In a moment the poor girl was once more enfolded in the arms of her faithful lover.

Not an instant, however, had they to exchange a word together ;—the vessel was rapidly filling, and every one was seeking the means of escape. There was a simultaneous rush towards the long boat, when Tom, feeling desperate at the situation in which they were placed, clasped Ellen in his arms, and thrusting several ruffians aside, he sprang with her over the side of the vessel, and reached the boat in safety. He was instantly followed by Richard, and amid the yells and execrations of the pirates,—several of whom fired at them,—the boat was unloosed from her hold, and in a moment was drifted by the fury of the waves far away from the fast sinking brig. An appalling shriek from the drowning wretches immediately afterwards convinced them that all was over, and that the pirates had met the fate which their crimes richly merited.

All three of the inmates of the boat were too much engrossed and appalled by the horrors of the scene which surrounded them, to suffer them to speak ; but Tom looked at his lover with an expression which was meant to inspire her with hope, and then directed his attention, with that of Richard, to the management of the weak vessel in which they were ; but all management, all control over the boiling billows, by which they were tossed as it were to the clouds, was entirely out of the question, and they were obliged to commit themselves to the mercy of Providence, suffering the boat to take its own course, and expecting every instant that they must perish.

Dreadful was the situation of the lovers and the boy Richard; but Tom sought all in his power to encourage the hopes, and to keep up the spirits of Ellen; and with the courage of a true sailor, he viewed the horrors by which they were surrounded, with a steady eye and calm demeanour.

"Fear not, my dear Ellen," he observed, "there is One who keeps watch above, and who will not suffer those to founder who place a firm reliance in Him, and are faithful to His command. At any rate, any fate is better than the one which we have just escaped."

"It is, indeed, dear Tom," replied the maiden; "and think not that I fear to die; no, Tom; rather would I share the same fate with you, then see you perish and survive myself."

"My poor, fond lass," ejaculated Tom, kissing her fervently, — "Heaven surely will not suffer you to meet with so untimely a death.

They could not say more,—for the attention of Tom and Richard was now called entirely to the guidance of the boat, which was tossed about in a terrific manner,—sometimes dashed mountains high, and the next moment buried deep in the bosom of the foaming billows. Every instant they expected she would capsize, and they were hurried along with the most furious precipitation,—the efforts of Tom and Richard to guide her being all but useless. The fury of the storm increased, rather than abated;—the roaring of the wind, the heavy peals of thunder, and vivid flashes of lightning, at intervals, were terrible to behold. They were drenched to the skin, shivering with cold, and in addition fast sinking with the great fatigue they had undergone. The honest tar raised his eyes towards

No. 16

Heaven, and mentally breathed a prayer for their preservation, and then, with renewed strength occasioned by the imminent peril in which they were placed, he applied himself to the guidance of the boat.

Richard behaved himself with a steady courage and composure which could not have been expected in one so young; and, indeed, his only care appeared to be for the safety of Ellen and her lover. Yet, to meet death under such circumstances, was awful, particularly when he thought of the heavy grief it would occasion Mat and his wife—a grief from which, he felt confident, they would never recover.

For more than an hour they were tossed about in this manner, every instant being placed as it were upon the very extreme verge of eternity, and excluded entirely from hope. It was truly awful to look over the fierce raging ocean, and watch the waves, with their white crests, as they soared to the sky, each one carrying a death with it. Wildly the sea-mews screamed; and the thunder's loud voice alone drowned their cries. At length they espied what they imagined to be land at no great distance from them, and with clasped hands, and expressions of gratitude, they returned their thanks to the Almighty, and prayed that they might be able to reach it with safety.

Aroused to fresh energy by this circumstance, they—that is, Tom and Richard—again plied themselves to their task, and they were rewarded for their exertion by observing that they rapidly neared what they hoped would prove the goal of their deliverance. As they approached it, however, they perceived that it was a rock, and they feared lest their frail bark should be driven so rapidly against it as to be upset.

Fortunately, however, this did not turn out to be the case, and they reached the rock in safety. The difficulty then was to reach the summit. It was very high and steep, and they were all so much exhausted by the uncommon fatigue they had already undergone, that it seemed scarcely possible that they could accomplish the task. There was very little time for consideration. They got the boat as gently as they could beneath the rock, and then Tom sprang from it, and with much difficulty clambered up the craggy sides, until he reached a small ledge, where he could rest. Here he paused for a second, uncertain how to act. Luckily there was a small coil of rope in the boat, which the sailor desired Ellen to fasten round her waist, and then to throw the other end to him, and commence the attempt to clamber up the rock, he assisting her all that was in his power. This was done, and Ellen, once more imploring the aid of Heaven, did as her lover requested her, and succeeded better than could possibly have been expected. Tom put forth the whole of his strength, which was nearly exhausted, and it was at length crowned with success. Ellen was drawn with safety to the ledge, and in the same manner she gained the others, until they ultimately reached the summit of the rock. Richard, with all the activity of youth, quickly followed them, and then they all three sank upon their knees, and in accents of sincerity returned their thanks to Omnipotence for their deliverance from the jaws of death. But their joy soon vanished, when they looked around them and beheld the wretched place upon which they had been cast. It was a barren rock, completely destitute of any signs of vegetation; and what hope was there for them of ultimately saving their lives, unless some vessel should pass near into which they might be received; no other prospect stared them in the face, but a dreadful, lingering death by starvation.

The storm had now entirely ceased; but they were perishing with cold and wet, and looked upon each other with despairing eyes.

"Alas! my poor Ellen," said her lover "never did your Tom expect to see such a day as this;—never did he think that his dear girl would be exposed to such danger. I care not for myself;—but to see you meet with so terrible a fate, tortures my heart to madness."

"Nay, dear Tom," replied Ellen," I intreat you not to give way to this sorrow; if it is to be my fate, you cannot avert it; and we should not arraign the will of the Almighty."

"Very true, Ellen," said the sailor; and he looked into her eyes with all that intensity of affection by which his behaviour towards her had ever been characterised;—"and to die together, loving as we have ever loved, and must continue to do with our latest breath, is some consolation. But, then, Ellen, to think that you should have been brought into this danger through my mad folly and headstrong conduct, racks me to the heart."

"Oh, Tom, do not upbraid yourself; do not reproach yourself for that which fate destined should take place," said Ellen. "Providence may yet deem fit to save us; and if not, we must endeavour to meet our fate with patience and resignation."

"You are a good, dear girl," said the honest tar, as he kissed the now pallid cheek of Ellen, and, in spite of his manly efforts to the contrary, could not resist the tears that rushed to his eyes; "you talk so like an angel, that even in the midst of this danger, it joys my heart to hear you. But as to that lingo about patience and resignation, why, you see, Ellen, it is much easier to talk about it, than to practice it, when I see you suffering in this manner."

"Your anguish only adds to mine, Tom," returned Ellen; "to behold you suffer, is worse to me than all the other troubles that can attend me."

"I know it,—I know it, my lass," cried Tom, fervently, "and for that reason will I endeavour to do as you desire. Surely, that Power which keeps watch over us, will not suffer us—or at least you—to die this miserable death!"

"If we put our trust in Him, Tom," exclaimed Richard, in a tone of fervour and sincerity, "rest assured He will not forget us; and if it is His will that this should be our end, we must learn to submit to it without a murmur. It is only for those we leave behind us, that I feel more poignantly than myself."

"Ah! my unfortunate parents!" ejaculated Ellen, in accents of distraction.

"My sister,—my poor, and now unprotected Rosina!" uttered Tom, in a voice of the deepest emotion.

Once more they fell on their knees, and supplicated the mercy of the Most High. Then Tom arose, and proceeded to some distance, to reconnoitre; but he saw nothing to appease his anguish on that desolate and sterile rocky island. There was no place to shelter them, and it was very cold; but Ellen bore up with her sufferings with the fortitude of an heroine, and in a manner which created the most unbounded astonishment in the bosom of Tom and Richard. She never uttered a murmur of complaint, and her countenance, in spite of the horrors by which they were surrounded, was expressive of hope, and eagerly did they cast their eyes over

the broad expanse of the ocean, in the vain hope of beholding some vessel which
might come to their relief. The storm which had but a short time before raged
with such terrific violence, had now entirely ceased, and a dead calm had succeeded. The billows which had lately boiled and foamed with wild fury, now
scarcely exhibited the slightest motion, and the huge mass of waters seemed to
slumber after the fierce battle they had been raging with the other elements.
They gazed across the ocean, however, in vain. Not the least signs of help
appeared.

Night rapidly approached, and as darkness began to veil everything around them
their situation became more appalling. At length, however, they huddled
together, to endeavour to keep themselves warm ; and in spite of the intense cold,
and the horrors of their situation, they were so overpowered with fatigue that they
gradually fell off to sleep. They neither of them awoke until the morning had
dawned, and the rays of the sun came warm and refreshing to them, after the cold
they had experienced the night before. It was a lovely day, and the deep blue
waters of the ocean were illumined with the sun's effulgent beams, while the clear,
cerulean blue of the sky, seemed to smile from the effects of his golden rays.

Tom looked eagerly upon his lover ; she was very pale and ill, but she smiled,
and endeavoured to conceal what she was really suffering. Tom, however, was
not to be deceived, and his agitation needs no description from us. And now
they all felt the gnawing pangs of hunger come upon them, and they had not the
least means of allaying it. It was then that they gazed upon each other with looks
expressive of the utmost horror, and their silence was still more awful than any
expressions of anguish they could give utterance to. But, in the midst of it all,
Tom's sorrow was for Ellen alone, and he endeavoured, by every means in his
power, to alleviate her distress. In return for this, the poor girl tried to appear
as calm and collected as possible, and still whispered words of hope. In the
midst of this, Tom, putting his hand into his jacket pocket, was delighted to find
a biscuit, which he had not known to have been there before. He cracked it,
and offered a portion of it to Richard and Ellen ; but the former, with that true
benevolence his nature was so characteristic of, refused it, and insisted that Ellen
should take his share. Ellen, notwithstanding, firmly refused this, and would
not take even a crumb of their scanty fare, unless Tom and Richard both partook with her. Their hunger was too great to suffer them to argue long upon the
subject, and they immediately eat the trifle which Providence had thrown in their
way, and which, of course, did not appease their hunger, any more than as if
they had not partaken of anything.

The day passed away like the previous one, and as night approached, and still
not the least signs of help met their gaze, their agony almost became insupportable. Notwithstanding all the efforts she made to keep up her spirits, Ellen felt
them gradually sinking beneath the sufferings to which she was exposed, and the
privations she had undergone for so many hours. Her throat and lips were
parched with thirst, and her hunger was so great, that it almost drove her to distraction. Her cheeks were deadly pale, her eyes sunk in her head, and she felt
altogether so ill, that she was unable to stand or walk about ; and the madness
which completely racked the brain of Tom when he saw this, and had no means
of relieving her, may be conceived, but cannot be properly pourtrayed. With the

air of a maniac, he rushed all over the place, with the hope of discovering a spring, so that they might at least quench their burning thirst, and in the most ardent terms supplicated the mercy of Heaven. But in vain was his search, and night again set in, and found them in even a more deplorable condition than they had been the day before. Sometimes they contemplated each other with looks that they all seemed perfectly well to understand, and they could read each other's thoughts. More than once did Gallant Tom half feel inclined to end at once his misery, by plunging into the dark waters of the deep; and such were the thoughts that momentarily would at intervals occupy the minds of his companions; but they quickly vanished, and they reproached themselves severely, by having, if only in bare thought encouraged such ideas.

At length, completely exhausted, like the previous evening, they fell off to repose, and did not awaken until day-break. They then found themselves so weak, that they could with difficulty rise, and could then only stand for a few minutes.

"Alas! my ill-fated girl," said Tom, "there seems to be no hope for us; we must all perish; but to die such a dreadful death as this, and you, my Ellen——"

"Think not of me, Tom," said Ellen, "but let us endeavour to prepare ourselves to meet that fate, which now seems to be inevitable, with becoming fortitude. It will not be long first. I feel weak, very—very weak, Tom. Oh! that I could but obtain only a draught of water to quench this intollerable thirst!"

"I shall go mad!" ejaculated the distracted sailor, as Ellen, unable longer to support herself, sank with her head upon his bosom. "Ellen! Ellen! my own fond girl, look up, and——Ah! she faints! What shall I do?—She will die, and I have not the means of rendering her the least assistance, Dick!—Dick!—for the love of Heaven, weigh anchor in search of water; although I could not find any, you may be more successful."

Richard had walked to some distance from Tom and his insensible companion, and just at the moment Tom spoke, he came running towards him, with a strength imparted by sudden joy, and shouted aloud,—

"Ah! see!—Providence hath heard our prayers!—Behold!—a sail! a sail!"

"A sail!" reiterated Tom, stretching his eager eyes in the direction to which Richard pointed. "It is true! I clearly behold the white sails of a vessel, which seems to be steering in this direction! Heaven send that she may turn out to be a fair craft, and we are saved!"

While he was thus speaking, Ellen recovered, and opened her eyes; and when she was informed of the approaching ship, she burst into a paroxysm of tears,—tears of joy and gratitude. Then they sank upon their knees, and solemnly offered up their thanks to Omnipotence.

Nearer and nearer the vessel approached, until Tom could discover her build, and he had very little doubt that she was a British ship, and a merchantman. She was also bearing down precisely in the direction of the rock, and, therefore, Tom saw every reason for them to encourage the hope of being rescued which her appearance had given rise to.

"Bear up, bear up, dearest lass," said Tom, as he vehemently kissed the lips of Ellen, "but a few minutes more, and we shall be saved!"

He tore the kerchief off his neck, and waved it above his head, as a signal of distress, and Richard followed his example, at the same time shouting with all his might. At length it was evident that the persons on board the ship had seen their signal, for they fired a gun, and when the vessel had approached nearer, they put off a boat with two or three men in it, which made for the rock to render them the assistance which they wanted.

At last it reached the rock and the men called to them to endeavour to descend it. This was a terribly difficult task, weakened as they were by hunger and fatigue;—in fact, Ellen was so much reduced that she could scarcely walk at all; and Tom and Richard, as may be expected, were both in a very little better condition. Tom, however, laid hold of her arm, and they began to descend the rock, which, after much difficulty, they accomplished, and were assisted into the boat by the men, who, as Tom had imagined, turned out to be Englishmen, and the vessel was a British merchant ship, homeward bound. Richard having followed them, the boat was pushed off and made for the ship, which they reached in safety.

They were received on board by the captain with much kindness, and upon being briefly made acquainted by Tom, of the misfortunes they had met with, he ordered them to receive every nourishment and assistance that his vessel afforded, and their distressed situation required. Ellen was placed under the care of the captain's wife, who was on board, and was a very amiable woman, and paid her every attention; while Tom and Dick, were well provided for by the orders of the captain, and were not long in recovering from the effects of their late suffering.

*　　　*　　　*　　　*　　　*　　　*

The miscreant, Saib, having discovered the retreat of Rosina, was determined that he would not lose so favourable an opportunity of gratifying his desires by getting possession of her person. He said nothing whatever to the earl, from whom he now frequently absented himself for long periods together; and he trusted that in less than a week the maiden would be securely in his power. How he exulted as these thoughts crossed his mind, and he laughed aloud in triumph.

" Proud, scornful beauty," he cried,—" yes,—thou shalt,—thou must be mine; nothing shall save thee! To obtain thee, I have run many risks, encountered many dangers; but have hitherto been foiled; but this time she is all but secure! Her brother is away; and, she has no one to protect her; all, therefore, favours my designs; and when I have gained possession of her, I shall even have the earl more securely in my power, and he will be compelled to resign her fortune to me!"

Fitzosbert felt uneasy that Saib absented himself so frequently from the Hall, and he scarcely knew how to act. He was fearful to give up the wealth of Rosina to his keeping, and yet he trembled at opposing the wishes of Saib, for he knew well, from bitter experience, the implacable temper of the African, and the revenge he would, in all probability, seek; he was completely in his power!—his life was in his hands, should he think proper to do so. Saib, who exulted in the anxiety and suspense he was undergoing, still avoided the Hall as much as possible, and when he did go thither, he did not let a sentence drop which could lead Fitzosbert to arrive in any way at the truth.

He watched constantly near the place in which the unsuspecting sorrow-stricken Rosina lived, but it was several days before the object which he longed for presented itself. At length his impatience increased to such a degree, that it was almost insupportable, and he could scarcely contain himself. Rosina was so distracted with the violence of her grief at the disappearance of her brother and the others, that she kept herself almost entirely secluded to the house, except when she visited the 'Old Commodore,' which was always in the day time, and when Saib was afraid to make any attempt to put his designs into execution. Several times had he seen her, and it was with the utmost difficulty he could resist the temptation he had to seize upon her, in spite of the almost certain defeat he would meet with. Every time that he beheld her she appeared more lovely than ever, and the passions of the hateful black became almost ungovernable.

At length evil fortune favoured the designs of the miscreant; he met her as she was returning from the inn in the evening, and across the wood. She had prolonged her stay at the 'Old Commodore' beyond her usual limits, and, buried in melancholy conversation, had not noticed its getting so late. As the villain beheld her approach, his exultation was so great that he could not repress a demoniac peal of laughter, and concealing himself behind a cluster of trees, directly in the way which he knew she must come, he prepared to seize her. Rosina passed the spot where Saib was concealed, and he let her proceed for a short distance, before he offered to obstruct her; then, stealing forth, he approached behind her with hasty but silent steps, and threw his arm around her, exclaiming in a voice which made the place resound again,—

"Now, proud beauty, thou art mine! Thou art in my power, and shall gratify those desires that have so long inflamed my breast! Thou art mine!— Thou art mine!"

"Oh! help!—Mercy!—Save me!" shrieked Rosina, struggling to escape.

"Thou callest in vain," observed Saib! "there is no one at hand to hasten to thy rescue.—Come with me, girl!—thou must with me, I say."

Again Rosina screamed, and tried all that her strength would allow her to escape from his hold; but her struggles were futile, and, overpowered by the violence of her feelings, she fainted. Saib then raised her in his arms, and had proceeded for some paces, when he heard the report of a pistol, felt himself wounded, and sunk to the earth, at the same moment that some one snatched the insensible form of Rosina from his arms, and a well-known voice smote the ears of Saib, exclaiming,—

"Take that, you infernal pirate! and, if that ain't enough for you, I have another ready for you!"

Saib looked up with astonishment, rage, and consternation, and his feelings may be readily imagined when he beheld Gallant Tom, Ellen, and Richard standing before him.

"Ah!" cried Tom, as he hung over the form of Rosina, "shiver my timbers, if it ain't Rosina, my sister! Why—why you damned first cousin to the devil, if I hav'n't a good mind to send another brace of bullets through your upper works! Rosina—sister—dear sister; oh, look up, and speak to me!—It is your brother returned to save you from the fangs of a villain, and to be your future protector."

Saib groaned aloud with the intensity of his mental and bodily agony, and staring at those who stood before him with looks of terror and incredulity, he ejaculated,—

"Powers of darkness! this cannot be real.—My enemies, whom I thought for evermore secure, returned ?—But, no, no ; it is only some infernal mockery !—My eyes must have deceived me !"

"But your eyes have not deceived you, you black shark," returned Tom. "It is, indeed, those whom you no doubt thought were gone to Davy Jones's ere this, and who have returned in the very nick of time to your confusion. This shall be the last trick of the kind you shall play, depend upon it ; for if the wound I have given you, and which appears to be an awkward one, does not do your business, the hangman shall for you !——Ah !—Rosina !"

At that moment Rosina recovered, and, staring around her, she ejaculated,—

"Ah ! that voice !—those well-known tones,—where am I ?—whither have you brought me ?"

"Rosina,—dear, dear sister," cried Tom, in a voice of the most indescribable emotion, "it is no dream ; it is your brother ; 'tis Tom, and Ellen, and Richard, who have returned in safety, and——"

A loud scream from Rosina, who had had her eyes fixed upon Tom, Ellen, and Richard, alternately, during the time the former was thus speaking, interrupted him, and giving utterance to his name, she threw herself into his arms, and once more became insensible.

The villain, Saib, lay writhing in agony and rage, and his eyes rolled fiercely, first upon Tom and the insensible damsel in his arms, and then upon Richard and Ellen. Curses and imprecations then rose to his lips, and he tried, but in vain, to rise from the earth. At that moment, Tom was placed in a dilemma, and knew not in which way to act, for he could not think of leaving the wretch, Saib, behind him,—and, how was he to take him from the spot without assistance ?

While he thus hesitated, pressing Rosina with the most unbounded affection to his heart, and imprinting warm kisses upon her lips, he heard the shouts of men outside, and looking in the direction from whence the sounds seemed to issue, he beheld several of his shipmates approaching that way, and the next moment they came up to the spot where the singular group was standing.

"Hollo !" exclaimed one of the sailors, " what's the meaning of this ?—Tom Clewline here, with a female in his arms, and that black fellow wounded and bleeding ?"

"The fact of the matter, messmates, is," answered Tom, " that this poor lass is my sister, and yonder black swab, is the same that you have heard me talk of, who endeavoured to fire the powder magazine, and has made several attempts upon the life of this lad. He would have borne my sister away, only I happened to steer this course, and bore down upon him just in time. I think I have given him a settler ;—but it is no more than he deserves."

"Why, shiver his black figure-head," observed one of the seamen, while Saib gnashed his teeth, and fixed upon him a look of the most diabolical indignation, "what shall we do with him, Tom ?"

"Just stow the lubber in some place of security for the present, messmates," answered our hero ; " I have a precious long account to settle with both him and his rascally master. Now, then, Ellen, my dear girl, see if you cannot restore this poor wench ; the sudden surprise has been too much for her. Oh ! I could willingly serve that wretch ten-times worse than he is already, for being the cause of all this trouble ;—but the time for his receiving his reward is not far off."

Tom gently placed his sister upon the stump of a tree, while Ellen, with the most affectionate solicitude, procured some water from a neighbouring brook, in a shell, and sprinkled the face and bathed the temples of the unconscious girl.

In the meantime the sailors, in compliance with the request of Tom, seized the wounded black, and in spite of his violent struggles, and hoarse muttered maledictions, raised him from the earth, and after having bound his legs and arms with their handkerchiefs, they were about to bear him away, when at that moment a tall figure in a dark mantle made its appearance before them, in whom Tom and Ellen immediately recognized the mysterious stranger who had sought shelter at ' The Old Commodore,' and whose strange conduct, and ambiguity of manner, had since been the cause of so much speculation among them. Richard no sooner beheld him, than he felt a peculiar sensation of unaccountable awe come over him, and he gazed at the stranger with the most intense and indescribable interest.

" Ah !" cried Tom, "this strange looking craft here again ?—What can he want I should like to know ?"

" Tom," said the mysterious man, "I am glad to see that thou hast returned, and in safety, for now will that vengeance, that retribution, which has too long slumbered, descend upon the head of the guilty."

The African fixed a look of wild scrutiny upon the mysterious form before him, whose face was concealed from observation, and his lips quivered fearfully, as he cried,—

" That voice ! that figure !—mysterious being who art thou ?"

No. 17

"Villain!" answered the stranger, in solemn tones, "the hour is near at hand when thou shalt know. Tremble!—Tom, let him be conveyed to a place of proper security, and now listen to me."

"Take the black rascal to the ' Old Commodore,' until we have finally settled what we shall do with him. Now, stranger, what is your business with me?"

Saib was carried forcibly away amid the shouts and scoffs of the sailors, and then the stranger, who seemed to have been contemplating the lad Richard with much emotion, said,—

"Tom Clewline, as you are called, Providence has made you the instrument of bringing about those events which, doubtless, will restore the injured to their rights, and bring shame and punishment upon the guilty ; and the hour is not far off when justice shall be done to every one, and Fitzosbert and his myrmidon meet with the reward due to their crimes. To-morrow, the usurper, little imagining what is brooding in the web of Fate, gives another masked fête ; at which I desire you and your friends, but more especially the boy, Richard, to be present. Do not hesitate to accuse Fitzosbert of the most heinous crimes ;—nay, of murder ;—I will be at hand and speedily bring about the result I have in contemplation."

" This is a mysterious business," said Tom, looking at the stranger with no little astonishment, " and, may I make so bold as to enquire who you are ?"

" That thou wilt know to-morrow," was the reply, " let it suffice for thee that I am the friend of virtue, and the mortal enemy of guilt ;—Wilt thou promise me ?"

" Why," returned our hero, " if one may judge by your words, you are an honest sort of a chap, and, therefore, I will do as you request of me."

" Enough, then, to-morrow we meet for justice !" said the man of mystery, and after approaching Richard for a moment, who had involuntarily knelt at his feet ; he raised his hands above his head, as if invoking a blessing upon him, bowed to Tom and the others, and immediately retired from the spot.

" Well," said Tom, when he had gone, " he certainly is a very rum fellow, and I don't know what to make of him.—How devilish fond he seems of Dick, too."

" I don't know how it is," said Richard, " but always when in the presence of that singular being, I feel a sensation at my heart such as I have never before experienced ; and, methinks, I could worship him !—What can this mean ?—"

" Why, it is very singular, Dick, as you say," remarked Tom, " but—ah ! my sister recovers !—Rosina,—sister,—dear, dear, girl ;—oh, look up ; your brother, Ellen, Richard, all your friends are restored to you."

Rosina passed her hand across her forehead, and then glanced vacantly around her ;—

" Where am I ?" she cried in accents of wildness ;—" where is he ?—The fierce that terrible man?—Ah ! is it possible ' No, no, the happiness is too great to be real ! My brother,—Ellen,—Rich——Oh, yes, it is,—it is true !—Brother !—brother ! Heaven, I thank thee for having thus listened to my constant,—my earnest prayers !"

Tom, Ellen, and Richard, embraced the poor girl with much emotion, until the former observed,—

" But, come, come, in some other place we will give vent to our joys. Let us immediately to the inn ; the poor old people must have gone almost mad when they were informed of our return, and we must not delay their joy any longer than we can help. I have got a rare lot to tell you, Rosina!—so, come; let us weigh anchor, and sheer off for the 'The Old Commodore.'"

With these words, Tom linked his arms in those of Rosina and Ellen, and, followed by Richard, they departed with all the speed they were able towards the house of old Mat.

We have informed the reader of the scene which took place between Toby Twitter and Cheeki, and which was overheard and witnessed by Patty; we have also described the indignation of the latter at the infidelity of that little man for whom she had run such risks, and encountered all the horrors of the ocean, and the terrors of the battle. Patty was a true woman, with all the foibles and weaknesses of her sex; what was more, also, she possessed all the ardent and sincere passions which usually prevail in the female breast, when they fix their mind upon any particular object; consequently, although Patty was very indignant at the improper conduct of Toby, and had made so many protestations to hate, despise and abandon him, her heart throbbed for him with a passion as warm as it had ever done, and she sincerely wished for an opportunity to effect a reconciliation, notwithstanding, she declared most positively, as many women placed in similar circumstances before her have done, that "she would not have him, if every hair of his head was hung with diamonds."

" The little brute!" she soliloquized, " the—the ugly little monster ;—to go to desert me for a black woman;—if she had been anything but a *black*, I might have thought it more *fair*,—but as it is,—oh, never let him come near me ;—don't let him venture to shew his nasty, ugly phizimigogomy to me, or I'll commit manslaughter upon him, or my name's not Patty !"

With this laudable resolution Patty walked out of the house, and, singular enough, took the very way in which it was more likely than any other that she should meet the object of her resentment.

Now, be it understood, that whatever failings Toby Twitter might possess, should be attributed more to the head than the heart ; and that, although the honied accents of Cheeki had come over him for a short time, he had his moments of remorse, and he possessed sufficient sense to be aware that he had acted very wrong to Patty, who had fully evinced the strength of the love she had for him, by following him to sea, in company with her mistress, and encountering so many perils and vicissitudes for his sake ; and, although he had in a moment of weakness yielded to the persuasions of his sable inamorata, in his serious moments he repented of the promise he had given, and would gladly have retracted it, could he have been certain that when he had done so, he should be enabled to effect a reconciliation with Patty.

" How shall I act," he ruminated ; " I am divided between love and gratitude ; black as she is, I must confess that I love this little Cheeki, and yet gratitude and honour demand that I should forget her, and place Patty on the throne of my heart. I am in a quandary ;—I am at a loss ;—let me see—*black's* a good standing colour, and——"

" Is it, you wretch ?" said a voice close to his ear, and its shrill, passionate accents left him no cause to doubt long from whom it proceeded ; he turned round, and beheld Patty by his side, who seemed as if she was inclined to commit summary punishment upon the abashed and flabbergasted Toby, for his infidelity :—" oh ! you vile man ;—oh ! you base deceiver !"

" Now, now, Patty," interposed Toby, in a mild, humble, and pacificatory tone, " only hear me."

" I won't hear you ;—I won't listen to you," cried Patty ;—" to go for to desert me for that nasty, ugly black girl !"

" Why," observed Toby, " I m ust admit, Patty, that that was a *black* piece of business ; but, then, you know, Cheeki has got money, and you have none, and, therefore, you could not but expect that such a thing would have its effect upon a gentleman possessed of a hindependent fortin of eight pounds, thirteen shillings, and a penny ha'p'ny *yearly per aniwum.* Hows'ever, to show you that I still love you with the ardour I always said I did, I am willing to make a sacrifice,—and a very great one you must own it is,—I am ready to discard Cheeki,—to sack my black diamond, and take to my jewel of inestimable price again."

" I'll not have you !" ejaculated Patty, wrathfully, although at the same time she was so delighted at what he had said, that she was almost tempted to throw herself into the arms of Toby, and agree to become Mrs. Twitter immediately. " Toby Twitter, Toby Twitter,—you are a—a—a wretch !—a brute !—a—a—a cannibal !"

" Blood of the Twitters !" cried Toby, " hear that,—she calls me a cannibal ! Hows'ever, Patty," he added, smiling at what he considered his rich wit, " I don't know that you are much out there, after all, for such a girl as you is enough to make any man *savage.* Besides, I had very good reasons for my conduct, for as you took to wearing the breeches before marriage, what could I expect you to do afterwards. So, you won't have me ?"

" No, I will not."

" Then," said Toby, hitting the crown of his hat, with much mock dignity,— " then I pity your want of taste.—I must come the independent here, I see," he added to himself.—" Well, Patty," he said aloud, " since it seems you are determined, so am I ; so I wish you a very good day, and I hope you may get a better chance than a husband with a hindependent fortin of eight pounds, thirteen shillings, and a penny ha'p'ny *yearly per aniwum,* that's all I've got to say about it."

As he thus spoke, he prepared to leave her, upon which, Patty thinking she had gone rather too far, and not at all disposed to lose him in that manner, said aside, to herself,—

" I am afraid he is serious ;—I must change my tone.—" Toby," she added, in one of her kindest and most insinuating tones,—

" Well !" he answered, with assumed fierceness.

" Toby, could you go to leave your poor, faithful Patty in this manner ?"

" To be sure I could," he replied, " didn't you refuse me ?—Didn't you call me brute, monster, cannibal ?'

" I'll acknowledge I did, Toby ; but I was in a passion then, and we women often say many silly things that we do not mean. Now, my dear, darling, good-looking Toby."

" Gammon," said Toby, as she placed her arm in a coaxing manner, round his neck, "I suppose these are some of the silly things that you do not mean."

" No, indeed."

" Then you are serious ?"

" Positively."

" And you'll never upbraid me after we are married ?"

" Never !"

" Nor want to wear the breeches."

" Certainly not."

" Then come to my arms, my duck of diamonds ;— these female *angels* are the very *devil !*"

They embraced fervently, and thus ended the quarrel of Toby Twitter and his faithful Patty.

We need not inform the reader that the vessel which had afforded Tom, Ellen, and Richard a shelter, after the danger and suffering to which they had been exposed, brought them home in safety, and the kindness of the captain and all the crew towards them, excited their utmost gratitude. But, how shall we describe the meeting which took place between them and Mat and his wife on their unexpected and sudden restoration to them ?—Language must fail ; and, therefore, we leave the task to the conjectures of the reader. Mat, however, seemed to feel little, if any surprise at the behaviour of the mysterious stranger ; and when he heard what he had said, and the promise Tom had made him, the old man exclaimed, while an expression of satisfaction overspread his venerable countenance,—

" Yes, my children, by all means obey the wishes of this singular being ; and something persuades me, that not only is the hour of retribution at hand, but that to-morrow will reveal certain circumstances, that will, doubtless, fill you all with the greatest astonishment."

" Hollo !" said Tom, " what's in the wind, now ?—Why, Mat, any one would suppose that you was on intimate terms with this strange craft, and were acquainted with all his secrets."

" To-morrow, as I before said," returned Mat, " will disclose everything ; till then, we will drop the subject."

Here the matter for the present ended, although every one present thought it was evident that he knew more than he thought it prudent to reveal, and their impatience for the arrival of the next day increased.

The miscreant Saib was confined in an out-house which adjoined the tavern, and, his wounds having been properly dressed, he somewhat revived, although the medical man who attended him stated, positively, that the wound he had received was mortal. Fearful that he would sink under his wound before the following day, and that they would thus be deprived of the evidence of the principal witness of the guilt of Fitzosbert, Mat and Tom several times visited him, and seldom left him during the night, hoping to be able to elicit from him a confession of his crimes, and of the dark deeds, in the perpetration of which it was suspected he had been connected with the earl.

Several times during the night he was delirious, and in those moments the wild ravings to which he gave utterance left them very little room to doubt the truth of their surmises. Towards morning he became more calm, and listened to their solicitations without evincing any impatience; and, at last, desiring he might be removed into the house, he promised to confess all. His wishes were complied with, and then, in a faint voice, spoke as follows :—

CONFESSION OF SAIB.

" Feeling the hand of death upon me, and stung with remorse and a guilty conscience, I wish to make all the atonement I can, by acknowledging the heinous crimes of which I have been guilty, and bringing retribution upon the head of him, who, by the tempting offer of lucre, first led me into villany and blood-shed.

" Lionel, Earl Fitzosbert, the elder brother of the present usurper, was my master, originally having purchased me from slavery in Africa, and brought me to England, where he educated me, and showed me all the indulgence that a master could show his servant. Alas! how did I repay him for his kindness?—The sequel will too plainly show,—My time is short, and my strength is almost exhausted; therefore, I must run over my narrative of blood as quickly as possible.

" Soon after the birth of a son, the Countess Fitzosbert died, and the earl became quite an altered man, abandoning that life of retirement in which he had before resided, and mixing with the political world, at the time when it was beset by the most violent storms, in which he became implicated. Towards his brother, who was his junior, by about two or three years, he behaved with the utmost affection and liberality, resigning to him a large portion of the property bequeathed to him by his late father, and insisting upon his continuing to reside with him; but, notwithstanding this, soon after I came to live in England, I could perceive that he viewed the earl with eyes of envy and hatred, and it was not long ere I discovered that my surmises were just.

" Robert Fitzosbert soon began to take particular notice of me, and took every opportunity of conciliating my friendship, by making me presents, and many other advances to my favour. Although I hated and despised him in my heart, his gold was tempting, for I was naturally covetous, and, by degrees he so completely won upon me, as to venture to confide to me his thoughts and wishes. It was then I discovered that his ambition was to become the possessor of the title and estates of his brother, and that he could see no other way of arriving at the gratification of his desires, than by the death of Lionel and his infant son, Julian. So completely had he lured me to his diabolical purposes by his accursed gold, that I was induced to listen to his proposals, and ultimately to become the panderer to his wishes. The assassination of the earl and his son was agreed upon, and an opportunity soon presented itself to put our infernal scheme into execution.

" The earl, having been accused of some political offence, deemed it prudent to quit his mansion for some time, and retire to the Isle of Wight. I did not accompany him, but it was agreed that I should follow after him, and meet him at a certain part of the coast. I did so. We got into a post-chaise to go to the place he had fixed on for his residence, and he had his child with him.

" I had managed my murderous plot ;—I had agreed with three ruffians (whom

I had become acquainted with on board of the vessel which brought me to England), to attack us at a certain place, and they did as I had desired them. The unfortunate earl, with the boy in his arms, was dragged out of the vehicle, and, with my own hands, I stabbed him in various parts of the body, and inflicted what I thought to be a deadly wound on the boy. After this we divided what money the earl had upon his person, equally amongst us, and drove the chaise into the sea, but left the bodies where we had murdered them, being alarmed by some persons who we thought were approaching the spot. I parted with the ruffians, and have never seen them since. Soon after this I returned home, and as it was not known there whither I had been to, suspicion never lighted upon me. In the course of a few weeks all inquiries after the earl and his son having proved unsuccessful, his brother, who had affected the most violent grief, took to himself the title and estates of Fitzosbert, which he has retained ever since. This is the truth, as I hope for mercy from that Almighty Judge in the presence of whom I shall shortly stand."

" But why was your hatred so excited against Richard ?" demanded Tom, "and why did you so often seek his life ?"

" Because," answered the black, " in him I discovered the son of the late earl Fitzosbert, whom I had imagined I had murdered, and the rightful heir to the earldom and property of Fitzosbert."

" Ah !" exclaimed Tom, in a voice of astonishment, " splice my timbers here's a discovery ! Bnt you are not spinning a yarn, are you ?—Oh, damme, if I didn't think that young Dick was born to be a great man !"

Saib repeated his assertions, and then becoming faint, they no longer thought proper to torture him with questions. In the course of the night, the unhappy wretch rallied, and he became not only more composed, but his pain seemed to be greatly alleviated. All chance of his recovery, however, was evidently at an end, and they were at times fearful that he would not survive until the following day, and thus frustrate a design they had in contemplation, by which the utter defeat of the villain Fitzosbert would be certain to be accomplished, and the innocent have ample justice done to them and be restored to their rights.

In the meantime, the guilty Fitzosbert had been informed of the attempt which Saib had made upon the life of Richard, and the consequences that had followed, and his horror and consternation were excessive. Should Saib in a moment of weakness betray the dark secret they had for so many years succeeded in concealing, ignominy and destruction would be his inevitable fate. He shuddered with horror at the bare contemplation of this idea, and he trembled with terrible foreboding. But yet he could not think that Saib would ever become so weak. A thousand times did he curse Tom for being the means of placing him in such a situation of imminent peril ; and then again he cursed the ill-fortune which did not make the mark of the sailor more certain, and kill the black on the spot, without affording him an opportunity of revealing those secrets by which his complete ruin would be certain to follow. Some confounded spell seemed to rest upon him, and all his evil designs ; for here, at the very time when he had believed Tom and Richard secure on board the pirate brig they had returned just in the very critical moment, and brought about a catastrophe, he could not think upon without the most indescribable agitation. In a state of distraction he sent down a peremptory order to Mat, to deliver up to him his servant, on pain of future proceedings ; and the old tar sent back an equally peremptory answer, stating that he should do no such thing ; and that, perhaps, ere many hours were over his (the earl's head), he might have reason to think that he did not care even the cracking of a biscuit about him or his boasted power. To this message Tom added another of the same description, and bade the earl prepare to give a little explanation upon certain matters, which he might consider anything but agreeable.

The rage and consternation of Fitzosbert, when his servants returned to the Hall, with these answers was extreme ;—he stamped and raved with passion, and it was with the utmost difficulty he could contain himself.

" Ah !" he cried, raising his clenched fist to his burning forehead, " my worst fears are all but confirmed ; the dastard knave Saib, hath disclosed all, and my crimes are made known to my enemies. But, psha !—what childish weakness is this that I suffer to come over me ?—I frighten myself without any just cause for so doing, and shall betray myself ;—I will shake off this cowardly feeling of apprehension and become myself again."

But, in spite of all his endeavours he found this to be a task it was quite impossible for him to accomplish, and that night he passed in a most wretched state of mind ; he now regretted that he had set the following day apart for a second grand fête, as his spirits would by no means be in unison with the festivities that would be going forward. He would have put it off ; but then again he was fearful that by so doing he would be the cause of exciting some suspicions that might ultimately be the means of bringing about the result he so much dreaded ; he, therefore, resolved that the fête should take place, and that he would endeavour by every means in his power to appear unusually gay on that occasion. The morning at length dawned, and at an early hour, the guests began to assemble at the Hall, eager to partake of the festivities ; but the attendance was not so numerous as it had been on a former occasion, no doubt many persons being withheld from going there on account of the mysterious events that had then taken place.

There was, notwithstanding, a very brilliant assemblage, and the mirth and gaiety that prevailed around, appeared to be universal. Yet, in spite of his endeavours, and the many deep libations he took, did the uneasiness of the earl increase, and he frequently arose from the festive board, and walked to some obscure part of the saloon, so that he might give free indulgence to the thoughts and feelings that tortured him. It was upon one of these occasions that he heard his name pronounced in accents he could never forget, and raising his head, he was horrorstruck at once more beholding the tall and awful figure of the domino that had haunted him on the occasion of the former fête, and who had more than once appeared to him under the most exciting circumstances. Fitzosbert started, and trembled in every limb, while his countenance turned ghastly pale, and he was unable to give utterance to a syllable. The domino stood for a second or two, and his eyes through the black mask which he wore, sparkled fiercely upon Fitzosbert, while in the same awful and sepulchral accents in which he had before addressed him, the former said ;—

"Robert Fitzosbert, thy time is nearly come ;—the injured are at hand to seek for justice ;—tremble !—"

As he thus spoke, the domino raised his mask, and again the guilty Fitzosbert gazed upon features that smote his soul with horror !—

"Avaunt! avaunt !" he cried, in frantic tones ; "I cannot,—dare not gaze upon you ! My blood freezes in my veins as I look upon thee !—Away, fiend,—spectre, avaunt !"

He staggered back to the table at which he had previously been seated, and covered his face with his hands in a state of agitation, we are at a loss to pourtray.

In the meantime the supposed phantom vanished amongst the numerous guests. Fitzosbert was soon aroused by receiving a salute from a heavy hand upon the shoulder, and, raising his head, his bewilderment and surprise were excessive when he beheld Gallant Tom at his elbows.

"Ah !" he cried, starting from his seat, "you here? — what means this intrusion ?"

"Oh, you will know all, presently," replied Tom, with the utmost coolness; "I thought you might not think my visit very agreeable but I have called to pay my *respects* to you, and to thank you for the kind service you and your sable dog did me, my Ellen, and young Dick, by getting us a berth on board the 'Nancy,' under that highly respectable individual, Will Barnsley. But I will introduce you to one or two more of your old acquaintances whom you did not expect to see."

No. 18

Thus speaking, Tom motioned to three female forms that stood close by, and immediately removing their masks, Rosina, Patty, and Ellen, stood before the wonderstruck and guilty Fitzosbert.

"Damnation!" he exclaimed, starting back, "Rosina!—what demons are at work to torture me?"

"You shall see," replied Tom, and waving his hand, in a moment, Saib, dying, was led in by Mat, and two or three others, and confronted his horrorstruck master.

"What means this?" demanded Fitzosbert, in a trembling voice; "Saib here!"

"The meaning of it, is this," returned Tom; "Saib has again been attempting the life of young Richard, and has met with the reward he merited. Since this he has become penitent, and confessed all his own crimes and yours too; and a very nice little lot they are."

"Ah! wretch!—" said Fitzosbert, his eyes glancing with a look of the most unutterable resentment upon Saib.

"The black man's career is nearly ended, and the implacable spirit he once possessed is broken;" said the African, faintly, "but on you, Fitzosbert who first incited me to crime, and made me the wretch I now am,—may my most bitter,—my dying curse descend.—Draw around," he continued looking at the guests and motioning to them,—"draw around, and listen to the tale of horror I have to unfold."

The guests did as he desired them, in the utmost amazement, and then Saib repeated that confession with which the reader has been made already acquainted. During this recital the rage of Fitzosbert exceeded all bounds, and he was with the utmost difficulty prevented from rushing upon the expiring black. Immediately after the latter had come to the termination of the guilty confession, he gave one dreadful groan of agony, and sunk a corpse upon the floor.

"Oh, believe him not," cried Fitzosbert, "the story he has told you is a base fabrication from beginning to end."

"Villain, thou liest!" replied a loud voice, and immediately the mysterious stranger appeared, leading in Richard by the hand; "the substance of that unhappy wretch's narrative is true, and thou knowest it;—but Providence hath preserved both thy much injured brother and his son; behold! to thy confusion, they both stand before thee!"

The domino threw off his disguise, and Lionel Earl Fitzosbert, and his son, Julian, hitherto known as Richard, stood before his guilty, conscience-stricken brother, and the astonished guests.

"My son!—my own dear boy!" ejaculated the earl, in a voice of the most uncontroulable emotion, and embracing Julian with the most delirious transport.

"Father," replied the lad, "and have I, then, one on whom I can bestow that endearing title?—Oh, Providence! Thy ways are, indeed, wonderful!"

"Tear them asunder!—it is horror to mine eyes!" cried the guilty Fitzosbert, his cheeks blanched,—his lips livid, and every limb palsied with terror; "do not let them embrace! Fools! why do you hesitate?—Nay, stand off;—do not dare approach them. Do you not see that he is not of this world?—Look, how the thick clotted blood stains his bosom !—Ah !—he is still there !—He mocks my anguish !—Retribution—retribution he demands !—There, do you not hear him ? —He approaches me !—do not let him grasp me !—will no one aid me against my ghastly foe ?—Off—off ! dread phantom of my murdered brother ?—I do acknowledge my guilt,—but I cannot meet thy reproachful gaze !—Oh, horror !"

Overcome by the power of his feelings, the wretched man sunk into the arms of two of the guests who were standing by. Suddenly, his countenance became frightfully distorted, and he appeared to be struggling for breath. He attempted to speak, but could not, and the next moment the blood gushed from his eyes, nose, and mouth; he had ruptured a blood-vessel, and was evidently dying. He was immediately borne into another apartment, and a medical man sent for, with all possible expedition; but, before he arrived, the wretched Fitzosbert was no more.

CONCLUSION.

Lionel Earl Fitzosbert was, of course, reinstated in his rights that had been so long usurped by his guilty and unnatural brother, whom he interred with all the pomp he was entitled to by his rank, and with him, he buried all recollection of the wrongs he had done him. On the night he had left the cottage belonging to the sister of Mat, for the purpose of taking a walk, he was seized by a press-gang, and, in spite of his remonstrances, and declarations of his station in society, forced on board ship. Not long had he been out at sea, when he was taken by an Algerine Corsair, and sold for a slave, from which he had but recently made his escape, after enduring great hardship, and returning to England with a resolution of seeking out his son. As has been seen, Providence directed his footsteps to the very place where Mat, and the long lost Julian resided. He immediately made himself known to the former, but thought it prudent not to make Richard acquainted with the strange surprise that awaited him, for the present, so as to enable him the better to accomplish the object he had in contemplation to bring about his own ends. How that plot was contrived, and in what manner it succeeded, has been clearly shewn.

The restoration of the earl to his rights was hailed with much delight by all who lived in the neighbourhood, and many gentlemen, who had formerly had the honour to enjoy his friendship, flocked to congratulate him on his fortunate escape from death, and the most miraculous manner in which his son had been restored to him. Richard felt none of that extravagant joy which might have been expected at his sudden elevation to rank and fortune, neither did he forget his former benefactors (on whom the earl fixed a handsome annuity) and he never called Ellen by any other title than " his pretty Coz."

Gallant Tom, as he still liked to be called, and his sister, Rosina, having now fully established their consanguinity, took a handsome house near that of the Earl Fitzosbert, with whom they were on terms of the most ardent friendship.

In about two months subsequent to the events we have been narrating, Tom, whom no change of fortune could alter, led his lovely Ellen to church, and fulfilled the vows he had so long plighted to her. A joyful day was that in Plymouth ; there were nothing but cheerful faces to be seen; and Tom invited the whole of his old shipmates to partake of his hospitality, and the festivities got up on that auspicious occasion.

We have little more to add : Tom rose to great eminence in the navy, and was as much beloved as an officer as he had been respected as a private man. He lived to see a numerous family around him, all inheriting their parents' virtues ;—and it is not many years since " he was called up aloft."

The earl Filzosbert lived to a good old age, esteemed by everybody, and was gratified by beholding his son nobly earn the laurel's that seldom fail to deck the hero's brow. He married a wealthy heiress of great beauty and accomplishments, with whom he lived a long life of uninterrupted happiness.

Rosina also was united to a gentleman who was every way worthy of her, and their days were passed in that felicity, which cannot fail to be the reward, when love and virtue are combined.

THE END.